"Hitchcock has once again crafted a delightful dance between intrigue and romance that I couldn't put down."
—Misty M. Beller, *USA Today* best-selling author of the Brothers of Sapphire Ranch series

"Delightful, charming, and witty. With a feisty heroine you'll secretly want to be, plenty of romantic chemistry, and secrets for days, *To Kiss a Knight* is an incredibly fun romp you won't want to end."
—Betsy St. Amant, author of *Tacos for Two* and the Magnolia Bay series

"With heart and humor, Grace Hitchcock will capture your imagination in her latest Regency novel, *To Kiss a Knight*. This second book in the Best Laid Plans series is sure to delight readers and keep them up turning pages to see how Vivienne will discover Sir Sebastian's true identity and join him in his noble cause."
—Carrie Turansky, award-winning author of *A Token of Love*

"Regency rom-com perfection! Grace Hitchcock brilliantly transports her readers to the Regency era in this delightful novel brimming with humor, faith, and romance. *To Kiss a Knight* was completely captivating and impossible to put down. Ladies, grab your smelling salts and prepare to swoon over Sir Sebastian Larkby."
—Rebekah Millet, award-winning author of *Julia Monroe Begins Again*

"An authoress fleeing an unwanted marriage, a chivalrous thief who is not as he first appears, and a marriage of convenience? Yes, please. Grace Hitchcock has pulled off another rollicking Regency with romance, danger, humor, and unexpected plot twists you won't want to miss!"
—Crystal Caudill, author of *Written in Secret*

To
KISS
a
KNIGHT

Best Laid Plans

To Catch a Coronet
To Kiss a Knight
To Win a Wager

A NOVEL OF BEST LAID PLANS
— TWO —

To KISS a KNIGHT

GRACE HITCHCOCK

KREGEL
PUBLICATIONS

To Kiss a Knight
© 2025 by Grace Hitchcock

Published by Kregel Publications, a division of Kregel Inc., 2450 Oak Industrial Dr. NE, Grand Rapids, MI 49505. www.kregel.com.

Grace Hitchcock is represented by and *To Kiss a Knight* is published in association with The Steve Laube Agency, LLC. www.stevelaube.com.

The persons and events portrayed in this work are the creations of the author, and any resemblance to persons living or dead is purely coincidental.

Scripture quotations are from the King James Version.

Library of Congress Cataloging-in-Publication Data
Names: Hitchcock, Grace, author.
Title: To kiss a knight / Grace Hitchcock.
Description: Grand Rapids, MI : Kregel Publications, 2025. | Series: A novel of Best Laid Plans ; 2
Identifiers: LCCN 2024059827 (print) | LCCN 2024059828 (ebook)
Subjects: LCGFT: Romance fiction. | Christian fiction. | Novels.
Classification: LCC PS3608.I834 T65 2025 (print) | LCC PS3608.I834 (ebook) | DDC 813/.6—dc23/eng/20241220
LC record available at https://lccn.loc.gov/2024059827
LC ebook record available at https://lccn.loc.gov/2024059828

ISBN 978-0-8254-4810-2, print
ISBN 978-0-8254-7087-5, epub
ISBN 978-0-8254-6988-6, Kindle

Printed in the United States of America
25 26 27 28 29 30 31 32 33 34 / 5 4 3 2 1

For Dakota—
angels sang the moment we met.

Casting all your care upon him; for he careth for you.

Be sober, be vigilant; because your adversary the devil, as a roaring lion, walketh about, seeking whom he may devour:

Whom resist stedfast in the faith, knowing that the same afflictions are accomplished in your brethren that are in the world.

But the God of all grace, who hath called us unto his eternal glory by Christ Jesus, after that ye have suffered a while, make you perfect, stablish, strengthen, settle you.

To him be glory and dominion for ever and ever. Amen.

1 PETER 5:7–11

Chapter One

England, Summer 1813

VIVIENNE POPPY HAD ALWAYS TAKEN pride in the fact that she had never fainted—not when her papa died, leaving her alone in the world, nor when her stepbrother promised her hand to the vilest so-called gentleman of her acquaintance. Of course she *would* faint during the most exciting moment in her life and miss all the potential story fodder that came along with being carted away on horseback by a masked highwayman.

But now, with her back pressed against the highwayman's solid chest and her head bent forward at an unnatural tilt and bobbing with each clop of the horse's hooves, she knew she had indeed fainted, and the moment he discovered she was awake, a battle would lay before her. She kept herself limp, despite the pain at the base of her neck, as the whispered warnings from ton mothers of what happened to unprotected maidens on the road flooded her pounding heart. She had already weighed that risk when she'd fled London before dawn, but she'd thought they were just stories. What was the risk of a supposed highwayman compared with certain imprisonment in a union of convenience that was anything but convenient for her?

This is salvageable. I can still have my new life. She had managed to escape her overbearing stepbrother and his waspish wife. She could outwit this brute of a man and emerge unscathed, with inspiration for her next novel. The only question was how to accomplish the feat. She dared to lift her lashes a hairbreadth, seeking anything that could help her plight in the rapidly fading light. The horse's long, strong strides along the dirt road hinted at the highest quality of horseflesh. The earth was too far from her perch to risk a leap. She might incur a broken ankle, and she didn't have funds to spare for the doctor.

Maybe feign an onslaught of violent illness brought on by hysterics? No man would take well to a woman casting up her accounts onto his leather saddle and shirtfront and would immediately dismount . . . but she hadn't eaten anything in a day of travel, as she hadn't dared to spend any coin on bread. A lot of good that did her when her precious coins were lining the bandit's pockets.

Indignation surged through her. Who was this man to pilfer her hard-earned money from her reticule? It had taken her ages to decorate her pretty bead purse and years to save her meager pin money, which she had foolishly carried with her in case she needed it on her journey. She would have to write another novel to replace the funds, for the reticule was no doubt emptied and in a puddle on the road between London and Bath. She could only pray that the horrid letter from her stepbrother, Lucius, was tucked in the highwayman's pocket and not on the road for him or—heaven forbid—her so-called fiancé to uncover and be given an inkling of where she had vanished.

Vivienne risked another peek. The man's strapping legs were clad in well-tailored black breeches tucked into polished black Hessian boots that glinted in the setting sun. A carved ebony knife handle poked out of his left boot just below her. *Perfection.*

If she was ever to get out of this mess, she needed to act now before he joined any associates and she could be overtaken. Judging from the solid mass of man supporting her, an escape would be problematic. But she had always been gifted in performing tableaux. Surely this was no different, even if the stakes were staggering. *Violent illness it is.*

She moaned, allowing her head to wobble from side to side as she clutched her stomach, her groaning frantic as she kept her lips parted in a show of rising hysteria. She allowed a bit of spit to dribble at the corner of her mouth to lend credence to the charade. "S-stop. I'm going to be ill!"

The man stiffened at once, drawing his horse to a halt. She barely kept her grin from appearing and betraying her. She moaned again and lurched forward, leaning over his left boot as if to cast up her accounts away from them. She wrenched the knife from his boot and whipped around, lifting the steel to his neck. "How dare you accost a lady. Who are you, and why did you take me?"

Clad entirely in black, her abductor wore a matching cloth mask over his eyes, tied above his striking golden queue that gamboled in the wind. His piercing blue eyes widened in shock behind his mask, and the corner of his mouth raised. The scamp was *grinning* at her, and dash it all if his breathing was even too.

Well, she supposed if one robbed stagecoaches for a living, daring was required. "What have you got to say for yourself? Are you to have no final words?"

"Not many can boast of tricking me," he said in a deep Scottish brogue. He rolled back his impossibly broad shoulders, which were emphasized by his layered cape, revealing a New Land Pattern pistol strapped to his chest . . . the reason for the sore spot on her back that would no doubt bruise.

From her book research, she knew it to be a firearm with a short range, but if his aim was as good as his horsemanship, she was in grave danger. He cut a handsome figure for a highwayman, with his sharp jawline and trim waist—mayhap he was not as smart as he dressed. "The Prince Regent will have your head for manhandling a lady of the court."

His brows rose. "The Prince Regent, eh? Seems I have absconded with the wrong damsel. A lady of the court even . . . one who travels by *stage*."

"Indeed you have." She lifted the blade to hide the lie that was surely reaching her eyes. She had never been good at misdirection, but proclaiming that one was a gentleman's daughter hardly held a threat, especially when she had no relation left who cared for her. She ripped the reins from his hand and tossed them over the horse's head. "Now, you will dismount and let me ride away, or I'll see you rot in prison."

He heaved a sigh. "While that is quite the tempting proposition, I'm afraid I cannot allow you to take my horse. I am rather fond of him." Using his legs, he guided his ebony steed in a supreme show of horsemanship, as the reins still dangled over the horse's head.

"And I was rather fond of my reticule. It is hardly compensation, but it is well within my right to have your horse, as you claimed my coin." She frowned at the horse's progress. "Stop directing him! I am in earnest. I will—"

His gloved hand flashed out and seized her wrist, twisting the blade away in a single motion as he appropriated it with the other hand, tucking it in his right boot this time, away from her grasp.

"Let us put that valiant attempt behind us, shall we?" He chuckled and retrieved the reins with ease.

She lifted her chin and flipped her long blond braid over her shoulder—hoping it hit him in the face—and pushed back the hair plastered to her perspiring temple, allowing the gentle breeze to cool her cheeks. She would not cry in her frustration and let this man think her any weaker than he already did. She was used to being underestimated. It was partly how she'd managed her flight, but she had not created this elaborate plan for freedom to perish before she took hold of her life. Perhaps if she hinted at there being anticipation of her arrival in Bath, she might be saved—at the very least, she could promise a ransom for her safe passage, paid for by her friends. While she traveled alone, she had Muriel and Tess. If Vivienne did not write to them by the end of the week, her friends would come looking—she had no doubt.

"Did I hurt you, my lady?" He grunted. "I am not used to dealing with the weaker sex. Forgive me if I bruised your wrist, but I did not wish to lose my head at your lovely hand."

"I hardly think you would care even if you did cause me pain."

"I may be a highwayman, but I am no brute."

"A nice sentiment, but it has yet to be proven."

He directed the horse from the main road toward a grove of trees, sending her heart racing wildly.

"What are you about? Don't you wish to evade the local constables and watchmen? I have no doubt they are following, after you were so bold as to rob a stagecoach bearing Sir Thomas Pomphrey and a lady."

"An unescorted lady, which begs the question as to why a member of the peerage would take a public coach instead of her own carriage." He slowed his mount as they slipped between the trees, the canopy of leaves shielding them from the road, the animal breathing heavily. "And my horse needs a rest. We will not be bothered here."

The rogue halted the horse, leapt from its back, and lifted his hands to her. She ignored his offer and kicked her feet free from her skirts. She gripped the leather saddle and skidded to the ground. Her limbs tingled from the cramped travel, and it was all she could do to hold on to the saddle to keep from collapsing.

The highwayman paid her no notice as he tossed the saddlebags over his shoulder and strode a few yards away. He dumped the contents of the bags, sorting through them, setting coins and pound notes on one side and the trinkets—most likely from Sir Thomas's and the driver's pockets—on the other. Her reticule fell out.

He has it! She released her breath. Her stepbrother would not find her on that score.

The man grinned at her intake of breath. "Ah, this must be Sir Thomas's purse. Lovely beadwork, I must say."

She crossed her arms. "There is little of value in there."

"I'll be the judge of that." He tugged open the reticule's ties and unceremoniously shook out her belongings—a letter, coins, a tight roll of pound notes bound with a thin red ribbon, a pencil, and her journal. He leafed through the journal, flipping it upside down while fanning the pages before setting it aside, whistling a lively tune as he added her money to his pile.

At least he would not humiliate her by reading her thoughts, notes, and sketches of her characters. It was a combination of a diary and ideas she was working out for her new story, an entirely lethal combination if ever lost to her, given her nom de plume was known only to her dearest friends. Others might disregard the content as musings of a love-addled girl. But in truth, if she did not make a love match, she wished to remain single all her days. She could have a good life living off her modest income as a writer and staying at her small apartment in Bath, which her father had bequeathed to her.

Even though a love match had not yet occurred and she was four and twenty and well on her way to confirmed spinsterhood, she was female and did, on occasion, develop fancies for a gentleman that were captured in her journal. No one had the right to read her innermost thoughts.

And as much as she feared what might happen to her on this adventure, she would most definitely be recording and sketching the highwayman's striking profile and features, the ones she could see at least, for future use in her stories . . . if she lived long enough to write more novels for her publisher and readers.

She patted the horse's mane, the highwayman's golden hair catching her eye once more. The color was unusually bright for a grown man, and the locks so thick they would make any woman jealous. She would sketch everything she could remember about him, guessing the placement of his cheekbones. Even with only her assumptions of how he looked beneath the mask, she would easily find him after she was safely at home in Bath by his stunning locks alone. She would see that he was brought to justice for daring to hold up her coach.

"Am I so admirable that you cannot take your eyes from me?" He grinned up at her as he rummaged through the pile. "I must warn you—many a maid is drawn in by my dangerous allure, but I am as difficult to catch as the waves upon the shore."

She rolled her eyes at his poor metaphor. "If by admiring, you mean preparing my description for when I hire a thieftaker, then yes."

"I wish you the best of luck, my lady. But as no one has caught me yet, I doubt you will be able to."

And yet I tricked you into thinking I was ill.

He stuffed a packet of letters into his waistcoat, and as the only stagecoach passengers had been herself and Sir Thomas, she knew they must belong to the older nobleman. But why did the highwayman bother with them? Perhaps she could trick him once more while he was engrossed with his loot. She eyed the horse, determining what it would take to get in the saddle unaided while he was distracted by his greed. There was a nearby low-hanging branch. If she climbed atop it, she could easily crawl into the saddle. She was a decent enough rider. She grasped the branch, hefted herself up, and scooted onto the limb, stretching her leg over the saddle to ride astride. She plopped down hard in the saddle, grabbed up the reins, and kicked the horse with all her might. "Yah!"

The beast kept munching the patch of grass. She kicked him again, but he did not budge.

"He answers only to me." The highwayman's eyes sparkled with mirth as he gathered the coins and notes. His gaze seemed to inadvertently rest at her stockinged calves for half a moment before he shifted back to his bounty.

At least the arrogant highwayman had some manners. She straightened her shoulders and kicked the horse again, using the reins as a whip, as she had seen him do. Nothing.

The man had the nerve to laugh, tucking the remaining loot into his saddlebag as he rose and whistled to his mount, who perked his ears and at once trotted to his side with Vivienne bouncing in the saddle and listing to the left.

"That's a good boy." He scratched the horse's chin, as if he were a devoted dog.

She gritted back a retort and, seeing no other way around it, moved her leg back over the saddle, tucking her skirts close and sliding from the horse's back. Her skirt caught the saddle on the dismount, and she lurched, splaying out her hands to brace her fall. He closed the distance in an instant, his arms encircling her waist while her face smashed into his waistcoat, which smelled of leather and woodsmoke.

"Allow me." He held her against him with one arm, his full lips inadvertently brushing her temple as he reached behind her and freed her muddied blue muslin skirt before setting her on the ground.

Oh my. Her cheeks flamed as she shoved herself away from him and his kissable lips, toeing the saddlebags he had abandoned to catch her. "Why do you care for those letters anyway? You tucked them in your waistcoat instead of casting them to the side."

He rubbed his jaw. "The gentleman protested at the time, saying they were from his deceased daughter. Mayhap I was too hasty in taking them from the man."

She blinked, hope blooming. "You have a heart after all."

He shrugged. "I can return them for a price."

"Of course. Mayhap you were too hasty in taking my money as well." She crossed her arms to hide her trembling limbs at her daring. "Do you feel guilty yet? Or should I wait an hour or so and inquire about your conscience again?"

"You will recover soon enough." He gestured to her ensemble. "You are quite fashionably dressed under all that mud you acquired when you fainted out the door of the stagecoach at my feet."

"And yet, as you have pointed out numerous times, I was taking a public stagecoach unescorted. Which means either I have no one who cares for my safety enough to send a carriage for me, or my family is too poor to accommodate me." She lifted a brow. "You seem gifted enough to fly from horseback to the stagecoach top without missing a beat, and somehow you miss this fact?"

"I would argue that your pelisse and muslin gown are cut in the height of fashion."

She gaped at him. "Y-you know muslin?"

He leaned against a tree trunk and gestured to his attire. "It takes a fashionable eye to look so dashing in my work. I had my garments specially tailored to fit my needs, such as leaping from a horse to atop a stagecoach, while also being swashbuckling."

"Pray, what is the name of your tailor, so that I may send my stepbrother to him?"

He laid a hand over his heart. "That I shall keep as closely guarded as my own name."

"Very well, Goldie the highwayman. You have managed to evade the constables. Are you going to release me now? I am fairly certain a passing wagon will take pity on me and give me a ride to the nearest village between here and Bath."

"Goldie?" He cringed. "Perhaps you should call me Bash after all."

"Mr. Bash?"

"Just 'Bash.' And what will I call you, my lady?"

"Just 'my lady.'" She looked about for a fallen limb to wield like a club. *As if that would knock him out.* She shook her head at her desperation.

"Fair enough. I could hardly allow you to wander about on the road, my lady, for anyone to find." He slung the saddlebags over the horse's rump, tying them into place. "You said yourself that a lady should never be unescorted."

She quirked a single brow. "Now you choose to be noble? I believe the time for chivalry has long since passed."

"Not all highwaymen are cads."

She snorted and stepped over a tree root, picking her way toward the road. "I think I would rather take my chances on the open road."

He swung up onto his horse and followed her, unaffected by her distance from him. "Dusk is nearing, and not all highwaymen are as gallant as yours. I would not leave you unattended, a helpless lady such as yourself."

"You presume much, sir. You are neither gallant nor a proper escort." She picked up her pace. Ten yards and she would be through the tree line. *Lord, let there be a coach passing nearby.* She broke into a run, leaping over tree roots and ignoring the branches snagging her muslin gown.

Hooves filled her vision as he raced up beside her and in a single motion lifted her into his saddle. His arm encircled her waist, pinning her to him, as if she were a butterfly in her nephews' entomology collections, fighting for freedom until her wings were tattered.

"After my mission is complete, I shall attend you to your destination. Now, can I trust you enough to release my hold on you? If you try to leap, I'm afraid you are in danger of being trampled under my horse's hooves."

She sagged against him. There was no use wasting her energy in fighting a man so strong and swift. She would have to outwit him. "I hardly think you could approach my home in Bath in a mask." She turned and eyed him, a hint of curiosity burning to see if his eyes were as brilliant as they appeared beneath the cloth mask.

He slowly released her, and seeing as she did not attempt to leap from the saddle, his arms kept a respectable distance from her. "Try me. I am quite good at what I do."

"Thieving?" she tossed over her shoulder. "I wonder how you got *good* at it. Gallant indeed."

"No. Becoming invisible," he whispered into her hair, sending a chill down her neck as he returned them to the spot in the clearing she had fled. "Now, we shall wait here until the moonlight guides our path. My horse needs to rest, and so do you. We have a long journey ahead of us."

"And if I yell the moment we are in a populated village?"

"While we are traveling, I will suggest that you comply with my demands. I would not wish to tell you what would happen if you yelled, but to begin, your reputation would be shattered. If you stay silent, I can at least save your reputation . . . as long as no one on the coach knew your name, and as you were traveling alone, I am assuming you did not wish to share it."

She pressed her lips into a firm line. The comely fiend had guessed correctly and had a point. She would have no choice but to comply until she found a means of escape.

Chapter Two

THE LADY'S HEAD LOLLED BACK onto his shoulder after hours of staying alert in the saddle in front of him. Sir Sebastian sorely regretted taking the lady's funds, along with the lady, but he had been under strict instructions from the Prince Regent not to be exposed in his mission—the political ramifications would be too great.

However, abduction had never been part of the plan. Riding with two to a horse slowed the journey considerably, but he couldn't rightly drop the lady on the side of the road. He was a knight and, as such, a protector . . . despite the fact *he* was the reason she needed protecting. But he had not lied. There were far more dangerous things than a ruined reputation, like leaving an unconscious lady in the same stagecoach as Sir Thomas without funds to see her safely home. And as he couldn't rightly leave her funds intact without raising suspicions of his true objective, the only way this maiden would arrive to her destination unharmed was to bring her himself . . . under the guise of abduction. Not his best idea in his nine and twenty years, but he was committed now.

He paused outside the open gate of a manor along the road to Bristol. Judging from the lack of light flickering in its windows, the staff had retired, along with the owner.

She stirred, her soft moan making him wish he could offer her words of comfort, but seeing as he was her captor, his words would have been fruitless.

Her body tensed, and she shot upright. "W-where are we?"

"Along the road to Bristol." He leaned into the thick Scottish brogue from his grandmother's clan that he used while posing as the highwayman. On the off chance he ever ran into Sir Thomas or others he had to visit on behalf of the Prince Regent, he chose to disguise his voice.

"Bristol! B-but I am to be in Bath." She groaned. "I was nearly there, and now I will be much later returning home."

"Did you not notice my horse deviating from the road to Bath? Or the change of mileposts?"

"I spent most of the journey in the stagecoach behind a book, and as you well know, was unconscious for a time, and heaven knows that I do not possess an internal compass that all you brigands seem to possess. I honestly had no idea where we were heading."

"That would explain your compliant behavior. I was wondering why you did not protest. I aim to make the remainder of our journey far more comfortable." He adjusted in the saddle, and the horse tossed its head. He petted the horse, who released a snort. "Peace, Brigand."

"Brigand? You named your horse *Brigand*?"

"He inspires me."

She snorted. "To be a man loyal only to himself and his horse?"

He glanced down at her, choosing silence over a lie. "You best remain quiet as well."

She mumbled an agreement, crossing her arms against the chill of the night.

They approached the stables, where a single lamp burned low, but no one was present. He crouched in the saddle as they ducked inside. He hopped off and quickly located a navy livery, which seemed like it would fit somewhat, and a worn-looking gig. He dug into his pockets and left enough coin to more than compensate for the items he needed.

She lifted her brows at this but said nothing as he reached up for her. His hands grasped her petite waist, and she obediently slid down. He loosened his grip too soon, and she fell against his chest. She pushed away from him, and he caught sight of a pretty blush creeping up her neck.

He grinned at the bloom in her cheeks, reached for the strap, and removed the saddle, stowing it in the gig before hitching Brigand. He dusted off his hands and reached for the livery. "Avert your gaze, my lady."

Her lips parted, as if ready to ask why, when her eyes landed on the clothes draped over his arm. She swiveled back to the horse. "So that's how you intend to escort me into Bath—Helios?"

"Helios? I would have thought Hermes was more in line with my work."

"With hair like the sun, it fits."

"That is a far sight better than being called Goldie, but I prefer Bash."

"I will call you Bash if you return my things to me."

"Call me Bash and I may return your book." He shoved his leg into the breeches, dressing quickly for fear the owner of the livery might appear at any moment. "In this uniform, I am simply a groom escorting his employer's daughter about town."

"That is not scandalous at all. And your mask? How will you explain that away? It is hardly covert."

"You shall pretend to sleep in the gig while I ride on the horse as a postilion. No one but strangers will see my face. I must change my shirt. Keep your eyes closed," he said from his place in the shadows.

"My eyes never opened after your first warning!" She fairly pressed her face into Brigand's side.

Sebastian replaced his black linen shirt before stuffing the clothing into the saddlebags and packing them next to the saddle in the gig. "It is safe now."

She turned, and he held a hand out to her. "My lady."

"Bash." She allowed him to assist her into the gig, tucking herself into the corner, but as the seat was small, it put little distance between them—a fact he found he enjoyed.

He wasted no time getting them as far from the manor as possible. The gig flew along the road, the moonlight illuminating every divot in the road. They had four hours left in their journey and two hours of moonlight left. Brigand was strong, but they could not make the journey without one stop. He gritted his teeth against the idea of tarnishing her reputation by keeping her out without a guardian, as ludicrous as that worry was at this point, but what other choice did he have? But if she was alone enough to take a public coach, perhaps no one would miss her if he was swift.

The jostling of the wheel awoke her. Vivienne stiffened. She had vowed *not* to actually sleep again, merely rest a moment. She cast a glance at him. In dawn's first rays, she spied his exhaustion in the redness rimming his eyes.

"Where are we?"

"I cannot rightly find us a room to rest while I wear a mask, and as I cannot reveal myself to you for obvious reasons, we shall take shelter here." He drew the gig to the side of the road and into a grove of trees.

She pressed her lips together, swallowing her protest.

The early morning light splayed through the greenery, casting a reverent glow as he directed them into the thick forest. With every turn of the wheel, her hope of escape sputtered. She was not skilled like Tess or strong like Muriel . . . but she was smart. She had to think of a way out of this situation. Despite the fact she had foolishly let her guard down by sleeping, he could not stay awake forever. She would act exhausted and see if he fell asleep, leaving her a chance to run. It wouldn't take much to act fatigued after the past few days.

"This should be far enough from the main road. It would not do for us to be discovered, for neither your reputation nor mine, so we are resting for the day. You will be home before dawn tomorrow, my lady. Now, we rest."

She crossed her arms. He would expect some argument from her over sleeping. "I rested."

"*I* did not." He climbed down.

"Well, you cannot expect me to actually sleep with you nearby and no longer occupied with directing the horse." She clambered off the side of the gig, hopping to the ground. Her shins stung at the drop.

"You do not trust me. I am aware, but we have a long wait ahead of us."

"And you do not think I will escape?" She hoped she wasn't taking her act too far. If she truly worried him, he might tie her up.

He shrugged, unhitching Brigand and releasing him to range free and take a drink from the creek. "I am a light sleeper, and I *know* you are not light on your feet in a forest." He strode away from the gig, leaves crunching underfoot.

She lifted her gaze to the canopy of the lovely forest. If she squinted, she might picture a medieval hero saving his lady love from the evil highwayman. She hid her smile as she stretched her tender back. This next novel would be fairly easy to write, as she could draw from her own life. Her fingers itched for her diary and pencil. "Are you not afraid of being found out in broad daylight?"

"I know these roads better than most travelers do." Bash knelt and gathered wood, building it into a neat pyramid and stuffing the inside with dry leaves. He removed a flint and his blade and methodically scraped it until a spark caught in the underbelly of the stack. He blew on the flame, encouraging the spark to life. He sat back on his heels, watching the fire grow. "We are far enough from the main road that we will not bring curious gazes from bored passengers. We shall appear as a husband and wife taking a reprieve from travel."

Husband and wife? She had long ago determined she would never marry for any reason except for love . . . a preference no one seemed to understand or respect. She had flirted with gentlemen in the past, of course, but never in earnestness after her writing began to sell. Some ladies had the good fortune to be heiresses and therefore had many choices in a husband. She had few, and poor ones at that. After her stepbrother's first few attempts to match her, she'd decided it was up to her to make her own fortune in life, saving her from the humility of a husband who did not love her. Her family had taken matters into their hands after her apathetic response to callers, which was when they'd selected the horrid Sir Josiah, who was worthy due to his rank alone. *Thank the Lord I am spared from that cad.*

She gritted her teeth, forcing her countenance to remain smooth. She had to wait only until Bash fell asleep before she made her move.

He spread out a thin blanket beside the fire. "Would you like to rest on the blanket?"

"I'm fine where I am, thank you." She planted her feet beside the tree trunk. She felt much more secure with her back to the bark and the metal at her thigh that Tess had secured in a leather harness for protection. It had been impossible to get to while atop the horse. If it came to it, she would defend herself at whatever cost. But despite her fears, she knew Bash would not harm her. This handsome thief held a strange code of honor, and she felt more at ease with him than she did in that public coach . . . *Which is why I need to run as soon as the opportunity presents itself.*

He reached into the saddlebags and withdrew a loaf of bread that he cracked in half. She winced at the stale fare. He tossed her a half as he sprawled on the blanket, his hand behind his head.

Even if he was a thief, he possessed a thoughtful heart to feed her. She rapped her knuckles against it. He may as well have handed her a branch to nibble on.

He grimaced as he bit into it. "If you imagine it is toast, it isn't so bad."

She chewed at the edges. "And if you close your eyes, I have no doubt butter would appear on it as well." She laughed and surrendered the endeavor after a few bites that endangered her perfect teeth. She tossed the bread back to him and dusted off her hands. "What enticed you to a life of thieving?"

He tucked the bread back into the bag and returned to relaxing, eyes closed. "I did not start out to thieve. I wished to lead a noble life, one filled with purpose as a knight of the Crown."

If she had been eating, she would have choked. "Yet here you are—a highwayman is about as far as you can get from a knight."

"Here I am. However, I do intend to remain noble." His thick lashes flickered open. "You need not fear on my account. You are safer with me than that Sir Thomas."

"Forgive me if I do not believe you." She had pushed out the words she thought he expected. It had to be the lack of food that was making this highwayman seem more noble than the fleshy, all too inquisitive Sir Thomas.

At a sharp cough, they both started. Three children watched them from the trees. They were clean, but their clothes hung on their thin frames, as if they had not eaten in days. Their eyes widened at his mask.

He slowly rolled to sitting and lifted both his hands. "You have nothing to fear from me," he repeated to them. He reached into his pocket and tossed them each a crown, no doubt from Sir Thomas's purse. "Fetch us four loaves and a hunk of cheese at the village. If you do and remain silent about our presence here, you may keep the remaining amount along with a guinea in my thanks."

They nodded, eagerness and ravenous hunger making their eyes wild as they scampered through the forest to do his bidding.

"You are giving them the money?" Vivienne crossed her arms, her golden braid spilling over one shoulder. "Or are you so cruel as to give them hope and then rob them of it the moment they return? It does not do you well to take advantage of the desperate, even if you are only a common highwayman."

"I am neither cruel nor common. As I told you, I am a man of honor, whether you believe me or not."

"Time will tell. But if you deceive these children, you are deceiving yourself." She slunk down to the base of the tree and closed her eyes, pretending to sleep but waiting for his steady breathing to alert her.

It seemed to take forever until she was confident, judging from his heavy breathing, that he was asleep. She rose, keeping her attention on him all the while. She stepped over the tree roots and bolted into the woods, not caring where it took her, as long as she was away from him. She pumped her arms, her side burning. She stretched her legs, imagining she was at that darling country cottage outside of Bath where no rules of etiquette applied—where she had spent her June months running through the woods or driving her pony cart across the green, as her father cared little for rules regarding what was too boyish for a girl to do while he was yet unmarried and only wanted to let a cottage and fish during the end of the busy season in Bath.

"My lady!"

She bit back a cry and ran faster, her hair pulling loose and drifting behind her in a torrential cloud of tangles. She spied a fallen log in her direct path. She could do it. She sprang and leapt over the log, her foot landing on a curled adder. It hissed, and she couldn't keep her scream inside as it lunged at her, fangs bared, aiming for her calf as a blade flipped through the air and pinned it to the ground.

Bash balanced on the log, panting. He bent and withdrew another knife from his boot and flicked it, ending the threat.

Trembling, she turned her eyes from the blood and lurched back. She twisted to catch herself. Her knee struck a root, the sudden, sharp pain bringing a bout of nausea. She closed her eyes against the stars lining her vision and against the throbbing. She felt herself caught in strong and, oddly, comforting arms.

"It's well. The snake is dead, my lady."

She put pressure on her knee, gasping from the agony. *How on earth am I to escape now?* His hand gripped her elbow. Her lashes fluttered open. The concern in his eyes touched her even though he had been the reason for her running through the woods.

"You're hurt."

"I only need a moment to collect myself and breathe through the pain." She shrugged him off and took a step, stumbling.

"You cannot possibly walk all the way back to camp on an injured knee." He swept her into his arms, the action drawing her arms about his neck. Realizing protesting against her captor turned hero would do little good, she rested her head on his broad shoulder and huffed a bracing breath. *Of course he smells divine even after a race through the woods.* She groaned.

"Does it hurt that bad? You may need to wrap it. I would do it myself, but I think you would consider it a grave impertinence."

"I would indeed, but if you have something I can use, I'll bandage it, because there's a little blood seeping through my once-favorite gown. I fear the only way to save my gown now is to burn it."

He cradled her until they reached the fire, and even then he held her as she trembled, slowly releasing her to rest on the blanket while he rummaged through his bags to retrieve a rolled length of gauze. He tossed it to her, turning his back to her. "You can either rip the bandage with your teeth, or I will cut the ends with my knife, as I cannot trust you with a weapon, given our first conversation."

"I shall see to it." She had no choice but to lift her skirts above her right knee, gritting her teeth against the gash. The root had torn through her stocking, and bits of dirt clung to the wound. She would need to have it cleaned soon, but for now she wrapped the gauze about it, using Tess's knife to slice off the edge. She returned the knife and her gown to rights.

She studied the man's strong back, attempting to put it to memory. The moment she had her journal, she would take down his likeness from all angles. He would be behind bars before spending a copper of her money. But it would be a pity for the handsome, noble thief to rot in some cell. She sighed. He should have thought of that before turning to a life of crime. "You may turn now."

He sank down at the base of a tree and crossed his arms and legs. "As you are unable to hobble away, I shall take this opportunity to sleep."

"And while you sleep, may I entertain myself with writing in my diary?" She widened her eyes, hoping to convey an innocent look. "With my knee injured, you can sleep in peace if I am entertained and, therefore, quiet."

His lips quirked in a half smile. "I shall not deprive a maiden of such an innocent pastime." He reached into his vest and lifted out her precious leather-bound notebook.

Her heart pounded as he flipped it open to the first page. "No! How dare you read my private—"

"'Belonging to Evie.'" He grinned. "At last I may call you anything but 'my lady.'" He brought it over to her with her stub of a pencil. "Write favorably of me, Miss Evie."

"No one calls me that anymore. That was what my father called me." She frowned and snatched them away from him. "To you, I preferred being called 'my lady.'" She flipped her book open to the first blank page and did not wait for him to return to the tree before writing furiously away. The moment he was asleep, she would sketch him. She scribbled, the story taking her away until at last she heard his deepened breathing. She flipped the page and worked on sketching what she imagined to be his fine Grecian nose, followed by a sharp jawline that she was certain he possessed, and his bright eyes. She was just adding the tiny flecks to them when rustling leaves woke him. She snapped the book shut.

The children returned, each carrying something—a loaf, a jug, a wedge of cheese, and some muffins.

He stirred, smiling as he awoke to the fare. "Well done, my friends. What wonderful treats you have brought us." He tossed them each another coin that they caught with grimy hands, their grins spreading.

Her jaw nearly dropped that he kept his word.

"Go with God, and tell no one where you found the gold. Better yet, hide it and take out only a small sum at a time, saving the guinea for last."

They scattered into the woods, as if frightened he would change his mind, and she did not blame them. Bash sat atop her blanket, tore the loaf, and offered her a piece. It was still warm and possessed a lovely crunch when she squeezed it. She inhaled it. She had not eaten since beginning this misadventure.

"Why is no one looking for you?" Bash asked as he cut off a piece of cheese and handed it to her, their fingers brushing.

"Why would you assume that?" She stuffed cheese into her mouth to gain enough time to formulate a question of her own.

"In our time together, you have not spoken of your family." He popped in a bite of cheese. "Or threatened me with a relative seeking revenge on your behalf, or even an offer of a ransom."

Seeing his kindness with the children had shifted something in her heart toward this man. He did follow a code, and he had never touched her in a way that caused her to fear. When he'd saved her from that adder, she had felt wholly safe for the first time in years. The ones who were supposed to love her, protect her, only wanted things from her—massive things, like marrying an unfaithful potato of a man.

For years, she had been her nephews' governess without pay, and now that they were finally old enough to be sent to school, she was no longer of use to the family. The first thing they did was send her a note and present her with an engagement to Sir Josiah, furthering her step-brother's objectives while crippling any hope of escape. Would it be wrong to trust this noble highwayman with the truth? She swallowed her mouthful. What did she have to lose?

"Because I am reckless and desperate."

His brows rose, obviously not expecting her honesty.

"I'm running from a marriage that would only benefit my step-brother."

He blinked, and if she wasn't looking so closely, she might have missed the chastened expression beneath his mask.

"And here I've taken your funds."

"Feeling guilty? I'll happily take my funds back." She flipped open her hand and wiggled her fingers. "With interest for the trouble I've been put through, please."

He laughed. "I can only afford to be honorable in my treatment of you—otherwise, the other highwaymen might take away my club membership to the Highwaymen's Guild."

Chapter Three

BASH PULLED BACK THE RIBBONS as the gig approached the outskirts of Bristol, the moonlight offering a glow upon the town. He shook out his stiff hands and looked to the sweet lady beside him. By chance they were thrown together, and despite his wish to remain focused on his mission, he could not help but be drawn to her.

Perhaps it was the knighthood flowing through his veins that moved him to chivalrous acts. The last knight had been his great-grandfather, but before him, the Larkby name had held the rank of honor and service to the Crown. Bash would see his mission through, and then he would see to it that this woman, who had begun to trust him, was protected.

Evie stirred and, with a gasp, sat up, blinking. "W-why did you stop? Are we not going into the city?" She whipped toward him. "Surely we are not going to take yet another rest in the woods, since I disturbed your sleep?" She rubbed her eyes, groaning. "Despite my best efforts, I keep falling asleep."

He grinned, knowing she was thinking of the spider that had crawled onto her pages and sent her to screaming, waking him. "I need to assume the position atop the horse, where you will not see my unmasked face and no one will suspect a thing of a man in livery driving a lady."

She smirked. "Do you not trust me enough to remove your mask after all we have been through?"

"It is not a matter of trust but of taking proper precautions for your sake as well as mine. If you are questioned, you will not be forced to lie on my account."

Her pretty lips turned down. "And why would I lie to save you?"

He reached out and brushed a curl from her face. "Because you are fond of me, my lady. You just don't know it yet."

She snorted. "Fond of the man who *stole* from me? You may be the most handsome man I have ever encountered, but you are delusional if you think that I hold you in any kind of regard—but I shouldn't be that surprised for a highwayman who claims to hold to a code."

"You think me handsome?"

She blew out her cheeks and crossed her arms. "You're incorrigible. That's what."

He chuckled, hopped out of the gig, and climbed onto Brigand, tugging off his mask and pocketing it. He directed the gig through the streets until he paused at the ramshackle house of a former Yeoman of the Guard. He climbed down, keeping his face averted from her. "Stay here and keep under the blanket."

"Why? Bristol is quite lovely, and I've never witnessed any sort of criminal here, present company excepted."

"We are not in a decent part of the city. Do not move and draw attention to yourself. If anyone bothers you, scream, and I shall come."

"I can take care of myself," she hissed, but out of the corner of his eye, he saw her nestling under the blanket.

He loathed leaving her outside alone at this time of night, but he had to deliver the letters to his most trusted former member of the Yeoman of the Guard, turned barrister, and he could not afford to have her take note of either of their faces.

He pounded on the flimsy plank door. Telford flung it open, glinting blunderbuss in hand, his black hair blending him into the darkness of the room beyond. His eyes widened at the sight of Bash, and he swung the door open, motioning him inside with the flared muzzle of his firearm. Once they had climbed the stairs and shut the second door, Telford broke the silence. "Another clandestine mission, Larkby? You might as well put me back on the payroll for all the help you have been requiring of me. You know I wanted to *retire* from service to the Crown, right?"

"And yet there is no other man I trust more than you."

Telford looped his thumbs in the waistline of his pants, rocking back on his heels. "I'll be sure to tell Wynn you said so. We've had a bet in the book at White's for years over who you considered your closest friend."

He shook his head, chuckling. "That is the most ridiculous wager I have ever heard." He handed the stack of letters to Telford. "See these are placed in the hands of the Prince Regent at once. I will return to my post as soon as I deliver another package."

"Another package?" His brows rose.

"It's in the gig."

Telford moved to the filthy windowpanes, brushing back the thick curtains that could do with a thorough washing. "Does the package happen to come in a lovely form?"

"How do you know? She should be shielded by the roof of the gig."

"Because she is climbing out of the gig and limping away as fast as she can."

Bash swore under his breath and raced down the stairs and out the door. He twisted about, searching for her. She had vanished. A lady alone would not last a single night out in the streets. He drew on his mask and closed his eyes, focusing his hearing. A clatter sounded around the corner. He bolted—daggers drawn and at the ready.

Vivienne stumbled back against the building as two men approached her, the rank contents of their tankards sloshing over their filthy hands due to their uneven gait. She reached for the blade strapped to her thigh. The action caused the men to pause long enough to appreciate her shapely limb, calling out phrases that burned her ears.

She flipped the blade over in her hand as she had seen Tess do on multiple occasions and nearly dropped it. She snatched it in the air and nearly sliced her palm. *So much for appearing foreboding.*

"I love it when they put up a good show," the shorter of the two drawled, his gaze roving over her muddied pelisse and torn hem.

She gripped the knife in both hands, pointing it at the men. "I suggest you leave me. I do not wish to cause either of you harm, but I will not hesitate to stab you should you refuse my safe passage. If you will excuse me, I will not keep you from your cups."

"You hear the tongue on her?" The taller snorted, running his hand down his scraggly beard. "Trying to sound like an educated lady, but what lady would be on our streets in a torn hem that shows so much limb?"

They ambled forward, grinning. She lunged and swiped the blade wildly, slicing the tall man's outstretched forearm.

He growled, dropping his tankard. "The little light-skirts nicked me."

The men's eyes narrowed, their expressions shifting from lust to anger.

The shorter one's maniacal grin flashed in the moonlight. "Seems like she needs a little more learning, and we are the ones to teach her."

Her pulse pounded in her ears, but she kept her stance as Tess had taught her, though the blade trembled in her hand.

Her attackers sprang at her, but instead of her steel meeting flesh, a thunderous roar and a flash of black sent her toppling into the mud. Her highwayman was between her and the lecherous men. He slashed his daggers at the men, slicing one in the shoulder and the other across the chest. The two pounced on him, and Bash was forced to drop a blade as he blocked a blow with his palm and struck the other across the jaw. She scrambled for his dropped dagger. She held it and her blade, which now looked ludicrously trivial compared to the heavy dagger.

The men pressed atop Bash, blocking his face from view. She started to run for help, but with the two on Bash, he might be overtaken. She gritted her teeth and aimed for the nearest fiend's broad back. She flung Bash's dagger as she had seen Tess do, and to her shock, it stuck in the man's calf. He howled. The injury was just what Bash needed to shove him off and deliver the blow that knocked the uninjured man out. The injured one clutched his leg as Bash brought down the hilt of his dirk to the back of the man's head. Bash turned to her, shoulders heaving as he wiped the blood trailing down his forehead.

Her knees weakened. If it hadn't been for Bash, God only knew what would have happened to her.

"Evie?" He held out his palm to her, keeping a wary eye on the men.

A sob caught in her throat as she wobbled toward him. He caught her about the waist, catching her dagger as it slipped from her grasp.

"Did they hurt you?" His voice was rough with what sounded like suppressed anger.

"You saved me. You could have let me fend for myself and you chose to save me, no matter the harm to yourself." No one had done that since her father died. No one had protected her like this highwayman had. Tears trailed down her cheeks.

As if of their own accord, her arms stole up his chest, her fingers grazing the side of his jaw before her hands wrapped about his neck and pulled him down to her, drawing him into a kiss that carried her away from the alley, from the stench of her fiancé, to a place filled with light and hope and . . . he didn't push her away as she half expected but held perfectly still, as if in shock.

What in heavens name was she doing? She was as bad as Muriel! No, worse. Muriel just proposed to a man and here she was kissing one that was not her intended and never could be! *And you're still kissing him!* She broke the kiss, her world spinning. *Not again!* She sank toward the mud. *My poor silk pelisse.* The last thing she heard was Bash calling out her name as his arms tightened about her. It sounded so lovely coming from his lips.

"Evie!"

The two cowards stirred as Bash held the limp Evie in his arms. He gritted his teeth as he laid her in the mud and lifted his remaining dagger to the men, gliding his feet into a ready stance. They had murder in their eyes as the one with the knife in his calf wrenched it out and tossed it to his partner.

"I wouldn't do that if I were you." Telford said, aiming his blunderbuss at the men.

"Took you long enough!" Bash chided Telford, glancing back at Evie. He needed to get to her, but he didn't dare turn the dagger away from the brutes until he was certain Telford had them under control.

"Had to find my boots. I'll see them to jail while you complete your mission. If they run, they will see the damage my rifle can do." He gestured with the barrel. "Put your hands where I can see them, good fellows, before my trigger finger slips and one of you loses a limb."

The men lifted their hands above their head, one dropping the bloodied dagger.

"That's better." Telford stepped around them, keeping the gun trained on the men while guiding them toward the jailhouse. He called over his shoulder, "Your package is stirring, by the way."

Bash closed the distance between Evie and himself. "Evie? Are you well?" He knelt beside her, gathering her into his arms. "Did they hurt you?"

Her lashes fluttered, and then she sagged into him in a faint once more.

He examined her arms, neck, and anything visible. Her gown was not torn in any fresh places, merely muddy. He lifted her into his arms, her form limp. He raced back to the gig and tucked her inside with the blanket over her, slapping the reins. He needed to get them as far away as possible from Somersetshire before anyone asked why a man in a livery costume was seated beside his unconscious employer and was driving like the devil himself was at his heels.

He paused at the edge of town and twisted in his seat to face her. He checked his mask and gently stroked her arm. She didn't stir, so he grasped her shoulders in his hands and shook her. Her head listed to the side. "What on earth is amiss? Why won't you awaken?" He grasped her delicate face between his hands. Her full lips spoke of the sweetness of the lady and, after that world-shaking kiss, of her tender heart as well.

He brushed back her golden locks. "My lady, I beg you to awaken." The pale hue of her skin made his heart pound in dread. Her pulse was faint, her fingers chilled, and her chest hardly moving. "Evie?" He leaned forward, pressing his forehead to hers, offering her all his strength and warmth. She was too still.

How did one wake a lady from a faint without salts? He raked his fingers through his hair. *How did knights in the past wake a sleeping beauty?* He'd heard that kissing stopped hysteria . . . Would it do the trick? A kiss had sent her into the swoon . . . would it get her out? He would be lying if he said he did not wish to kiss her once more. But he was a knight and a man of character, and he held himself to the highest of standards. He shook his head. *Kissing is the solution of fairy tales— and poorly written ones at that.* If she did not wake soon, he would need to consult a doctor, and he couldn't wear a mask for that. His entire mission would be at stake, and the Prince Regent would not save Bash, or his title, if he was discovered.

He tried gently shaking her again, silently begging her to wake, to no avail. "Forgive me, my lady, but I see no other course but to try to shock you awake." He reached for his canteen and dumped the entirety of its water on her head.

"Oh!" She gasped, sputtering as she jerked upright. "W-what was that for?"

He gritted his teeth against the admission. "You were unconscious. I couldn't wake you, and I—"

"And you thought *dumping* water on me would be the best course of action?" Her voice rose an octave.

"It was a better idea than kissing you awake. It seems to have done the trick." He ran his hand over the back of his neck. "My sincere apologies for the forwardness, but you did not have any smelling salts in that reticule and—"

"But nothing." She crossed her arms, her cheeks puffing. "I think I would have preferred kissing you again to being drenched and potentially catching a cold from all of your bright ideas."

"So you dream of kissing me again, do you?"

Her cheeks flamed even in the moonlight, and he felt a pang at teasing her over the lovely kiss.

"I-I did *not* say that. Besides, I never carry smelling salts, as I take pride in the fact that I never faint . . . or rather, I *did* take pride in that. Since meeting you, I've swooned twice in two days."

He crossed his arms. "I'm beginning to doubt your word on the matter."

"It's the truth. And my fainting never would have happened if you hadn't had the audacity to take me in the first place," she shot back.

He bowed his head. "Again, I extend my sincerest apologies for the inconvenience. Please be assured that I tried everything I could think of to rouse you, and I feared you may have been concussed. I did not wish to bring you to a doctor until I had exhausted the possibility of waking you by other means. It would have meant revealing my true identity."

She snorted. "Some highwayman of *honor* you are. You would rather keep your identity secret than to see to my welfare?"

Where was all the tenderness of only moments before? "I may be a man with a code of honor, but I am no fool. Besides, you would not have fainted again if you had listened to me in the first place and stayed put inside the gig." The moment the retort exited his mouth, he knew it was incorrect.

"Because *you* abducted me."

"True." It was *all* his fault. He was desperate to right the wrong, but as the highwayman, he had to protect his true identity or lose everything. It was all so muddled now. The plan had seemed simple at the time.

"Honestly, Bash, have you never taken someone against their will before? It would be unnatural for a lady *not* to run away." She huffed, sending a curl spiraling away from her forehead.

"I have never taken a lady before and pray I never will have to again, given all the trouble you have put me through. You almost had me killed when my objective in Somersetshire was supposed to be straightforward."

She frowned. "Not that I concede that any of this is my fault, as I did not create this situation, but because of your actions, it is good for you that I, beyond reason, trust your word—a fact that should see me in Bedlam should anyone hear of our adventures and of my kissing my abductor in a moment of weakness. Were you successful in your . . . objective? Or shall we call it what it really was—a handoff?"

"My part is finished, and I am free to see to your needs now." He gathered the reins.

"Good." She brushed at the mud caking her pelisse. "Put me on the next stagecoach to Bath. There is no need for you to return me to Bath."

"In your current state? No, it is not safe, especially as not all highwaymen are as gallant as I."

"As you have stated before." She pressed her lips into a line. "However, I am not eager to give you my address."

"I fear I have no other option of seeing you safely home. I will not abandon you in the city after this night, and those cads nearly put their hands on you."

"But is it wise to give you my address?" She eyed him. "I fear you will rob me the moment I open the door to my home."

"I give you my word that I shall not." He placed his hand over his heart. "You said you trusted me—after saving your life, I might add, yes?"

"I'm a fool, but yes. Take me to the Circus terrace homes."

He released a whistle as she mumbled the house number. "Fancy."

"Do not crow until you see it." She motioned to his mask. "Are you going to wear that the whole way?"

"If I do not, will you promise not to fall in love with me? I'm considered quite dashing."

"I see you have been gifted with great modesty as well."

He grinned. "At the very least, promise you will not have me arrested?"

She rolled her eyes. "Would you believe me if I did promise?"

He chuckled and slapped the ribbons. "It was worth asking. We shall be to your townhouse before sunrise, my lady. Try to rest. After your fright, I do not think it will be difficult."

The pair rode in silence until they reached the outside of the city of Bath, where Bash dismounted, removed his mask, and rode on Brigand with Evie in the gig, as he had in Somersetshire. He directed the horse into the city, glaring at anyone who dared to look too long at Evie. The streets were not busy, but as some parties yet continued, the risk of Evie being recognized pressed on him. He'd ruin her fragile reputation if he did not make haste.

He halted his mount before the impressive terrace home that bore no flickering lights in any of the windows. He kept his face averted as he dismounted and held the reins, facing the grove of trees in the center of the Circus even though he longed to look upon her as they parted . . . but the risk of her seeing his face was too great. "Unfortunately, my lady, our time together is at an end."

"So it is."

She seemed to be waiting for something—an apology? "I do not enjoy stealing from women. My sincerest apologies for robbing you, my lady."

"Sincere enough for you to return my funds?" The gig shook in her attempts to gingerly dismount, and she grunted at the jostling.

His body pushed him to aid her, but with all the flickering lamplights, he could not risk being seen without his mask. He planted his feet and dared to glance over Brigand and caught her running her hand over her skirts, whacking away at the mud caking them. "Not quite." He looked away as she crossed her arms and glared at him from the sidewalk.

"What of my beaded reticule? I doubt a lady's emptied purse holds interest for you."

"I consider that reticule a treasure," he teased. He reached into his livery coat pocket and tossed her the small reticule over the horse's back. "But if that is what it takes, consider us even."

"Hardly." She retrieved the key from her necklace, limped up the steps, and fitted the key to the door. She smiled over her shoulder at him and opened the door. No servants awaited her, it seemed, but from the dim light of the flickering streetlamp, he spied a pile of trunks at the foot of the stairs. She glanced back at him, and he shielded his face with his shoulder.

"You can hide your face from me now, but know that I will find you, Bash."

He dared to peer around Brigand's mane, keeping his hat pulled low to shadow his features. "You are most welcome to try, my lady, but as I said, I am quite good at hiding unless I wish to be found."

"Believe me, we shall see each other again, as I will see to it that you pay for your crimes . . . one way or another." She closed the door between them.

"And after that kiss you bestowed upon me, I most heartily wish to find you once more," he whispered. "But duty is waiting." He sighed, stripped off the livery coat, and slipped into his black coat before snapping the reins and vanishing into the night.

Chapter Four

SHE SHOT THE BOLT OF the front door and leaned against it with a sigh, clutching the diary that was nearly complete. Her stomach churned at the thought of how close she'd come to losing it. But even if she had, she'd never forget Bash the highwayman. She had never been a swoony type, but if she were, she might swoon over Bash. *That kiss.* Oh, that kiss was so different than she'd ever imagined kissing to be. She would have to revisit her current work in progress and revise the couple's first kiss—she had no idea that one could leave their body whilst kissing. She lifted her fingers to her lips, feeling the gentle pressure yet.

She moved to the sidelight, watching him watch her house. His hat cast a shadow across his face. She *should* provide a sketch of what he looked like for the authorities, but it would take time . . . given she had not actually seen his face. The one she had created in the woods had taken too dreamy a turn to share. Her heart sank. Must she turn him in? He hadn't caused anyone physical harm . . . and he had protected her from those horrid drunkards and even saw her home. *But he did take my money, and I wouldn't have been in the position of needing saving if it wasn't for him abducting me.* Yes, abduction and thieving were the thoughts she needed to keep close when she marched to the authorities . . . later. She rubbed her eyes and groaned at the thought of her lost funds. In desperate hope, she tugged the strings of her reticule. Her funds were gone, but Bash had left her that horrid letter from her stepbrother.

She would have to dip into her meager savings. She had only enough to pay for food. With Bash taking the money she had hoped to use to hire a maid, she feared her dream of supporting herself was in peril. If she did not severely retrench the financial aspect of her best laid plans, she might have to lease the house to perfect strangers.

Her father had received multiple offers for selling the home after his marriage to Mrs. Hart, but because of Vivienne's begging, he had kept the property as a secured inheritance for her. She had made it clear that she would much rather own the lovely building than to hand over her money to a future husband, and besides, she doubted the money would have made it to her pockets if he did sell it. Her stepbrother did not take kindly to her having anything he considered family money. She was, and always would be, the outsider in his relations. To explain away the royalties from her novels, she claimed to have rented out the apartment in Bath to Lady Larkby, her nom de plume. It was only because of Mrs. Hart that Lucius did not try to take the funds from Vivienne, but with each passing year since Mrs. Hart's death, Vivienne knew it was only a matter of time before he demanded the funds be given to him.

Not for the first time did she wish her situation had been a mirror of Muriel's. While Vivienne possessed good birth, she did not have the true riches of earth—a loving family. Her father had been everything to her, and the moment he'd died, her world had shifted. She had gone from beloved daughter to burdensome stepsister and stepdaughter. She unfolded the letter from Lucius Hart, as she had done whenever her resolve to leave her life in Chilham wavered.

This time she crumpled it in her fist. She'd never give in to his demand that she marry Sir Josiah. Her stepbrother couldn't make her, no matter what his waspish wife demanded of her. It was fortunate Lucius had no idea where she was, given she had used her secret nom de plume for the whole of her flight. She had her pen and her father's terrace home to provide her with a good life. What else did she need? Not her family. She tossed the note to the marble floor.

She was more than another mouth to feed or a body to clothe. Despite what her stepfamily thought of her, she would prove that she could make her own fortune—*without* the husband they had carelessly selected for her. Pedigree was all they desired to further their place in society. The man's character was not important enough to even warrant a discussion. When she had delicately mentioned Sir Josiah's ladybird in Dover, she'd been met with dismissal and scoffs at her naivete.

She shook the morose thoughts from her head. "It will not do to dwell upon the past. And at least I am here and whole, with a story provided by the very man who stole from me." The ordeal had been terrible, but she couldn't help but delight in the story she'd write. She dared to peek through the sidelights once more to catch a glimpse of the handsome muse. *Gone.* She shivered, feeling the void of his protection—as ludicrous as it was to feel protected by a highwayman. She should check the servants' entrance and make certain it had been locked again after Muriel's staff had delivered her trunks and cleaned her home.

She eyed her surroundings. A taper sat on the foyer table with matches beside it. She struck it, lighting the wick. She shielded the flame and darted down the hall to the servants' entrance. She stumbled a bit as the wood floors turned to brick, and at last she found the rear entrance and tried the doorknob. *Locked.* Her breathing settled into a less frantic pace as she strode back to the marble foyer to her row of trunks.

She hadn't even thought to ask the deliverymen to bring them upstairs. She would have to unpack each item and climb the stairs with as much as she could carry in one arm. Then, she might drag the mostly empty trunks up as well. She groaned at the feat that seemed nigh impossible given her knee. The scullery maid should be arriving in a week or so, as well as a part-time cook, but that seemed too great an extravagance now. She would have accepted Muriel's offer for staff, but her pride did not allow it—not when she had already accepted her friend's offer of having the terrace home cleaned. Vivienne stared at the staircase. "And we all know how much pride aids a breaking back."

She had best get started now. If she flagged, she'd use her pride to bolster her injured knee. "The most important of belongings first." She flung open her trunk of books and removed her little travel writing desk, her heart speeding at the worn wood. Every time she held it, she felt close to her father. No matter the years between the last time she had held her father's hand or sat at his feet as he'd penned his correspondence, she could still hear his soothing voice as the nib scratched across the parchment. She hugged it to her chest. "To be home again does my heart good, Father."

She brought her treasure to the small sitting room with a pleasant window that had a splendid view of the Circus. She would write her musings while looking out onto the street. Strangers always made for fascinating muses. She crossed the hall to her father's library, peeking in through the open door. At the tomes lining the shelves, happy memories flooded her being. However, she dare not linger in her fatigued state, lest she give way to the tears she had been holding back since the moment she'd entered this dear house where her father's touch appeared at every turn.

Flinging open the lid of the second trunk, she gathered her paper-wrapped clothing in one arm while balancing the taper and her hem in the other, and then she slowly climbed the steps to the first floor, which held the master suite with the adjoining rooms. Vivienne did not remember her father ever sleeping here. He chose instead to give the master suite to Vivienne as her bedroom and the adjoining one for her governess and her nursemaid. He had taken residence in the larger of the two guest rooms on the second floor. At least she wouldn't need to face Father's room yet.

She opened her childhood bedroom, with its pretty papered walls and the canopy bed that called to her. She set the clothing on the coverlet and swiped her finger over the bedding, sighing in relief that everything had been laundered. How delightful it would be to fall asleep on a feather bed. But sleep would have to wait until the trunks on the ground floor were unpacked and her own gown changed after she lugged up fresh water from the kitchen for a sponge bath. The tasks before her had her head spinning.

Your pride saw your funds taken and no staff awaiting you. Your pride shall have to provide the means of getting your things in place. She pulled back the curtains to let in the dawn's light and, setting down the taper, cracked her knuckles. It was time to make her house a home once more, or as much as her knee would allow. A nap and then writing would be her reward. And with said writing, she would allow herself to dwell on that kiss once more—for research purposes, of course. Once she regained the full use of her mind over her heart, she would have to see the constable to report the handsome highwayman. *Such a pity.*

After abandoning the gig on the outskirts of Bath near a questionable stable, along with a penciled note, torn from his little leather notebook stashed in his saddlebags, that stated to which manor the gig belonged, Bash tugged on his black riding breeches once more, trusting the color to shield him from all until he returned to his apartment. He rode hard for hours. In the unlikely event he was followed, he bypassed the road where he'd robbed the stagecoach and put a few villages between them for good measure.

The stolen funds pressed against his calf inside his Hessian boots. He knew too well the peril of traveling with such heavy funds in his purse—even a highwayman could be robbed. Bash planned to donate it to the church as usual, but he had no time to stop, as his shift as Yeoman of the Guard was slotted for the morrow's eve. He would have to donate the funds later.

Despite the pangs of guilt that plagued him for robbing Evie, he looked forward to hearing the Prince Regent's relief for the return of the letters. For generations, the men in Bash's family had served the Crown, but only a few had been granted the knighthood like Bash— revitalizing the old title of *Sir* Sebastian Larkby of Lark Manor. Years of serving the Prince Regent and going on covert missions such as this had earned him the title—one he risked every time he donned the mask on behalf of the Prince Regent. For if he was caught, the Prince Regent would not be pulled down into the mess.

He rode until he grew stiff in the saddle. He took a few breaks for

Brigand's sake but pressed on until the sun began its descent. Eager for a cot after the trial it had been to retrieve the letters, he turned his mount into The Blue Fox, a rather ramshackle country tavern that boasted of rooms to rent for the night.

He dismounted in the yard as a hen darted across, squawking at the dog nipping at her feathers. Bash was rubbing Brigand's mane when a rail-thin boy with a shock of black hair appeared in the stable doorway.

"Do you need your horse boarded, mister?"

"For the night and a good rubdown, as well as oats." Bash released Brigand to the stable boy and tossed the lad a shilling, a small price to keep pickthanks at bay. "For your silence. What's your name, boy?"

"Yes, sir. Thank you, sir. Name is Noah, sir." The boy bobbed his head and stuffed the shilling into his pocket before leading the massive stallion into the stall for some much-deserved care. The boy glanced over his shoulder thrice, as if afraid Bash would change his mind and demand the tip be returned.

Bash shoved open the heavy plank door. The scent of meat stew hit him first, closely followed by the stench of copious spirits and unwashed bodies. His eyes adjusted to the dimly lit tavern. A few patrons were clustered around a table over a game of cards beside the fire. All looked up at his arrival, then quickly shifted their attention back to their cards. Bash was well aware of the dangerous figure he cut. He commanded respect first by his appearance and second by his fist.

He approached the stout man behind the bar. "Lodgings for the night and a tray sent up to my room." He slid a coin to the innkeeper.

The man bit the gold piece, revealing a missing canine and rotting teeth. With a satisfied harrumph, he fished out a tin box from under the counter, found the key, and tossed it to Bash. "First floor. Second door on right."

Bash climbed the creaking stairs and swung open the plank door. He tossed his hat on the back of a lone chair in the corner, which also served as the stand for the chipped water basin. He tugged off his boots and, stuffing the funds into his waistline, sank atop the rope bed, pulling the filthy blanket over his head. The stench from under the bed made his eyes water, and he wondered when was the last time the chamber pot had been given a scrubbing or even been emptied.

A gentle knock at the door pulled him from the bed, and the same lad from the stable stood there with a tray balanced between his filthy hands. *Mucking stalls and serving guests?* They were working this young man to skin and bone. He nodded his thanks and closed the door without a word. He made quick work of the stew and drained the stale water. He stowed the loaf of bread in his saddlebags and crawled into bed.

The clattering of pots being scrubbed downstairs awoke him. Bash squinted in the sunrise splaying through the dust-coated window-panes and groaned. It was far later than he had anticipated. He had a long journey ahead of him to reach the Prince Regent by nightfall. He swung his feet to the floor, scratching behind his ear as he did so. He stumbled to the washbasin, splashed murky water from the pitcher to his face, and ran water through his golden hair. The itching in his scalp did not relent. *Oh no.* He gritted his teeth against the realization. He glanced at the filthy bed and groaned.

The Prince Regent would not allow Bash near if lice were anywhere on his person, not with the Prince Regent's fine wardrobe and own hair at risk. Bash sighed and reached for his knife. *You are a Yeoman of the Guard, not some foppish dandy. Best to do it sooner rather than later.* He flipped the knife in his hand and gripped the worn handle, slicing off a handful of hair at a time until he'd cropped it as close to his scalp as possible, where no louse could hide. If he kept scratching, he'd risk sores that might get infected, keeping him from his work.

He made quick work of devesting himself of the fiends, tossing his shorn locks into the chamber pot. He scrubbed his head and what little remained of his hair in the basin of water. Satisfied the lice had not made their way into his spare set of clothing, he dressed.

Despite the familiar attire, his shorn locks were not something easily disguised. He did not need unnecessary questions regarding his appearance. He looked out the window. He could manage it. He tossed out his saddlebags, crawled out and gripped the sill, and, stretching out his body, dropped to the ground, rolling on his shoulder to his feet to break his fall. He trotted across the yard to the stable.

The stable boy was asleep in a mound of hay in Brigand's stall, brush in hand, as if he had fallen asleep as soon as he had taken care of the horse. In the night, Bash had thought Noah was thin, but in the daylight he looked akin to starving. Bash reached into his boot and from the purse withdrew a sovereign. He knelt and set it in the boy's palm.

His eyes flashed open, arm lifting as if to block a strike. "No!"

Bash dropped back to his heel and lifted his hands. "Never fear. Check your palm."

Noah's jaw dropped at the coin, his fingers trembling. "I-I didn't take it. I swear—"

"It's a gift for looking after my horse. His coat is shining."

His eyes welled. "I've never had so much in my life. Probably won't have it for long once the innkeeper finds out, but I thank you, sir." He moved to saddle Brigand.

Bash frowned at this bit of news. "The innkeeper takes your funds?"

The boy hefted the saddle over the horse's pad, giving Bash a second look, betraying that he'd noticed Bash's shorn locks. "Says I eat more than I should and I owe him that much."

Bash's brows shot up. "I would venture a guess that you do *not* eat much. Does he beat you if you do not give any tips to him?"

Noah frowned and tightened the girth, his silence telling Bash all he needed to know.

"Do you know how to get to Bath?"

The boy narrowed his gaze. "Why?"

Bash shouldn't allow himself to be distracted by anything other than his work for the Crown—and to have a boy remember him was dangerous. *But he never saw your mask. He may think you are only a traveler.* "There is a lady along the River Avon at Lark Manor who needs a stable hand. Tell her that her grandson sent you, and you shall be taken care of."

"Y-yes, sir. Thank you, sir."

Bash reached into his saddlebag and broke the loaf in half, tossing a hunk to the lad, then finished readying Brigand. "Leave on foot now, and you should be there by night if you set a good pace. Keep your sovereign in your boot until you can spend it on food in Wells." He mounted and drew on his hat.

"God bless you, sir."

"Make haste and God be with you, Noah." He nodded to the boy and charged out of the stable.

Chapter Five

THE INCESSANT RINGING IN HER ears would not end. Vivienne snapped her head up from the desk, wincing at the scrawled diagonal line across the page that she must have scratched as she fell asleep. Paired with the drying puddle of drool, she would have to copy the entire page again. She rubbed the sleep from her eyes and collected the pages into a neat stack, keeping the spoiled page out.

The ringing was back. *A visitor? Where are the servants?* She groaned at the realization that *she* was the servant for now. She checked the clock above the mantel that, of course, was not working. It was, no doubt, calling hours, but she had been in Bath for nearly a week and had no visitors to show for it . . . Of course, the home hardly seemed in use, as she was alone. It was only because of Muriel's thoughtfulness in stocking the larder that Vivienne had not had to venture out to market alone yet—something she felt wholly unprepared for but that was inevitable. She trotted down the stairs, her hair flowing to her waist after she'd relieved all the pins from her chignon early this morning while writing a particularly trying scene.

She flung open the door to find a footman in the navy-and-gold livery of Draycott Castle, holding an overlarge hamper as he stood beside the carriage. Turning from an unmarked carriage with a basket on her arm was Muriel's abigail and friend.

"Charlotte Vale?" Vivienne gasped in delight, clasping her hands before her skirts. "How wonderful to see you! What on earth are you doing here?" She peered over the woman's shoulder, searching for Muriel.

Charlotte laughed and cast a glance to either side. Finding no neighbors or servants nearby, she answered, "The duchess knew you would never agree to her supplying a little help for your townhouse, but she insisted, as it would be helping *me* out also to come to you in Bath, as well as Brexton." She nodded to the footman, still balancing the hamper.

"Oh?" Vivienne was no duchess, this was no castle, and there was nothing she could offer this sweet maid that Muriel could not. "Is Muriel making a cake out of mud pie and being overly kind in what I can offer?"

Charlotte smiled. "Not this time. I'm to be your companion. If you agree?"

"If I agree?" she echoed. She grasped Charlotte's hand. Having Charlotte as a companion would be a pleasure, and it would indeed improve the former maid's position. She would find some way to pay Charlotte and Brexton—perhaps she should finally agree to write that serialized story for the *Bath Chronicle*. She would send a note at once to accept. "I would be most honored to have you as my companion in my new home, dear Charlotte."

"Thank you, Miss Poppy." Charlotte motioned for the footman to come closer.

"And, Brexton, what did our duchess offer you to entice you to come to Bath?" Vivienne nodded her greeting.

He grinned. "My sweetheart is in Bath. I was happy to join your household to be near her, if you are in agreement?"

"Most heartily. Anything I can do for young love."

He nodded his thanks and, at her gesture, disappeared into the house as the driver unloaded the trunks attached at the rear of the carriage.

"I will also see to dressing your hair should you have need." She eyed Vivienne's wild mane and sucked in a breath through her teeth. "Which I believe you do. Are those bits of branches in your hair?"

Vivienne gritted her teeth. "I thought I got them all out. Honestly, my hair has been impossible to manage for the past week, so I've been wearing it in a bun most of the time."

"I'm almost afraid to ask how it came to pass that you have nature in your hair, but seeing as you are the duchess's closest friend, I shouldn't be surprised to see you follow her grace's tendency for mischief." Charlotte giggled. "Let's get you inside before word spreads that Lady Larkby prefers to wear her hair down and wrinkled gowns while sporting ink on her fingers."

"I wasn't able to do much on my own, but give me time and Lady Larkby shall make her first appearance at the pump rooms." Vivienne glanced down at her poplin. It was a sight, but it was far better than her spoiled traveling gown of blue and the once-darling pink pelisse that now wasn't fit enough for the charity basket. It was still in a heap in the basin in the kitchen, where she had been soaking it . . . for days. The mud would not be scrubbed away. She worried her bottom lip thinking of her spotted poplin cream gown. It was fashionable enough for a Chilham maiden, but the country ball gowns she had in her dressing room would hardly be worth notice.

"Perhaps we should do a bit of shopping on Cheap Street and breathe some fresh pieces into my wanting wardrobe?" Her stomach twisted at the thought of how much she would need to spend for a wardrobe befitting a noblewoman. She should have considered that when selecting her nom de plume. At the time, she'd thought the title lent her an air of mystery and romance.

"Actually, the duchess saw to that." Charlotte grinned as Brexton slid past them. She gestured to the trunks the footman began toting into the house, lining them along the wall near the stairs. "The two larger trunks I brought with me are for you." Charlotte nudged her into the foyer. "Did you not suspect when we brought four? The medium is mine, and the small is Brexton's."

Vivienne laughed. "I thought they were yours. Muriel is too generous."

"She's always been so." Charlotte lifted a lock of Vivienne's hair. "Shall I see to your hair while you have something to eat and a cup of tea? I've been thinking of hot tea and scones for the whole of the journey."

"I have no one to ring for food in the kitchen and was not able to find the tea leaves."

She lifted the basket on her arm. "The duchess baked your favorite just before I left, and I've brought a tin of my favorite tea leaves. As for the making of the tea, we shall take care of it." Charlotte laughed and passed along the need to the footman before following Vivienne upstairs and seating her at the dressing table. She then removed a napkin piled with scones.

Vivienne inhaled the vanilla treats. "Our baker duchess is a saint. How are she and her new husband faring?"

"That is partly why she sent me." Charlotte pushed half of Vivienne's hair to the side, dipped the comb into the basin of water, and then began to work with the less tangled section. "She and his grace are going on a holiday in his ship, but he did not say where as it was a surprise. She thought that, as I do not enjoy sailing, I might look after you in her absence and obtain some experience as a companion, as she has long known that secret desire of my heart."

Vivienne shook her head. "Our mischievous Muriel looking after us both in the kindest way possible."

Charlotte's gaze fluttered to a crumpled note on the floor beside Vivienne's untouched bed. "Are your characters eluding you again?"

"That's the missive from my stepbrother in Chilham. After a particularly trying journey to Bath and arriving to an empty house, I needed to read it yet again to refresh my memory. The state of the note is due to my memory having been sufficiently refreshed."

"And the state of the bed?"

"My memory being refreshed allowed me to realize that I need to work harder to earn my living. I cannot afford to let a single day pass without writing—besides Sunday, of course." She shook her head. "But I must confess that during the most trying of services, my mind does tend to wander to storylines."

Charlotte finished combing both sections and then pulled the back half of Vivienne's hair into a top knot. "The duchess said your stepbrother promised your hand to that blackguard Sir Josiah Montgomery." She grimaced. She knew full well of the duchess's former fiancé's inclinations toward ladybirds. "Does your stepbrother care so little for your happiness that he would have the banns read in church on Sunday against your will?"

Vivienne gritted her teeth at the news, fighting back her rising anxiety. She was thankful she had not suffered an attack of anxiety during her ordeal, but *his* name was worse than any highwayman.

Charlotte clasped her hand. "Did you not know?"

She shook her head and squeezed Charlotte's hand as she drew in a bracing breath, counting to ten. *Lord, help me to trust You to keep me safe.* "I-I do not know why Lucius dislikes me. Perhaps it was because his mother remarried. But if it hadn't been my father, the widow Hart would have married someone else. She was not meant to be alone. But it seems that all my stepbrother cares about is putting me in my place and reminding me that I am the unwanted stepsister he inherited by his mother's demeaning marriage. So yes, he is determined to see me unhappy, which is why he had the banns read without even asking me."

Charlotte expertly plaited the front of Vivienne's hair, taking time to weave in a gold cord to make her hair shimmer before she looped the braids back and tucked them neatly into the bun.

Brexton knocked on the open door, keeping his gaze firmly on the tray of tea he gripped. Charlotte took the tray with a nod of thanks and Brexton shut the door. She made quick work of pouring them each a cup. "What if we find another match for you while you are here in Bath and, therefore, cut all ties with your stepbrother?"

"Finding a husband after the banns have already begun for my match with Sir Josiah? Not likely." She blew out her cheeks and accepted the cup. "No, this calls for something more drastic than finding a husband." She glanced at Charlotte. "No offense to our dear duchess, but she was seeking a good match. I am seeking freedom."

Charlotte finished pinning Vivienne's hair into place and took a sip of her tea. "None taken. I do realize that not everyone is fortunate enough to find a handsome privateer turned duke for a husband as our Muriel Beau. What is your plan?"

"I shall remain the enigmatic Lady Larkby and stay single all my days to keep my secret safe."

"But weren't you raised in Bath until your father's remarriage? Won't people recognize you as Vivienne Poppy?"

"It's been more than a dozen years since I've lived here. Since then I've grown a foot and have learned a thing or two about fashion, along with having help arranging my wiry curls. There should be precious little resemblance left."

"Very good. And with your identity concealed, your living is secured and Sir Josiah will not be allowed to succeed in entrapping you in a loveless marriage."

"Correct." Vivienne reached for another of Muriel's perfect scones and handed it to Charlotte. "The last time Tess, Muriel, and I planned something this drastic, it ended quite successfully. And now that I have you, I have no doubt that the four of us can see this plan to a victorious end. As the latest member of our friendship society, I shall defer to you on our first order of business."

Charlotte broke off a corner of the scone. "I believe our plan should begin with a trip to the Pump Room to stir curiosity from your readers, which I think will help the sales of your newest novel."

Vivienne laughed and dusted her fingers free from the sugar. "To the Pump Room!"

A thump outside the door followed by a knock saw Brexton with a pile of trunks behind him.

"Perfect timing, Brexton." Charlotte smiled up at him.

Vivienne caught the spark in the footman's eyes at Charlotte's praise, but she did not press her yet. She had time enough to discover if a romance was brewing, with his mention of a sweetheart in Bath. Together, the ladies readied themselves, which took longer than they would have wished, but it was diverting to sort through all that Muriel had sent, which ranged from sweet morning gowns to a masquerade costume, all in Vivienne's tastes.

Charlotte cooed over the costume and sighed. "Heaven help me if we actually attend a masque . . . My costume is, to put it delicately, hideous, but as I didn't want to spend my money on it and refused to allow Muriel to purchase a new one, Tess was kind enough to offer me an old mask of hers."

"They truly are the kindest of friends." She had never felt so seen as she had with her dear friends, and this wardrobe was proof that Muriel knew her better than anyone else. Though Muriel had not been raised in high society, they'd been friends since girlhood. Muriel now was well aware of all that was required from the ton . . . a hard-won lesson, and Vivienne hoped to avoid a few lessons of her own.

In the end, she decided upon a lovely white muslin with a single ruffle on the collar, paired with a striking sapphire spencer with a white collar and lapels. Charlotte assured her the result was simple but elegant when paired with the sapphire parasol and silk-trimmed bonnet with its white plume and her gold earrings with the golden pearl centers.

By the time they strolled through the Pump Room door, they were both eager for a cup of the curative waters. The spacious Grand Pump Room hummed with conversations beneath a high-domed ceiling supported by decorative Corinthian columns. A line of people awaited to take the waters in one corner of the room, where two servers handed out glasses of the warm mineral water from the fountain. An orchestra played softly in another corner, adding to the opulence of the gathering. At the end of the hall stood the statue of Beau Nash, the hall's first master of ceremonies, with guests milling beneath him. It was as stunning as Vivienne remembered from her visits here as a small child with her father before he had wed again.

It had been such a happy time. Vivienne's father believed quite differently than other parents. He wished to have his daughter at his side wherever he went, inviting her as one would a treasured friend. He had valued her opinion and company. Because of him she'd learned how to manage a household with his supervision, how to balance the books, and most of all, she'd discovered the gift of story.

For it was through her father's ardor of recounting the stories of her parents' devotion that Vivienne had learned what true love looked like. She had never known her mother . . . Her father had scarcely had time with her himself before she'd died giving birth to Vivienne, but the time her parents had spent together had been beautiful. Their terrace home had been part of Mother's dowry and had been Vivienne's haven until Father had married the visiting Mrs. Hart, who'd been established in Chilham in a country manor.

It had been difficult leaving Bath for Chilham at the delicate age of ten. She had been loath to leave it, but the idea of gaining a mother and a stepbrother seemed to be worth the sacrifice. It was only by Father's insistence and Vivienne's begging that Mrs. Hart not sell their home in Bath, instead keeping it in Vivienne's name, that Vivienne was able to have a home at all now. Father had hired a local family to clean it every season, preparing it in the event they took a holiday. Regardless of the drain of funds to see to its upkeep, Mrs. Hart had been a kind soul and never challenged her husband's wish. But they'd never seemed to have any time to take a holiday to Bath, and then he'd died and all talk of such a trip ceased. The house had remained closed.

Mrs. Hart had been kind. But based on the stories Vivienne's father had told about her mother, it appeared the second marriage was more so one of companionship and need than one of those destined to be together.

But companionship isn't so bad.

As much as she disliked admitting it to herself, Bash had filled her thoughts all week. The memory of his lips on hers made her wish for his second appearance. She still hadn't found the time to walk to the constable's office to give her witnessed account. Well, if she were honest, she'd had more than enough time. She just didn't have the heart to report any more information on the thief who was mentioned in the newssheets by Sir Thomas. The account was factual but lacked feeling.

A thief who cared for the poor and a lady's honor *was* a conundrum. Everything about him was manly, strong, and all she had ever written about in her heroes. Never before had her head been so turned by a man, but she suspected it was because of the impossibility of anything coming from it that she allowed herself to dream. She shook her head over her foolishness. She had no time to dream about a man who'd stolen her funds. She needed to ensure her future, and dwelling on the handsome highwayman was not beneficial.

Charlotte touched her arm. "Lady Larkby? Would you like me to fetch some curative water? You have a distant look in your eye. Is it the crowd?"

"I'm only deep in memories. A cup of mineral water would be lovely, with a couple of pastries to go along with it." She opened her reticule and handed Charlotte a coin. She couldn't buy treats every time she visited the Pump Room, but it had been so long since she had been here, and she needed to mark the occasion with the sweets that she and her father had so enjoyed.

"Of course, Lady Larkby." Charlotte strode away.

Two ladies nearby had their heads bent together, whispering. One lady nodded to Vivienne, approaching with a tentative smile. "Pardon my breech of etiquette, but did I hear your companion address you as Lady Larkby? Are you the famed authoress?"

Vivienne inclined her head, ignoring the fact that she had never been recognized out in public before. She offered a smile, imagining that Lady Larkby would act far more gracefully and confident than Vivienne Poppy. "I am."

"How fortuitous. I am Mrs. Pickering, and my friends and I meet every other Friday in Sydney Park and discuss our favorite novels over a picnic breakfast. We would be honored to have you join us, as we have only just completed *A Knight and His Lady*." She fluttered her fan to beckon a friend who was arm in arm with a gentleman. "Mr. and Mrs. Cheslyn are readers in our little book gathering as well!"

The feather in Mrs. Cheslyn's hat stood at an impressive height, but it kept brushing against her husband's nose. He patiently swatted it away with a dazed expression directed at Vivienne. "Lady Larkby, I cannot describe the joy I derive from reading your books. Pray tell, what is your next book about?"

"My next novel, *The Privateer Takes a Bride,* is already in with my publisher, but I'm now writing about a highwayman and a lady he robs at gunpoint, only to find that it is his heart that is stolen."

The women clapped, giggling. "How daring, Lady Larkby. You simply must come this week and speak with our group."

They chatted a few moments more, and as word spread about the Pump Room, many couples eyed her with interest, the gentlemen smiling appreciatively her way. Charlotte brought her the curative drink as their new acquaintances promised to send round proper invitations at once for meetings and even a dinner party. Charlotte gracefully led her away with a ready excuse, handing her the confection.

Vivienne closed her eyes and took a bite, the sweetness coating her tongue, memories filling her heart. She had missed Bath. Her throat constricted with emotion. "Shall we return home? Maybe go to the coffeehouse on the way back?"

"You need never ask when there is a refreshment in question." Charlotte wrapped her hand about Vivienne's arm and wove through the crowd. She beamed as they strode through the Pump Room's doors and into the abbey churchyard, pastries in hand, whispering with a hint of glee. "Not even socializing in Bath for a full day, and people are already taking notice of you. It seems our plan is working already! You are a novelty that everyone wants to show off at their parties, which will secure your future."

"Lady Larkby!" A footman trotted up from behind. He bowed and presented her with a note before folding his hands behind his back and dropping his gaze.

Vivienne paused in the musing shadows of the Gothic abbey and opened the fine paper to discover a personal invitation from a Lady Delamere.

"What does it say?" Charlotte peered over Vivienne's shoulder.

"It is from a lady whom I have not met."

"A lady? What does she want?"

"My address for a formal invitation to attend her daughter's birthday ball tonight." Vivienne tapped the letter against her palm. "Well, we are in for a penny, in for a pound. It appears we shall be attending a masquerade ball in the Upper Assembly Rooms as Lady Larkby and guest."

Of course, Bash would get head lice before his return to Bath, but given what he had done to the poor Miss Evie, he supposed it was a fair penance. His hair was unfashionably short, but what else was there to do than to crop it until it was barely visible? He could wear a wig, but having that upon his head reminded him too much of being on duty, and if he wasn't sporting his red uniform and white stockings, the style was outdated. He'd stick out even more.

And vanity was no reason to keep himself from purchasing some curative waters. Bash tugged his coat into place, squaring his shoulders as he entered the Pump Room. His grandmother would appreciate his bringing her a mineral drink, and he meant to do whatever possible to ease her pain whilst he had a month off from his duties as Yeoman of the Guard . . . and to distract her from his hair, or lack thereof.

The Prince Regent had been most gracious in his thanks over the letters. So much so that he had granted Bash's request for the month off to attend his ailing grandmother. But Bash suspected that was more from the Prince Regent's revulsion of Bash's recent encounter with head lice than excessive gratefulness for carrying out his duty.

He stood in line at the fountain, and at the brush at his shoulder and a lady's askance eyeing of his hairstyle, he cleared his throat, barely refraining from running his fingers over where his thick golden locks had been—the hair that had caught many a lady's attention before. *Vanity. Get in, get the curative waters, and get out.*

"Lady Larkby is in Bath!" a woman whispered to her companion. "I overheard from Lady Thalia Jennings that she was going to invite her to her annual party at the Sydney Hotel."

His senses bristled. *Lady Larkby?* He frowned. No Lady Larkby existed as of yet. The ladies of the Pump Room whispered behind their fans, and even a few gentlemen seemed enchanted with the idea of this woman whom everyone clearly knew. But how could she hold the title of Lady Larkby when she would have to hold the position of his wife to obtain it? And he most certainly did not have a wife.

He reached for two corked bottles of the curative water and paid the attendant, pocketing the glasses as he followed the gazes of those about him to a pair of ladies across the room with their backs to him, one in a sapphire spencer and the other in a drab brown spencer. They appeared to be heading to the front door. Was one of them the interloper?

"Do you think she would mind if I sent a servant with an informal invitation for my masquerade ball?" A young woman near his elbow whispered to another. "I'll mention it is for my birthday . . . Perhaps that would persuade her. Imagine if I managed to have her before the marchioness. Everyone in Bath would be in attendance." The young woman coaxed the lady, who appeared to be her mother judging by the marked shape of their thin lips. "Do say I can, Mother?"

"It isn't usually done, but as it would be great fun to be the first to host her, I shall discover her address and send a note with the formal invitation, apologizing for my tardiness." The mother waved at an attendant, beckoning him near. "You there! I need paper and pencil to send a note to Lady Larkby. She is most likely still in the churchyard. She's in a stunning sapphire spencer. I will need her address."

It had been her. Bash easily looked over the heads of those nearby, but the two ladies would have been lost in the crush even if they were in sight. He attempted to follow, but the surging crowd kept him from reaching the supposed Lady Larkby. He would have to secure another means of finding out the identity of this woman who was parading as his wife.

He approached the lady who'd finished jotting down a note, folded the paper, and shoved it into the footman's hands, shooing him away. In the press of the crowd, he managed to relieve her of her purse without her noticing, dropping it at her feet. "Pardon me, my ladies. Did one of you drop your reticule?" He bent and scooped it up, as if just finding it, and offered it to the mother with a short bow.

"Oh my word! My, what a gentleman of honor . . . whom I have not had the pleasure of meeting." The older lady nodded graciously to him. "Because of the magnitude of your service, I suppose we may forgo the lack of etiquette with you speaking first without an introduction."

"Allow me to rectify my error." He bowed once more and retrieved the master of ceremony, informing him of his title.

The man performed the introductions of the lady and her daughter with fanfare, stamping his cane twice before bowing and sauntering back to his place.

"Sir Sebastian Larkby?" Lady Delamere crooned. "How fortuitous! I just sent an informal invitation to your wife for our masquerade to-night. The footman is acquiring your address now for the formal one to arrive within the hour."

"Did you? I had not planned to return home until nearly supper. But where is your ball? I can change at my club and be there before the dancing."

"Oh dear. If you will not be home to fetch your invitation, allow me to write down another informal invitation to see you are admitted." She snapped her fingers at another footman, asking for another slip of paper and pencil.

Lady Arabella clapped. "How romantic it will be to have *the* Lady Larkby and her husband at my first season's ball. Is it not marvelous that she dedicates all her works to you?"

She does what? It was quite the charade this woman had created. He inclined his head. "As the inspiration of her heroes, I attempt to be worthy of her adoration." His response had the two ladies tittering and their fans flapping.

If this author was going to create a fake marriage, why cannot our marriage be one that was written in the stars?

The ladies pressed their hands to her chests, fluttering in delight at his words. With the informal invitation to Lady Delamere's ball tucked into his pocket, he bowed to them and wove through the crowd. It was a risk to entrust his title to Lady Delamere on the off chance the supposed Lady Larkby heard he was in town and decided to run away instead of facing her lies, but he did not have time to waste if he were to prevent this Lady Larkby from circulating word of her marriage to him further than this masquerade ball tonight. He and his family were not well known about town, as he and Grandmother had always preferred their country estate and occasionally visiting with their neighbors to circulating with the ton. A fact he never thought would come back to haunt him.

Of course, he could have followed her trail, but this seemed so less taxing, and it would give him a chance to take a repast in a tavern and rent a room there for the afternoon. He didn't dare return to Lark Manor, as he needed to end this woman's ruse before his ailing grandmother heard and rejoiced over his marriage that had most certainly not occurred. And it was the perfect excuse to check on the vivacious Evie. She had been on his mind nearly every moment since he had left her—a fact driving him to distraction.

He mounted and directed Brigand to the Circus terrace apartments. It was foolish to return so soon as she might recognize him, but he had to see her and make certain she was well. He had thought of her too often in the days following his mission—Evie had plagued his dreams. He needed to find a way to see the funds returned to her without her knowledge, but he had no idea how.

In the daylight he could much better see the tall circle of narrow houses with their three terraces boasting columns in Doric, Ionic, and Corinthian, with a stretch of unique frieze gracing the ground floors just above the thresholds.

He reined his mount in the green beneath the row of trees that hid the reservoir in the center of the circle of terrace homes. He dismounted and purchased a hot bun from a vendor, savoring it as he watched Evie's house. At last two ladies knocked on the door, and he spied movement in the parlor window. Evie's golden hair made his heart skip. A footman opened the front door and showed them in.

His shoulders sagged in relief. At least she was able to keep some staff. She might not be as poor off as he imagined if she was entertaining callers, but the guilt still stung. He sighed. He was not going to solve any problems staring at her from across the street like some lovelorn puppy. And as it was a masque tonight, he needed to ride to Cheap Street to find something to wear as well as purchase a copy of this woman's work to find out more about her.

He took one last glance at the golden-haired creature sitting by the front window, sipping tea. Perhaps he should leave a package tonight for her to discover in the morning. Perhaps he could catch a glimpse of her without her knowing. The idea made him grin. He'd don his mask one more time and this time see that he brought good to Evie instead of stealing from her.

Chapter Six

VIVIENNE CLUTCHED CHARLOTTE'S HAND AS they entered the Upper Assembly Rooms from the corridor, having handed her invitation to the footman at the vestibule. She supposed that if anyone dressed in masque, they could join the ball uninvited if it weren't for the footman guarding the entrance. He bowed and motioned them inside. She held her shoulders back, confident that the lovely creation Muriel had sent would stand up to any ton costume.

Lord Delamere bowed over her hand in the octagon antechamber. "Such a lovely butterfly. Might I beg to know her name?"

Vivienne smiled from behind her black netting mask. "Vivienne—"

Charlotte elbowed her, as if already knowing that Vivienne was about to say her real name.

"Vivienne *Larkby,* my lord, and this is my companion, Charlotte Vale."

"Ah, the famous authoress. Welcome to our ball, Lady Larkby. I hope you and your companion enjoy your evening. My wife was thrilled that she managed to let the place for our daughter's birthday for her debut season. Please enjoy refreshments in the tearoom. There will be musicians in the gallery as well as, of course, in the ballroom to your left." He smiled and beckoned them inside, urging them to enjoy the party.

"That was close," Vivienne whispered as they strode into the tearoom first, her blue crepe dress with its black-lace overlay and white-trimmed cape fluttering behind her and giving the illusion of a butterfly.

Charlotte leaned to her. "Such splendor."

"In all the fun, I nearly forgot that this is your first ball." She threaded Charlotte's arm through hers, keeping her close in the crush of guests. "And what a marvelous one to begin with."

The Delamere family had decorated the Assembly Rooms with clusters of greenery in the corners and pale-blue linens with gold runners over the refreshment tables.

They paused by the punch table, and Vivienne was grateful she could take a drink without removing her mask like Charlotte, with her cumbersome horse's head that acted as both costume and mask, had to.

Charlotte declined the drink from the servant and nodded to a group of gentlemen studying them. "The mystery already begins."

"Are you certain they aren't looking at you, dear Charlotte?"

"I'm wearing a horse's head as a mask. No, I do not think they are looking at me. Her grace did apologize that she didn't have anything else for me to wear. Tess wore this one time and refused to wear it a second." Charlotte adjusted it to see Vivienne better through the horse's netted snout, mumbling, "I can see why."

"You are always lovely, horse's head or not."

Charlotte smirked. "Thank you for that obvious yet kind falsehood regarding my hideous costume, but I am here for you and no other, so it is neither here nor there if I mind wearing it." She squeezed Vivienne's arm as a man approached.

"Good evening." He bowed. "As you are masked, I cannot say if we have been properly introduced or not. If we have not, forgive my forwardness, but I would be honored to claim your first dance, my lady."

Under normal circumstances, Vivienne would never dance with a stranger . . . Well, she'd hardly had the occasion to dance with a stranger in Chilham, as she'd known all the men since their boyhoods. But a masque did lend certain liberties to the strict rules of the ton. She looked to her companion.

Charlotte inclined her head. With the horse's head, it was quite the dramatic gesture.

"Thank you, miss. Should I have my friend fetch you a carrot as thanks?" He snickered, offering his arm.

Vivienne gasped and clutched Charlotte's arm. "I believe I was mistaken. We have *not* been introduced. Please excuse us." She guided Charlotte away from the cad.

"He only meant it in jest," Charlotte whispered, excusing the man's behavior.

"It was a poor jest."

"But since you refused him, you won't be able to dance all night." Charlotte sighed. "And it is such a pity, as I know you dearly love a dance."

"No one insults my friend like that. Can you unpin my train?"

Charlotte bent and swiftly released the pin holding Vivienne's skirts up, allowing the small train to flow behind her. "You three ladies were always so kind to me even when I was only a maid. The duchess told me that you would look after me, and here you've gone and sacrificed your dancing for me."

"It is nothing. I would much rather chat with you at my side than make conversation with an uncouth stranger."

"What do we do if you are not to dance?"

"We circulate." It had been too long since she'd circulated, especially without Tess and Muriel at her side. But a fierce sense of protection filled her at the thought of Charlotte's discomfort. She felt that Lady Larkby would be confident. If she were in attendance, she would take a turn about the room, feeling no sense of discomfort without a male escort. Vivienne held her head high and, taking Charlotte's arm, surged through the crowd.

Behind his golden half masque, Bash studied the tearoom swirling with costumed guests, bright colors filling his vision. As Yeoman of the Guard, he often attended balls, but never as a guest and always in his

GRACE HITCHCOCK

crimson-and-white uniform, keeping watch just behind the Prince Regent. More than once tonight he had moved to adjust his white wig to ensure the golden curl was in place at his forehead, as he was required to wear it when in uniform, but all that met his fingertips under the wig were fine, short bristles. He shoved aside the twinge of regret at having shorn his hair.

He reached for a refreshment at one of the tables, nodding to the footman extending the punch to him. "Have you seen Lady Larkby?" he called over the string instruments.

"Yes, sir." The footman pointed above them to a woman standing at the rail on the first-floor musician's gallery with her back to him. "She is the one dressed as a blue butterfly, speaking with Sir Anthony, Mr. Monroe, Sir Gordon, and Mr. Oswald. The guests are most enthusiastic over her arrival in Bath, and I must admit, so are some of the staff."

"Thank you." He downed his punch. She seemed familiar. Her height was moderate, and he could tell even from her profile that she was fair of face by the graceful curve of her neck and high cheeks—that and the crowd of men eagerly surrounding her, plying her with questions. His chest burned. How dare this woman make use of his good name and title to further her own agenda. He reined in his ire, set aside his glass, strode up the stairs, and approached the group.

The lovely woman turned to him. A shimmering black netting served as her mask, and he jerked back at the familiar wide green eyes. He grasped her hand. "I cannot believe it's you."

Her cheeks flamed beneath the netting as she pulled her hand from his grasp. "Forgive me—you may know me, but I most certainly do not know you, and therefore, I doubt I gave you the liberty of taking my hand."

The gentlemen surrounding her scowled at him, one going so far as to clutch his fists. All murmured over his breach of etiquette. The woman in the horse's head beside her tilted her head back and narrowed her eyes at him through the snout, the only part of her face visible behind the costume.

He swallowed back his explanation. The ire from only moments before dissolved into pleasure at seeing Evie once more. *What are the odds that the woman who has consumed my thoughts is standing before me now . . . parading about as my wife?*

Of course she didn't recognize him. He couldn't rightly proclaim himself to be the highwayman, as the Prince Regent's secret mission must be protected at all costs. Besides, he doubted anyone in attendance was even aware of the Larkby family having a residence on the outskirts of Bath, given his grandmother's decades-old inclination to avoid town at all costs.

Dressed as a butterfly, this Lady Larkby was resplendent, and he wished for nothing more than to shoo away the gentlemen flocking around her. He bowed low. "I beg your pardon, Lady Larkby. I've read your works for so long, it seemed as if I knew you. I offer a thousand apologies for such impertinence."

Her eyes sparked, her lips pursing.

That certainly had not been the thing to say, but how else could he explain his familiarity? "What I meant was, may I have this dance?"

Her companion slid her arm protectively through the curve of Evie's elbow.

"I believe that cannot happen, as you have not been properly introduced, and as you can see, my train is not pinned up." Evie lifted her chin, as if preparing to give him the cut direct.

"Allow me to rectify my mishap at once." He bowed, clicking his heels together, and turned about, spotting Lord Delamere at the head of the receiving line. Bash trotted down the stairs to the host's side. "My lord! I know we have only just met, but might I beg an introduction from one of your guests?"

Lord Delamere laughed, whispering his excuse to his wife. He slapped Bash on the shoulder. "Find yourself a lovely lady? Well, I'd say that our debt to you in the rescuing of my wife's purse has been paid in full."

"There was never any debt, but I am most appreciative, my lord, for your assistance."

"And who is the lady of your soon-to-be affection?" He waggled his brows.

"Lady Larkby."

The gentleman grinned. "Why, Sir Sebastian, what a lark to have me introduce you to your wife."

"We met in a ball, so I like to keep up the tradition." The lie slid easily from his tongue. After all, a fictitious wife required a fictitious romance.

"I expect nothing less from a knight who so gallantly returns a reticule to a perfect stranger in the Pump Room." He inclined his head. "Would more gentlemen woo their wives thus. I should take a page from your book. Mayhap it would earn me forgiveness for the gambling habit that Lady Delamere is forever scolding me about."

"Perhaps. I think most gentlemen would find their wives more forgiving if they spent a little more time pursuing them even after marriage." Evie certainly had forgiven him after her abduction, in her kiss. She may not have admitted it, but he sensed it.

Bash paused in front of Evie, unable to keep his smug grin from spreading as Lord Delamere bowed, the gentlemen in the tight circle stepping back to allow their host inside.

"My lady, may I have the honor of introducing you to a gentleman who is enchanted by you."

She fanned herself, releasing a soft laugh. "Enchanted? My my, such praise."

"May I present Sir Sebastian of Lark Manor." He winked to Bash.

She curtsied, obviously not understanding the connection as she bestowed a smile upon him. "A pleasure to make your acquaintance, Sir Sebastian."

Bash bowed. "And an honor to meet you. While your skirts are not pinned, I cannot help but ask if I may have this dance?"

She whispered to her companion and inclined her head to Bash, extending her hand to his offered arm. He guided her down the stairs and through the crush to the ballroom.

"I must say, it was a surprise to see you here, my lady."

TO KISS A KNIGHT

"My lady?" She twisted to face him, her lips parting as she gasped. "My lady! Did you think I would not recognize that phrase?" She fairly growled and wrenched him behind a cluster of potted trees.

Bash nearly toppled from the force of her jerking and releasing him at once. "My lady!"

"You!" She ripped the mask from his face, along with his wig.

Chapter Seven

THE GOLDEN HAIR DID NOT tumble from the powdered wig. Nothing tumbled from the wig. His hair was cropped. And he was the most handsome man she had ever beheld—almost too handsome to bear. And here she had ripped his wig from his head and *growled* at him. Her heart tumbled. *What have I done?* "Y-you are not the highwayman?"

"My lady, whatever are you about?" He snatched the wig from her hands. "I admit, I didn't put much thought into my costume, but I most certainly would not dress myself as a common thief for a masque." He repositioned the wig and tugged his coat, returning himself to rights. "I am a nobleman—a knight."

She pressed her hands to her burning cheeks, and she turned to the window, mortified. *Thank the Lord I had the good sense to hide him behind the greenery before accosting him.* "I am so sorry, Sir Sebastian. I-I thought I recognized you." What possible explanation could she give other than the truth, even though the truth would cause a scandal?

"And this is how you always treat your friends at a masque?" He chuckled, grasped her elbow, and turned her to face him.

He was a striking fellow with his broad shoulders and seemed so familiar, especially with his deep timbre . . . If she had paused long enough, she would have realized he did not possess the Scottish articulation of the bandit. And then there was the matter of his cropped hair. Bash had run his fingers through his hair often enough that she knew he was proud of it. Why would a gentleman crop his hair so? Perhaps he wore a wig most times. But it was out of fashion for his age. "Again,

I thought I recognized you. I do not possess many gentlemen friends, so my answer would have to be no. I do not make a habit of accosting my friends."

"Oh dear. That would make me not a friend then, and I had hoped to get to know each other." He settled his mask back in place. "Shall we continue to our dance? I believe the minuet will give us ample time to converse and perhaps rectify the situation of us not being friends?" He grinned.

"My train—"

"However, I suppose a hidden place such as this is more conducive for a private conversation."

She could hold her train for a single dance—especially for one as boring as the minuet. She inclined her head and allowed him to lead her onto the dance floor, her blue wings fluttering as they took their position in line toward the middle, the guests about her murmuring. If Muriel had not blessed her with a thoughtful trunk holding fashionable gowns, including a costume for tonight, they might be murmuring for another reason altogether.

"So, Lady Larkby. How is your husband?"

He kept her hand in his, their arms spread as they waited for their turn to perform the slow, graceful steps of the minuet, but as they had seven couples before them, it would be a while, which was why she did not care for this old-fashioned procession. "M-my husband?" she called over the string orchestra.

"Yes, how is he doing these days?"

She blinked. She did not know her husband's first name—fictitious though it may be. She hadn't thought this part through. Living in Bath, as the famed authoress, surely her readers would wish to meet the man to whom she dedicated all of her books. Should she allude to being widowed? It *would* explain the lack of a husband in her terrace home. She had skirted as many questions as she could tonight, playing the enigmatic eccentric noblewoman. Her stomach twisted at the thought of what she might have said during those initial few moments of sheer panic at the first batch of interested gentlemen. She honestly could not recall the conversation. She would need to become more fluid in her lies regarding her name, but after a single evening parading about as some titled lady, she was reconsidering being out in society. She could not afford to surrender her nom de plume, but to lie constantly about her name? She would rather be considered a recluse and refuse all invitations. She would need to consult with Charlotte though, as it affected her as well. After her first ball, she might wish to attend more.

"My husband is no longer with us," she choked out.

"Well, this is all quite a shock to me." He shook his head, as if clearing the clouds from his eyes. "I-I can hardly believe he is gone."

Her belly churned—and not because of the oysters she had consumed—and the ballroom began to feel impossibly warm. "D-did you know of my husband?"

"Know of him?" He pulled his lips in and shook his head again. "He was closer to me than any man on earth, and to find he has a bride—and now that he has passed." He closed his eyes and turned his head, lifting a fist to his mouth.

He is going to cry. Lord, help me. He is going to cry in the middle of the dance floor. She thought she had done significant enough research to determine the title was no longer in use. And here she had proclaimed herself the widow of the man. The oysters were definitely threatening a second appearance. "Sir Sebastian, I beg of you, escort me from the dance floor at once and we can further discuss this in the corridor, away from the crush."

He bowed his head to her, and she shot an apologetic smile to the nearest lady, placing a hand over her stomach and hoping to convey that she felt ill, which she did indeed.

Sir Sebastian led her toward the corridor. He rubbed a hand over his jaw, his shoulders shaking. He was clearly overcome with emotion, and it was *her* fault. A gentleman would never display such emotion unless he was devastated. She couldn't have felt worse than if she had collapsed on the dance floor and been trampled by each couple performing the minuet. *Lord, give me the courage to tell him the truth, and let him keep silent.*

The moment they were within the corridor, with the moonlight shining through the glass dome upon his tear-filled eyes that . . . were no longer tear filled? His eyes hardened, and her heart skipped with dread. "Sir Sebastian?"

He tucked them behind a colonnade, keeping her between him and the wall, and lowered his voice. "You must cease your falsehood at once."

"Falsehood?" she squeaked.

He lifted his brows, folding his arms over his broad chest. "I happen to know that the gentleman of that title is very much alive, which leaves little doubt that you are not who you say you are. What is your real name?"

"What?" Her lungs tightened. "W-what do you mean you know the gentleman?"

He gestured to himself. "Imagine my surprise, when I returned to Bath to visit my grandmother, to discover I have a wife I did not wed."

"Sir Sebastian *Larkby* of Lark Manor?" She pressed her hand to her throat. "Good heavens." The room spun, and she crumpled.

Bash lunged forward and caught her before her head struck the column. She looked too pale beneath the netting. What if she did not awaken like last time? He didn't dare dump water on her again, lest she remember him as surely as he remembered the searing touch of her lips. He knelt with her, holding her up against his chest. Her head listed back, her ivory neck gleaming in the candlelight.

He shouldn't have teased her so. The moment he knew it was Evie, he wasn't even angry about her taking his title. After all, he had taken her funds. He hadn't known at the time that Evie was an authoress using his family's name. She had simply been Evie. If he had taken a moment to discover her identity, he would have ascertained what she was about, but he had been in such a rush to return to the Prince

Regent that he hadn't done his due diligence in discovering whom he had abducted. But he couldn't address her as Evie until she told him her name, and yet he couldn't go about calling her Lady Larkby either.

She moaned, stirring in his arms. She clasped his lapel.

"My lady?" He gently shook her. He really should carry smelling salts to revive this maiden who supposedly never fainted yet kept collapsing in his arms.

Her full lips parted, her thick lashes blinking slowly as she focused upon him. "Why am I in your arms . . . What happened?"

"You fainted, my lady."

"Fainted? That does not sound like me." She attempted to rise, but groaned. "I never faint."

He begged to differ, but as he was not playing the role of the highwayman, he suppressed the urge to correct her and held her fast. "There is a first time for everything." *And in your case, a third time.* "Perhaps it would be best to take a moment. I have found that when ladies swoon, it is best they catch their breath before rising."

"But what would people say if they saw me in your arms on the floor of the Assembly Rooms corridor?"

"We are married apparently. No one would think a thing of it. Speaking of which, I think it might be best you cease using my title before it's too late." He lifted his brows.

"Oh my heavens." She slowly pushed herself from his arms.

She looked frail. Not at all like the girl from the stagecoach who was all fire and courage. Had his robbery and their adventure caused her to fall ill? Another stab of guilt pierced his gut.

"I-I can't." Her breath shallowed, and she flipped open her fan, flapping wildly. "My nom de plume is how I make my living."

He nodded. "I discovered that you were an authoress when I heard the rumors of my having a wife, but you must understand my point of view. Surely you have family that can support you?" He knew she had a stepbrother, albeit one she was running away from, as well as a marriage. He gritted his teeth. Bash was a cad for what he'd put her through. He would see to it that he returned her funds this very night, with interest, for her to find upon awaking. He did not care if she thought it strange. This woman was desperate, and he'd played a part in that desperation. He took her small hand in his. She was trembling. He had brought her to near panic.

She gripped the neck of her fan and inhaled a bracing breath, calming herself. "A family that considers me burden enough to promise me to one of the worst sorts of men."

He stiffened. They had been together for a day and yet she had never once confessed that the gentleman she had been fleeing was evil . . . He had assumed she only wished for a love match. *This complicates matters.* "Do you not have enough from your living to sustain you until you find a suitable position? Perhaps as a governess?"

"One cannot simply become a governess any more than any gentleman should become a clergyman because he is a second son. It is a calling as well as a vocation, and I can assure you from firsthand experience with teaching three little terrors that I am positive I am not well suited to the job." She rested her face in her palms. "La, what am I going to do now?"

It was his fault again. This woman had done nothing to him and yet he had robbed her stagecoach at *gunpoint*, a fact she most likely did not recall, given her tendency of swooning around him, and now he was robbing her of the use of his name. But what else was he to do? He had determined not to marry. As a Yeoman of the Guard, he was placed in nearly as many dangerous situations as those on the front line might encounter, since the Prince Regent trusted him with important matters of state that sometimes needed to be kept off record. And if he were ever caught, he'd potentially lose not only his title but funds that any wife and children would require. The only reasonable solution was to not marry, for he had no intention of retiring until he was too feeble to be much good.

But even if he didn't intend on taking a wife, it was his grandmother that he was worried about. He could not disappoint her in her final days by refuting the news. "I understand your dilemma, but I believe the only course would be for you to retire that name and find another more suited."

She snorted. "Everyone buys my books under that name—it's a novelty for a highborn lady to be an authoress. But when they find out that I am untitled and only a country gentleman's daughter, I have no doubt the romantics will become disenchanted. They might even be so angry that I lied they would refuse to buy another book under any other name I choose." She shook her head and bit her bottom lip. "I did not intend you harm. Perhaps if you allow me to keep the name, I'll put yours in a book and immortalize you in the written word. It is not much to offer in return, but it is all that I have."

"I have a bedridden grandmother who is very hopeful about my providing her with grandchildren. I cannot give her false hope. If she hears of this, it would be her undoing."

She sighed. "Can you at least allow me until the end of the week to formulate a plan before I write to my publisher and end the career I have spent my life dreaming of and years building?"

"That is too long. My grandmother still has one friend in Bath who will no doubt be writing to her the moment she hears your title bandied about the city. I shall give you until the morning. Shall we meet for breakfast at Sydney Park?"

"That is highly improper—"

"Bring your companion if you wish, but as all think we are married, I doubt a breakfast with your supposed husband will ruin your reputation." *Any more than spending time in the company of a highwayman.*

"Oh my goodness gracious! Whatever has happened here?" A lady in a silver gown hurried to their side, calling for help over her shoulder, bringing the lord and lady hosting the event to their side.

Evie turned wild, fearful eyes on him. He nodded once. He'd promised he wouldn't give her away, and he would not. As much as he wished to aid the lady whom he had robbed, he feared he had little choice but to take the title away from her. Some knight in shining armor he had become.

Chapter Eight

SIR SEBASTIAN WAS TRUE TO his vow to see that her secret was safe until the morrow. He played the part of a concerned spouse as he escorted them to the left of the building to the colonnade for sedan chairs, paying to place her and Charlotte in the chairs, despite her protests. It was only a few minutes' walk to reach her home. But he insisted and dutifully strode behind them until they reached her home.

He was regarding the terrace home as Vivienne stepped out of her sedan chair. She was thankful to see lights flickering in the windows, welcoming her home after such a horrid night. She nodded to Charlotte, who slipped inside, leaving Vivienne with Sebastian, who tipped the men that had carried them home.

She hadn't needed the ride, and the cost was more than she wished to pay. "Thank you for escorting us home, Sir Sebastian. If you wait here a moment, I can fetch coins enough to reimburse you."

"There is no need."

"There is every need. A gentleman should not pay for a woman's way unless—"

"Unless they are married, and until tomorrow we are." He smiled sadly. "I'm afraid I have not changed my mind on the timeline, but may I ask where you hail from and what is your real name?"

She glanced back at the front door, where Charlotte stood watching from the sidelight. "I am reluctant to share such information with a perfect stranger."

"I think I have earned that right, and besides, how might I find you after you retire using my name if someone directs mail to my place of residence? I promise I have no ill plans toward you."

"I doubt that will happen, but you are correct that you deserve to know." She sighed. "I am Miss Vivienne Poppy of Chilham, in the county of Kent. My stepmother is the late Mrs. Hart-Poppy. My stepbrother, Lucius Hart, resides in Chilham, but forgive me if I do not volunteer his address. I have little wish for him to be alerted and even less for him to come fetch me."

He lifted his hat. "Your confidence will not be cast aside, Miss Poppy. Until tomorrow."

She nodded and slipped inside, her shoulders sagging in defeat as her friend embraced her. "Oh, Charlotte, what are we to do now?"

"We pray for a miracle."

The lights were out now. Bash affixed his highwayman mask, tying it low enough to hide it under his collar, and tugged on his wide-brimmed black hat to disguise his missing locks. He directed Brigand to the back door, which had a ledge wide enough to secure a foothold if he grasped the windowsill above it while Brigand stood beneath it. The transition from standing atop his saddle to the doorframe was fluid. He at once pivoted and reached for the first-floor windowsill. He shoved it open and climbed through, his boots landing lightly on the hardwood floor. He paused. The house was silent.

From his time watching her home before, he thought she lived on the first floor. He padded down to the room he believed was hers and paused outside the door. He might just leave the funds at her door, but dare he trust such an amount with servants about? He pushed open the door and, on the tips of his boots, strode inside her bedroom. The curtains had been left wide open, the window cracked, allowing fresh air and moonlight to fill the spacious chamber.

Her soft snoring came from under the mound of covers. He swal-

lowed a chuckle at her being sprawled across the bed. It was little wonder she could not sleep out of doors on the ground if that was how she
usually slept. He strode to the window seat and set the purse on her
book, the coins rattling. Her snoring jolted, and he stilled, waiting for
her breathing to even again. She jerked up in bed, eyes on him.

"Bash." Her tone was even, as if she wasn't surprised to see him in
her bedroom—nor afraid.

"Evie."

"So you did return to rob me again." She sighed. "I knew I should
not have given you my address."

He grinned. "To trust a highwayman is never encouraged."

"Indeed. I spy a leather purse on my window seat." She slipped from
her bed, drawing a blanket around her shoulders to cover her thin
nightgown. "Pray, what are you stealing from me now?"

He did not move away, letting her approach him . . . How could he
bolt when he had thought of little but her since their parting? Tonight
they had held each other's hands as they'd stood together for the minuet, but it was not with the familiarity of the highwayman and his lady,
as he had wished.

"You are not afraid I shall scream?" she whispered. She stood before
him now, gazing up at him with those wide eyes.

"The rules from the other night still stand." He grinned. "I trust you
would not wish to risk your reputation by alerting all to the man standing in your bedroom."

She laughed softly. "Nay. My reputation is all I have left." She lifted
the purse and plucked the rolled note in the knotted string. "'From
your honorable highwayman.'" She shook the bag. "And yet from the
sound of this letter, it does not seem you are stealing my jewels. What
are you about, Bash?"

"I decided I did not need your money." He leaned against the window frame, crossing his arms as he studied her.

"The pouch is far too heavy to be my money alone." She looked up at
him through thick lashes.

He shrugged. "It was your idea. For the trouble I put you through,

I've added a small sum. Consider it a lesson on investment opportunities. Some adventuring pays in dividends, and others in disaster."

She opened the bag, gasping. "One would think you are sweet on me. There is enough in here to see me through the year!"

"One would be right in assuming so." He dared to reach out and brush a curl from her cheek. She did not jerk away. Was it his imaginings or did she relax, as if she missed his touch as much as he did hers? "Do not give my weakness away. I have a reputation of my own to uphold in the underworld."

"I will not." She leaned into his palm, her voice strained. "I thought calling yourself a noble thief was an impossible promise, and here, you have proven me wrong with a generosity I have not experienced from a man since my father's death."

He swiped his thumb under her lash, capturing a tear. "Not all noblemen wear finery, my lady." He tossed open the window and hitched his right leg over the sill.

She gripped his arm. "Whatever are you about? You'll fall to your death if you do not take care."

He grinned. "Have you forgotten my talents already?" He released a low, sharp whistle.

The clopping of hooves brought a smile to her cheeks. "Of course. Brigand is your partner in every situation. You are fortunate that I have only two people under my roof and they are even more exhausted than I." She moved to the side table and lifted the lid to a small china pot. "I didn't clean up after tea." She grasped his hand and dropped sugar lumps into his palm. "Thank him for me."

If he leaned forward, her lips would meet his. At her flushing face, it seemed the lady was not opposed. *But what kind of knight would that make me?* He pocketed the lumps and tipped the brim of his hat. He swung his left leg through the opening, gripping the sill as his feet found purchase at the ridge.

"Bash," she whispered, leaning out of the window.

With her braid spilling over her shoulder, she was fairly impossible not to kiss. "Yes, my lady?"

"I have not turned you in, and after tonight, I may not yet."

Her smile nearly made him forget he was perched on the ledge. "Farewell, my lady. May God bless you." Gripping the colonnade with one arm, he released the window. Stretching out his body, he dropped to the first-floor ridge. From that ledge he repeated the action and was face-to-face with the frieze and its triglyphs and emblems. It was an easy drop onto Brigand, who was standing at the entryway.

Bash glanced up to see her leaning through the window, her golden hair still spilling over her shoulder as she observed him. He voiced his hope. "Until we meet again, my lady." He wheeled Brigand about and into a trot.

Bash removed his mask the moment he faded from Evie's view. Once through Bath, he urged his mount into a gallop. He would be home at Lark Manor within the hour, as it was only a few miles outside Bath. The ride was shorter than he remembered . . . but that was likely due to his mind being occupied with thoughts of the lovely Evie Poppy.

The manor was alight yet, and just the sight of it made his heart pound with longing to be within its walls once more. He had loved growing up here. His grandmother had taken the place of his sweet mother after she had passed when he was but six years of age. It would be a wonder to see Grandmother again after nearly a year apart. He hadn't intended to be gone for so long, but being a yeoman left little room for family visits, especially when the Prince Regent kept him so busy.

He passed through the iron gates and dismounted, his boots scattering the gravel underfoot. He left Brigand's reins over his back, trusting him not to wander too far. He rang the bell and waited at the door, shifting from foot to foot, wondering what was ailing Grandmother that kept the servants up so late.

The butler answered. Ladd's eyes widened before he stepped aside to allow Bash entrance. "Sir Sebastian? Thank God you arrived home in time."

Ladd's tone halted Bash's greeting. His stomach sank. He should've never delayed his arrival for a masquerade ball, even if it had been for the sake of protecting Grandmother. "What's wrong? Has she taken a turn?"

"This afternoon, sir. We feared the worst had come, but she received a correspondence two hours ago that brought a bloom to her cheeks, and she was able to drink some broth." His words were tinged with newfound hope.

Bash dropped his hat in the butler's ready hands and raced up the steps two at a time, his greatcoat fluttering behind him. As he halted outside her door, his breathing coming quick, he bowed his head. *Lord, please, I cannot lose her. Please don't let me lose her. She's all I have left.* He slowly opened the door. The fire crackled in the hearth, and in the massive bed was a form too small to be the grand lady he knew and loved. How had she weakened so in only a year? He crossed the room, his throat catching at the sight of her gray skin and her lovely silver locks spread over the silk pillowcase. A letter rested in her hand. He sank onto the side of the bed, making the mattress dip, and took her free hand in his. Her pulse was impossibly faint. "Dear heart, I am home."

Her stubby white lashes flickered, the aging blue eyes at once lighting in recognition. "Sebastian, my sweet boy. You've come home to me at last." Her withered, mottled hand reached for his cheek, stroking it tenderly. "And without your hair it seems. Whatever possessed you to part with it?"

"Necessity." He smiled, then leaned into her papery hand and pressed it to his lips. "How are you feeling, Grandmother?"

"The good doctor thought I would be gone by now." Her words came in pants, as if even speaking was trying for her. "B-but I surprised them all."

"What does he know?" His voice sounded rough to his ears.

"A great deal, but there is one thing he did not take into account." Her eyes sparkled as she lifted the paper an inch toward him. "The power of a dream long since dreamed."

He relieved her of the letter but did not take his gaze from hers. "What do you dream?"

She lifted a shaky hand, pointed her finger, and weakly jabbed it into his chest. "You. My dear friend s-said that she heard . . . a *Lady Larkby* has made quite the splash in Bath. You have given me a new life, my sweet boy, with the hope that I might live to meet her before I go home to my Lord and Savior." She seemed to gain vitality as she spoke and looked beyond his shoulder. "Where is she? Where is my new granddaughter? I-I long to hear about your whirlwind romance from a female."

The hope in her voice pierced him. How could he tell this sweet woman that her hopes were in vain? He lifted her hand to his lips. Indeed, it was impossible. "It was undeniably a whirlwind romance. She is from Bath and is packing her things as we speak. She will arrive to Lark Manor on the morrow." *God, forgive me, but surely, this is the nobler path, yes?*

Chapter Nine

"SURELY THE OCCASION DOES NOT have cause for you to dress in black." Charlotte removed the bombazine-and-crepe mourning gown from Vivienne's arms and instead selected a darling blue morning frock.

"Lady Larkby is such a significant part of me now. To see her taken away . . . It feels much like losing a dear friend." Vivienne followed the black piece with her eyes.

Charlotte nodded. "I know it does, but your readers will follow you to a new name. Perhaps it may even cause a sensation."

"Sensation?" She snorted. "My dear Charlotte, I think you meant to say *scandal*."

"Whatever it is, news is news. Why don't we try to come up with new names for you?"

Charlotte continued her attempts to encourage as she finished helping Vivienne before heading down to the kitchen to pack a breakfast. Vivienne drafted letters to her publisher regarding her new pen name, but nothing sounded so beautiful as Lady Larkby. At Charlotte's call from the bottom of the stairs, she gratefully tossed aside her latest attempt.

She took the traveling tea service leather case from Charlotte, and they made their way toward Pulteney Bridge and across to Sydney Place's hexagonal pleasure gardens, showing the man at the front their brass admission token. He allowed them through. They passed the Sydney Hotel and their garden dining booths, where members of polite society dined on Sally Lunn tea cakes and a repast of cold meats, cheeses, and hot beverages.

Beyond the hotel's garden dining, couples lounged atop luxurious oversized blankets in the pleasure garden while the elderly in attendance reclined in chairs brought by servants, propping their fine-china dishes on their laps. Beaver hats and parasols abounded, with flashes of bright-colored clothing and the clink of silverware on china and glass goblets. Charlotte and Vivienne shared a glance at their meager basket and tea service case and then back at each other, bursting into giggles at their country feast.

"Shall we return home and see if Brexton can bring something for you to sit upon?" Charlotte whispered. "Most of these ladies are sitting on feather pillows."

Vivienne nodded to the basket and blanket draped over Charlotte's arms. "I am not above sitting on a plaid, especially as my title of Lady Larkby is about to be stripped away. I am plain Vivienne Poppy of Chilham, and I might as well act the part now."

"You are the daughter of a gentleman, and there are benefits that come from such birth," Charlotte reminded her, helping Vivienne spread the blanket upon the grass.

The ladies set out the fare of lovely pastries and meat pies, which the footman had fetched this morning from the bakery, and the hot tea. It had been a splurge, but when one was about to undergo the worst sort of embarrassment, indulgent food was necessary to endure the coming conversation. As Charlotte adjusted the three plates, a gentleman in a striking, well-tailored hunter-green coat approached them from the tree-lined path.

"My ladies, what delightful fare. I trust you rested well?" Sir Sebastian bowed to them before sitting cross-legged on the now-too-small blanket.

His knees grazed Vivienne's, but there was nowhere else to scoot. She squinted in the morning light, studying him. His eyes were red, the dark circles beneath nearly gaunt from strain.

She handed him the plate of pastries. "Please have something to eat, Sir Sebastian, and tell us how your grandmother is faring."

At the mention of his grandmother, he ducked his head. "The doctors haven't much hope, and I have to admit—" He cleared his throat and brushed at his eyes with his fist. "I have to admit that I do not hold much hope either. I fear she will be gone within the fortnight."

Vivienne's stomach twisted from shame. She had been selfishly planning on pleading her case one last time, and this man was losing the closest person in his life. She rested her hand on his arm. "I am so sorry. I well know the pain of loss. I shall keep you and your grandmother in my prayers throughout the days ahead."

His piercing eyes met hers, the desperation there shocking her, along with a flash of something familiar. But perhaps it was her own desperation that made her conjure any sense of familiarity with this man on whom all her future hopes rested.

"My lady, you said that you depended on my name for your very freedom."

She blinked at the sudden change in topic. Was he changing his mind? Had his grandmother's state rattled him so much that he no longer cared? *He did say his main objection was because of his grandmother's eagerness for grandchildren.* Her heart careened toward hope. "I do."

He tore the chocolate-filled pastry and popped half into his mouth. She resisted cracking her knuckles as she waited for what he would say next.

He tossed the remainder of the pastry onto his plate and dusted off his hands. "As I feared, my grandmother heard of my supposed marriage to you."

"No." She pressed her hand to her mouth. "Oh, Sir Sebastian. I am sincerely sorry for all the pain I've caused—"

He lifted his hand. "I have a plan that will prove mutually beneficial."

Surely he wouldn't propose an actual binding marriage? Her stomach churned again, and she clutched Charlotte's hand even as the tendrils of hope sprang to life in her heart. "P-pray tell."

"When I arrived last night to find her so frail, I expected her to pass in the night, but when she saw me, she lifted a letter at her side. Her friend wrote to her, telling her of the arrival of Lady Larkby in Bath. Grandmother was aware I was on my way to visit and took the word of her friend to heart. She thinks you are a surprise for her—to bring her light in her final days on earth."

She pressed the back of her hand to her neck to cool her skin. She had not meant her nom de plume to cause such a stir—to cause a dying lady to have false hope. "I never meant for any of this to happen. I beg you to believe me that I am in earnest. I thought the title was long out of use."

"I'll admit, I did not believe your intentions were pure when I first heard of a lady falsely bearing my title . . . but rest assured, I do see that you are speaking the truth." He rested his hand on hers for a second before drawing back and taking his teacup with him, as if he had been reaching for his cup all along. "The staff said that after reading the letter, she had color in her cheeks that her maid has not seen in months. I hope you understand that I cannot take away that spark in her final hours."

"What are you asking, Sir Sebastian?" Vivienne lifted her linen napkin, fanning herself. "I am appalled that I have caused such a stir, but I-I *cannot* wed a stranger."

"No!" He interjected so emphatically that a few about them turned to survey him. He cleared his throat, lowering his voice. "No, Miss Poppy, I am asking that you merely continue your charade as my bride . . . at Lark Manor."

Charlotte gasped, and Vivienne dropped her napkin. "Sir. As much as I wish to aid a dying woman, I cannot—"

He lifted his palm once more. "I know. It is beyond scandalous to even utter a plan such as this, but you have your companion. Miss Vale can act as a protector of your reputation. I give you both my word—this arrangement is only until she passes. After . . ." He cleared his throat and paused as he gathered himself. "After she goes to our heavenly Father, I vow that I shall not protest you using my name."

"B-but what of a future wife? Even if you haven't met her yet, you must consider what this would do to her feelings. She would protest such a plan."

"I have no plans for marriage, as I serve the Prince Regent as a Yeoman of the Guard."

"A yeoman . . . I suppose that does add some credence to your character." Charlotte brushed a piece of grass from the edge of the blanket.

"Indeed. I've never met a guard to royalty." Vivienne eyed him. This explained his broad shoulders, his impossibly large muscles that only Corinthians sported. This man was no simple sportsman but a knight in every sense of the word. And if he was a yeoman, they would be safe to entrust him with their well-being.

"Because of my position, which I have no intention of releasing until I am too old to bear the role, you may have the use of my name without fear of any future wife laying claim to it."

She dipped her head, her mind whirling. *This is utter madness. Foolhardy, but . . .* The possibility of having control over her future was so close, if only she would have the courage to seize it. *Seize, or take leave of my senses. In this instance, they are one and the same.* But she had already been out in Bath society as Lady Larkby. Everyone knew she had a husband. It was a wonder she had yet to meet anyone who knew of Sir Sebastian, given that Lark Manor was just a few miles outside the city. *I suppose it helps that most of Bath society only stays for a season.* However, the more time she spent in society, the more likely she would hear of someone who knew of Lark Manor. If she did this, no one would ever suspect she was not married—except perhaps Bash, if he returned. But he was a highwayman, and he had no room to judge her.

She could have the independence offered to a married woman, along with the supposed protection of a knight. No one would dare harm her. This might be the greatest blessing ever placed before her. This could work. *But I need Charlotte to agree.* "Sir Sebastian, would you mind taking a turn in the gardens for a moment? I need to ask Miss Vale her thoughts."

He rose, tipped his hat, and strode toward the path that led to the bridge near the labyrinth.

She turned to Charlotte, cheeks warming at the prospect before her. "What do you think?"

"I think you have been offered a gift . . . but it is so risky, Miss Vivienne." She twisted her hands. "Perhaps you should send for Miss Tess Hale? She would better protect you with her skills with a blade."

Vivienne shook her head. "I would not accept Sir Sebastian's proposition if I did not trust his conduct and word as a gentleman. Besides, even if I possessed skills, a knight of his caliber would be able to evade them."

"You trust him? We've only just met him," she reminded her. "I do not wish for your desperation to cloud your judgment."

"I am desperate, which is why I am trusting you to help me decide. I have a feeling about him, *and* he's a knight."

"A handsome one at that," Charlotte added and packed away the empty teapot. "Yes, and it is because of his position that I am considering this wild scheme—and that his grandmother's heart is involved. I am not certain how you may remove yourself from this current situation without giving her unnecessary heartbreak." Charlotte pinched the bridge of her nose. "This is my first time as a companion. I've longed to better my position, but I selfishly fear if I let this occur and it goes awry, I will never be awarded another position after you eventually marry and no longer have a need for a companion."

Vivienne grasped Charlotte's hand. "I have no plans of marrying anytime soon, my dear Charlotte. And if the miraculous happens, you will have a position with me for so long that even if there is a small scandal leading up to said miraculous union, everyone will have long forgotten about it by the time you wish for a new position."

Charlotte sighed, reaching for the last bite of her pastry and tucking away the plate. "I hope I do not live to regret this moment."

"Trust me, the feeling is mutual." She lifted her hand to Sir Sebastian, motioning him over. She grinned up at him. "Sir Sebastian, it appears you have yourself a bride."

He clapped his hands, rubbing his palms together. "Excellent, because I already told Grandmother I was coming to fetch you and your things."

GRACE HITCHCOCK

"You were confident I would agree?"

"I was confident in your need for my title." He knelt and handed his dish to Charlotte to pack. "How fast can you ladies be ready for staying a week or two at the manor?"

"I can have Lady Larkby packed in an hour, but before we go rushing off to the manor, I think you two might need to have a chat."

They turned to Charlotte.

She rose, basket in hand, as she motioned them off the blanket. "You are supposed to have had a whirlwind romance. It would be for the best that you have your stories in tandem and that you learn about each other before your bride meets Mrs. Larkby and the entire plan unravels."

Vivienne scooped up the front corners of the blanket, with Sir Sebastian taking the opposite ends and helping her fold it—an unexpected act that touched her. She handed it to Charlotte. "What would I do without you?"

"Ruin your reputation all on your own?" She shook her head. "You will be safe enough to take a promenade back to the apartment while I hurry home and see to the packing."

Sir Sebastian extended his hand to her. "Lady Larkby, shall we explore the labyrinth? I heard it is nearly a mile long."

"As we are just beginning our acquaintance, let us stroll to the bridge in plain view of all."

Bash had missed having Evie in his company. While she had been rather rude at times with him as a highwayman, he knew that was not her true nature—especially when she'd confided in him in the end. He had caught a glimpse of her heart, and it was lovely. He would have to sift his motives for helping her—among the guilt, pressure, and excitement at the prospect of taking her to Lark Manor, he also had a sense of obligation . . . and interest.

She paused on the bridge, leaning over the rail to watch a couple in a rowboat glide underneath as thunder rumbled overhead. "Sir Sebastian, I do not know quite how to transition to such an intimate topic that I feel needs addressing, so I simply shall begin."

That brought him up. What intimate topic was she considering? At her all-encompassing blush, he swallowed. *Ah, that.* He ceased holding her arm and leaned on the railing to join her in watching the boats. "I shall reiterate that I am a nobleman and a God-fearing man. I would never—"

She held up her hand, her pretty cheeks flaming even deeper. "*That* is not what I was going to ask. I wished to know how we fell in love."

"Fell in love?" His heart thudded in his chest, thinking of their time together on the highway—of her kiss that had awakened his heart. He hadn't considered himself in love, but the all-consuming thoughts of this woman echoed the name that was forever etched on his soul.

"I have several ideas, of course, but would like to seek your counsel to see if they would match your true character, or if to make this believable, to take you out of character because you are besotted with me."

He grinned in sheer relief to see her shoulders easing. "Pray, how did we meet?"

She steepled her fingertips, drumming them against one another. "I suppose it is rather devious to take pleasure in creating such a tale, but it is what I do, so forgive me. You and I met on the road to Bath."

He stopped short. Did she recognize him? "W-what? How could that be? I only just arrived to Bath, and you've—"

She rolled her eyes. "This is a fictionalized history. Surely you cannot have a problem with it already?"

He scrambled to explain his odd reaction. "What I meant is, we should have met sooner, perhaps in a ballroom in London?"

Her eyes brightened. "Excellent. There's the spirit, Sir Sebastian. Yes, a ball in London would be just the place. We danced thrice, causing all sorts of talk of your affections. I left for my home in Bath, and you followed me, only to come upon me being taken by a handsome highwayman."

He swallowed a grin. "Handsome? Not a rogue with mottled teeth and bad breath? Wouldn't that be more believable?"

"But not so much fun to talk about. I picture him as a devil-may-care fellow with flowing locks that shimmer like gold in the sunlight." She looked off into the distance, as if imagining Bash, the highwayman. "Perhaps it aroused a fierce protectiveness in you, as well as jealousy, but only a hint of jealousy, as a jealous man would be tiresome to deal with day in and day out. That jealousy awoke you to the depth of your devotion for me though."

"Handsome he will be, then." Bash gently grasped her hand and tugged her down the bridge, trying not to be too pleased with the fact that she had considered him handsome and obviously had been thinking on him. He had been thinking of her hourly. He looked down upon her as they strolled through the pleasure gardens. How could he not? She was positively charming. And now, to have her on his arm, pretending to be his wife? It was nearly too much. He waited for the usual sensation of needing to bolt back to his position in London, but only a deep contentment settled. He was drawn to this fiercely independent young woman who broke away from the conventional socialite in so many ways. An arrangement of convenience should not be this amusing. "What happens next in our journey to matrimony?"

"You fight the highwayman and rescue me, winning my heart and my hand. We, of course, must have courted for at least a fortnight, and we wed over the anvil."

He nodded to her bare finger. "We had best stop at the jewelers and find you a ring."

"Such a thing is not necessary." She dipped her head.

He halted her, taking both her hands in his. "A token is expected, and as a thank-you, you may keep it."

Evie gasped. "I couldn't possibly. Such a gift—"

"If you are to hold my title, as per our deal, you should indeed keep it as proof of your claim. There is a jewelers only a few minutes out of our way on the walk back to your terrace home." At the thunder crackling, he gritted his teeth. "Or perhaps I should hire us a coach?"

"I love being out of doors before a rain. Though, it does tend to make my hair as wild as it was in my girlhood."

He would like to see her hair wild again. "Shall we walk?"

She nodded and allowed him to guide her out of the park toward Great Pulteney Street. The amble to the jewelers on Milsom Street was filled with snippets of information passed between them as a fine mist began to fall, and he found himself needing to be careful not to show how much he already knew about her.

He held the door for her as they entered the jewelers. Her eyes widened at the selection, but her gaze was at once drawn to a small display of citrines, even though she kept bringing her observation back to the more sensible silver pieces in the corner.

The rail-thin man behind the counter inclined his head to them, eyeing Evie's wild curls. "May I be of service?"

Bash patted Evie's hand. "I am in need of a ring for my lovely wife."

"We have some pieces in a simple design that might interest you." He reached for a collection of gold bands.

Bash lifted his hand. "I was thinking something with citrines."

She twirled around to gape at him. "Truly?"

He caught her hand in his and pressed a kiss atop it, her eyes widening at the gesture, but she schooled her mien. "For a lady of golden locks and a heart of gold."

The bell over the door jingled once more, and a buxom woman in a scarlet pelisse strode inside.

Evie jerked her hand back, her cheeks blossoming. "Oh no. Oh no," she muttered.

"Whatever is—"

"My dear Miss Poppy?" The woman approached Evie, her arms open, and pulled her into an embrace. "I'd recognize those wiry golden curls anywhere. You never were able to tame them in your childhood, and now I see they have grown even more unruly. I didn't think that was possible." She held her at arm's length, smiling. "Your features are so manly still that I knew you were Mr. Poppy's daughter. At least your sense of fashion has improved to bring out your feminine graces." She released an energetic giggle, looking to Bash. "I cannot tell you how many times I caught this girl in nature-stained, torn dresses, driving her pony cart pell-mell across the green—such a wild little thing without a mother to guide her."

He instantly disliked the woman. Evie was all grace and beauty. While she might possess her father's likeness, a fact he would never know, she was all womanly curves. As for the driving, he was eager to witness her prowess.

"Mrs. Zander. How wonderful to see you after so many years. You have not changed a bit." Evie's voice and smile were strained.

"Such flattery will not distract me from the striking gentleman kissing your hand for all to see." She eyed the citrine the jeweler had in his hand. "And a gem being selected? Do I hear wedding bells?"

Evie sent Bash a look, begging him for help.

He swept her hand into his, kissing it once more. She jerked out of his touch. He had misread the situation—at least she did not wipe the back of her hand on her skirts. He bowed to Mrs. Zander. "Indeed, the wedding bells have long since sounded. I am Sir Sebastian Larkby."

"A knight? My my, you have done well in the world, Lady Larkby." Her eyes brightened, recognition widening her impossibly broad smile. "Why, you couldn't be the famed authoress? How long have you two been married if the authoress has been publishing these three years and you are just now buying a jewel?"

"It is an anniversary jewel," he supplied, even as he felt Evie squirm under the lies, or perhaps because of the fact that Mrs. Zander knew her as Vivienne *Poppy* and word might very well get back to her stepbrother. This truly was getting out of control. He had not taken into account that Evie might still have friends in Bath from her childhood. The fictional romance would have to be adjusted to reflect the timeline. Perhaps they could say it was a secret marriage? He gritted his teeth. *That does not seem scandalous in the least. And as for the stepbrother, one dilemma at a time.*

"Well, I hate to be the bearer of bad news, but I have had my eye on that very gem. The jeweler can attest to my seeing it yesterday, and I did not have enough on my person to purchase it. Today I do." She jingled her reticule, giggling. "You do understand, don't you, dear? Citrines are so rare, especially one with such vivacious clarity." She moved to cut before them and held her hand out for the jewel.

"I'm afraid that I do not agree. My wife is quite partial to citrines, and not only do we wish for the ring, but the matching necklace and eardrops as well."

Evie seized his arm. "Dearest, I had no idea you were going to purchase the set." She lowered her voice. "The surround is gold filigree. It is too costly."

"It was going to be a surprise for you." He lifted his purse and paid the jeweler. "Shall you wear them out, my love?"

"In broad daylight? How vulgar." Mrs. Zander tsked, her cheeks puffing at being bested.

"It is permissible to be a little vulgar on one's anniversary." He motioned for Evie to come closer. He pulled the sash of her bonnet and removed her silk-lined piece. He set the eardrops in place, his fingers brushing her neck as he did so. He fixed the necklace, and at last, he lifted the ring. She stared up at him, her full lashes wide, and he had the urge to kiss her then and there as he slid the ring on her finger. *It is an act, man! Remember she is* acting, *as you are.* He was a fool to spend so much on jewels, but at this moment he considered it the soundest investment to be the reason behind her smile.

Chapter Ten

SIR SEBASTIAN LIFTED HIS HAND to her, assisting her from the coach. She clutched her skirt and stepped down onto the limestone gravel drive. The manor was situated before the River Avon and proved to be a stunning estate, far more vast than she had imagined. Vines crawled up the two-story manor house of checkerboard limestone and knapped flint, a lovely pattern that fit perfectly into the hillside that nestled it beyond the walled gardens with avenues of trees that would lend to a shaded walkway along the river. Roses abounded, sprawling on all sides of the manor, giving a romantic air to the estate.

"What an enchanting place to live."

"My grandmother has made it her home since her marriage to my grandfather, who passed many years ago. He planted the roses for her. He said that every bloom was a kiss from him to her for all eternity."

She pressed a hand to heart. "How romantic. I've never heard of a gentleman doing so for his lady."

A butler, four footmen, and two maids appeared at the door, lining the path to the house, hands held stiffly at their sides as they smiled at Vivienne. She nodded at the servants, offering them all smiles as she strode to the grand hall boasting a wide staircase. She cast a glance about, catching sight of the lovely furnishings and rooms that promised comfort and elegance. She itched to explore.

Sebastian paused at the threshold by the butler. "How is she, Ladd?"

"She's holding on for you and the lady." He bowed to Vivienne. "It is an honor to welcome you to Lark Manor, Lady Larkby."

"Thank you, Ladd." Her cheeks warmed at the kind gazes. Charlotte grasped her elbow, silently telling her to be strong.

"My lady." Sebastian offered her his arm.

She placed her trembling hand through it and allowed him to lead her up the wide stairs to the first floor. The hall was carpeted in emerald, which was splendid against the gold frames that lined the walls. She would have to find Sebastian's painting in the gallery.

He led her down the hall, pausing outside the first door on their left. "Grandmother Larkby will be somewhat disoriented, but smile and say how happy you will make her grandson."

"Make her a grandson?" Vivienne's voice squeaked at the expectation.

"No! How happy you will make *me*." He ran a hand over his jaw, as if to block a laugh. "Obviously, *I* am her grandson."

"Oh, of course." She swallowed, the guilt gnawing at her belly with the act to come. But wasn't this an act of the greatest charity? To send a dying woman to meet her Maker with a light heart over her grandson's happiness? "Sir Sebastian, are we doing the right thing by her?"

He gritted his teeth. "I know. I have been having second thoughts as well, but it is too late, my lady. Before my grandmother you must call me Sebastian as a sign of your affection."

"Yes, Sir Sebastian."

He sighed, giving her a pointed look.

"I mean, *sir*." She pressed her hand to her forehead, groaning. "Sebastian! I'm sorry. I am just so nervous, and I am not very skilled at telling a falsehood with ease."

"It speaks well of your character." He gently grasped her elbow, smiling down at her. "How about if you called me 'my darling' to avoid confusion?"

She blinked.

"It would be easier to remember than not adding my title before my name. It does not flow from your tongue, but it will save you from stumbling."

"I suppose that would be acceptable." She straightened her shoulders and followed him into the dimly lit room, where a frail woman lay in a four-poster bed propped up on a silk pillow, her frilly mobcap fairly swallowing her head. Even though her eyes were sunken and her skin pale, her lovely smile brightened the room and set Vivienne's racing nerves at ease.

"Sebastian, my dearest one. You've brought her." She held her hand out to Vivienne, tears swimming in her eyes. "My, what a lovely bride you have found. Please, both of you kiss my cheek."

Vivienne did so, catching the scents of strong medicine and sweet lavender. "It is an honor to meet you, Mrs. Larkby. M-my darling has told me so much about you."

Her smile deepened. "He is darling indeed. What a relief to know that my Sebastian will be taken care of and loved by a woman who sees his worth." She patted Vivienne's cheek, her coloring heightened and her eyes brighter than only moments before. "Sebastian tells me you are an authoress. My eyes have not been as strong in recent years, or I'm certain I would've read your works before now. My lady's maid does not read, and I did not wish to burden a companion with my company. If you would be so kind as to read to me, I would like to hear your stories, for it might help me get to know you better before I'm called home."

Vivienne's eyes filled. "I would be happy to." Seeing Mrs. Larkby sparked within her a glimmer of a memory from her father's last days. Some would consider the time too hard to dwell upon, what with him being so weak, but she cherished those days when she had spent every waking moment at her father's side, gleaning his wisdom in his faith. When her father had first taken ill, her own faith had been rattled, but seeing him praise the Lord despite his circumstances had sent the sputtering spark of her faith into an inferno. She bowed her head. *Lord, let me bless Mrs. Larkby in her final days as my father blessed me in his.*

"I-I do have one question." Mrs. Larkby beckoned Vivienne closer with a flick of her gnarled finger. "Do you have any grandbabies on the way?"

Sebastian coughed, and Vivienne's cheeks burned at the loud whisper. "Such a question, Mrs. Larkby."

"*Grandmother*," she corrected Vivienne with a smile. "Well, with two people as handsome and lovely as you, beautiful babies will soon be on the way, if they are not already. It's only natural."

Vivienne looked about for Charlotte, who had been in the doorway only moments before. "I best find my room and help guide my companion as she unpacks my trunks for me. Excuse me, Grandmother Larkby. I shall return with a book for us to read together."

She fled, pushing aside thoughts of having beautiful babies with a beautiful man like Sebastian. That was not her future—unfortunately.

Charlotte came around the corner with a stack of Vivienne's books in hand. "I heard Mrs. Larkby ask for your books, so I took the liberty of retrieving your five titles from your trunk."

"Thank you, Charlotte. I'll store these in the library."

"There's a library?"

Vivienne gestured to the manor. "How could an ancient place such as this not possess one? I'll find it, one way or another, and hide there until I'm ready to face Mrs. Larkby again."

"It grew more awkward after I left?" Charlotte guessed, stacking them in Vivienne's arms.

"There was talk of beautiful babies on the way and a handsome husband."

"La, my lady." Charlotte's cheeks paled. "Such questions are far too intimate."

"I know." She nodded to the stack of books. "I shall be in the library for an hour if you have need of me. I intend to visit with Grandmother Larkby after I set my emotions to right." She needed to find a stack of paper and an inkwell to lose herself in her new tale, along with the painful, uncomfortable present.

The familiar scent of leather-bound books enveloped Bash. In the far corner of the library, the billiard table from his youth still stood, the cues racked and waiting. He needed time to think, and what better way to do it than to play a game? He lifted his favorite stick and moved to the table, removing the rack from the balls on the green fabric.

Vivienne popped up from the floor behind the settee, blinking in the afternoon light spilling through the curtain's opening. "Oh! I must have fallen asleep writing." She smoothed back her hair, which was spilling from her coiffure in an appealing manner. She rose and shook out her skirts. "Pardon my appearance. I am told that I am quite the wild sleeper, which gives my hair too much freedom."

His chest bubbled in laughter at the memory of Evie sleeping in the gig. He could attest to her fitful sleeping. "You look lovely as always, Vivienne, but I must ask why on earth you would be writing on the floor when a desk stands in the corner?" It was strange to call her so, but if he wasn't careful, he would be calling her Evie and risk being found out.

"Unlike many believe, writing is not always done at a desk or in one spot. I prefer to move to different places about a room to keep my mind sharp, and every now and again, I need to act out a certain scene to be sure I have it written in the best form." She shoved back a lock of hair, leaving an ink smudge on her forehead. "I was working out a scene of a fight in an alley." She motioned to the settee. "It provided an alley of a sort. After I worked out the scene whilst on the floor, I must have fallen asleep."

An alley? He grinned. She was capturing the entirety of their adventure on paper. "Sounds exciting."

"It is." Her smile dimmed as she stretched her neck from side to side. "I fear I'm neglecting my duties though." She snatched up a book from a small stack on the writing desk and hurried past him toward the doorway.

"I came to play billiards while Grandmother slept. You are neglecting no one." He set his stick down and caught her creamy wrist, gently staying her as he reached into his pocket and withdrew a handkerchief. He pressed it to her forehead, wiping at the mark, but it held fast. "It seems the ink on your forehead doesn't want to depart."

Her cheeks bloomed as she stepped back from him, and he released her wrist. "Thank you. I'll see to it. I often forget that I have ink on my fingers after writing."

"My lady, you have no need to feel uncomfortable in my presence. I know my grandmother may ask some things that are . . . forward, but the elderly tend to set aside conventions in their final days. Know that I think nothing of such questions. I am forever grateful for you being willing to help me, and I shall stand by the terms of our arrangement."

"We both have much to lose, and she is a kind soul. I can see why you would go so far to see her happy."

He picked his stick back up, struck the white billiard ball, and sent the balls scattering. "I would do anything for her. She is everything to me."

Vivienne clutched the book to her chest. "I shall be in Mrs. Larkby's room, waiting for her to awaken, if you have need of me."

He glanced from her retreating form to the stack of books atop the writing desk—all bearing *his* title. Lady Larkby was quite prolific for having been published for only three years. He picked up a title and flipped it open, sinking on the window seat. The bookstore had been sold out when he had attempted to discover more about her before the masquerade—which felt like an eternity ago.

He cringed at the romance, but the story itself wasn't terrible and the writing was melodic. There were so many bouquets being given in the book, he finally sighed and tossed it aside, deciding he had best take a cue from Evie. *Vivienne.*

He strode out into the rose gardens, gathering one bouquet for his grandmother and a second for his supposed bride. If he were to keep up appearances, he would need to give each woman a token of his affection.

"Excuse me, Sir Sebastian?"

He turned to find the boy from the inn stables—looking considerably less scrawny in the short time since Bash had last seen him. Grandmother must have taken one look at him and instructed the cook to empty the larder and pantry in an effort to minister to his health. "I see my grandmother gave you a position." He nodded to the lad's livery. "You look well, Noah."

Noah puffed out his chest, grinning. "The best I have ever felt. I-I would never seek you out, b-but I wanted to thank you. I was grooming the horses when you arrived—otherwise I would have told you then."

He shook his head. "No need to thank me. I may have seen you awarded the position, but it is your hard work that will see that you keep it. Are you happy here?"

"Yes, sir. Very, sir. Mrs. Larkby has been kind to me. She even let me have the mornings off to attend the local school. If there is anything you ever need, you let me know and I'm your man." The boy scampered back to work, his movements stronger than they had been not too long ago.

He would have expected nothing less from his grandmother to see to Noah's mind as well as his body's needs. She always did have a soft spot for motherless boys. Bash climbed the stairs with his two bouquets, noting the laughter floating out from his grandmother's chamber. The two women had apparently bonded much while he was out. He strode inside to find the windows open wide and Evie sitting on the edge of the bed with a book in her hand and his grandmother . . . in tears? He paused at the door, blooms in hand, assessing the situation. He was not skilled when tears were involved.

"My dear Sebastian, come in. Your bride is a delight. I have not laughed so hard in years." Grandmother's gaze shifted to the roses, and she clasped her hands to her heart. "Oh, what lovely blooms. Thank you, my boy. I miss such thoughtful gestures when you are away. And yet knowing that you are living your childhood dream makes my heart take flight."

He bent, kissed Grandmother on the forehead, and rested the blooms on the blanket where she might enjoy them as the maid fetched a vase. He turned to Evie, uncertain. He had never given a young lady flowers before. He bowed and extended them to her. The small gesture felt monumental.

Evie's fingers brushed his as she accepted the bouquet with a smile and buried her nose in the blooms, breathing deeply. "How kind of you, my darling."

He found himself wishing that she meant the pet name.

As if sensing his longing, Grandmother scowled. "Aren't you going to thank your husband properly? You're a writer of romance and adventure, but I've yet to witness either from the two of you."

Her cheeks flamed. "Grandmother Larkby, such a thing you ask. You have been too long out of society if you think such a thing is acceptable to ask."

He grinned, liking the sound of Grandmother Larkby's suggestion, but he gave her a teasing grin and chided, "Grandmother, I hardly think such a display is—"

"You would deny me such happiness as bearing witness to a sweet romantic moment at my advanced years?"

He grasped Evie's hand and helped her to stand, his heart pounding as hard as Brigand's hooves. She was a lovely woman. It wasn't as if the thought of kissing her again hadn't crossed his mind. But kissing with an audience, who was already giggling in delight at his discomfort, was hardly how he'd imagined their second kiss. He lifted Evie's hand to his lips. "There. You mischievous girl." He winked at Grandmother.

She snorted. "Sebastian Gray Larkby, you look like a chicken with that peck."

"No one has ever dared call me a chicken."

"When one kisses like that, it is warranted. If you think that is a kiss, it is a wonder that you got her to the anvil."

His brows rose.

"I told your grandmother about our romantic marriage over the anvil in Gretna Green." Evie sent him a strained smile, begging him to play along.

"Ah yes, our marriage." He claimed Evie's hand in his once more. "I wish you could have seen it, Grandmother. Vivienne hardly ceased kissing me long enough to say the vows."

"Sebastian!" Vivienne gasped, walloping his chest with the roses, a handful of petals bursting free. "I did *no* such thing."

Grandmother lifted her roses and caressed a bloom. "Do not fear my judgment, dear girl. Sebastian's grandfather was the most romantic man I have ever met. Surely some of his romance has passed on to his grandson, making him irresistible to you." Grandmother coughed into her handkerchief. "Go ahead and kiss her then. Do not be shy on my account, Sebastian. Lord knows, you were never shy in any other instance. Why, I remember you pretending to be an Olympian as a boy, tearing across the lawn in nothing—"

He drew Vivienne close to him, assessing her for any signs of unwillingness. Chewing her bottom lip was a mark of contemplation. Did she want him to kiss her? It felt too long since their kiss, but would she recognize his touch? He slowly lowered his lips toward hers, giving her ample time to signal him.

She darted under his arm, laughing. "You are quite naughty, Grandmother Larkby, goading my Sebastian into a kiss, but I shall not kiss a reluctant knight. Now, if you'll excuse me, I have some writing to do. I shall leave you with your Olympian."

Chapter Eleven

THE MAID PAUSED BEFORE THE open door, hands folded before her skirts and head bowed as Vivienne and Charlotte ambled into the bedroom that was to be Vivienne's for the fortnight. The massive four-poster bed was dressed with robin's-egg damask curtains that brightened the silver-papered walls and would do well in protecting one from the harsh chill of winter. The fireplace was, of course, dormant, and in place of a fire, a lovely basket filled with dried lavender brought color and a delightful scent.

She traced the chair rail with her finger and paused before a door opposite the bed. *Please be a closet and not a connected dressing room.* She opened it and found her trunks in the far corner, along with a washstand and the necessary. Her heart pounded at the sight of a second door that surely adjoined her room with the master's—Sebastian's. She shut the door and schooled her voice along with her features. A bride of three years, even one with a secret romantic union such as Sebastian had explained to the staff, would not show such trepidation. *Only a single morning at the manor, and the lies are already suffocating me.* "I thought Grandmother Larkby was staying in the master bedroom?"

"She likes the one facing her husband's roses and the river," the maid said.

Vivienne glanced at the window that overlooked the front gardens, and while it was pretty, she understood why Grandmother Larkby preferred to overlook the river, which would give her beautiful views year-round. If Vivienne were the lady of the house, she likely would do the same.

The maid tittered. "Besides, you are Sir Sebastian's wife, and she insisted you be given the adjoining suite meant for a couple."

Yes, his wife. She grasped Charlotte's hand. Thank the Lord for Charlotte, who would never leave her side day or night. Vivienne trusted Sir Sebastian—she would not have agreed to this scheme if she did not. And yet she had this niggling inclination that she had met him before. She had been drawn to him. Perhaps it was her romantic side taking over her sensibilities. Who wouldn't be overcome when encountering the gentleman who was supposed to be her counterfeit husband and who then proceeded to pretend to be said husband when he rescued her from making a fool of herself in Bath? *"Counterfeit" being the key word, Vivienne Poppy. He is not and will never be yours . . . just like a certain handsome highwayman.* "My companion and I shall see to the unpacking."

The maid's brows shot upward, but she pressed her lips into a thin line and bobbed a curtsy. "If you have any need, pull the bell cord, my lady."

Vivienne groaned at the click of the latch and sank onto the window seat, staring out upon the drive. "Oh, Charlotte, what have I gotten us into?"

Her companion rolled her eyes, not exactly the comfort Vivienne was seeking. "No one ever listens to me, so why should you? You have gotten us into exactly what you planned, my lady."

"I admitted folly. This was not my best laid plan, but must you rub salt into my wound?" Vivienne crossed into the dressing room and flung open the trunk lid.

"Sometimes being the one in the right, it is impossible to stay silent on such matters." Charlotte relieved Vivienne of the morning gown, setting it in its proper place. "I'll put this and the rest of your things away, my lady. You had best acquaint yourself with the manor during the daylight to prevent further disasters should you desire some night writing in the library and find yourself somewhere you shouldn't be."

Disasters of the reputation-destroying kind. She squeezed Charlotte's arm in thanks.

Carrying her small book of poetry, her notebook, and a pencil, she took to the halls to explore every open door. The first few proved to be dusty guest rooms, but at the last room on the left, she paused, guessing this must be Sebastian's old room. The familiar flare of curiosity burned in her belly. She gave a light tap on the door on the off chance he was inside. She counted to twenty, glanced both ways, and pushed open the door. She dashed inside and softly closed the door, her heart pounding at her unspeakable daring.

The masculine scent of leather and peppermint enveloped her. On the wall were decorative daggers, swords, and even a pike. She smiled. It had to be Sebastian's room . . . well, his room before his supposed marriage to her. She dared to step inside further, feeling like an intruder. She ran her fingers along the spines of books stacked on his desktop. She didn't recognize any of the titles, each about some form of weaponry, fighting, or history of battles. Judging from the weapons surrounding her, Sir Sebastian was a formidable foe. *She'd* be well protected under his care.

She shook her head at that thought. He was only her ally for a fortnight. After which she would be on her own again—as always. She would have to learn to be her own protector . . . despite the fact she was the reason she was in this predicament in the first place. After this misadventure, she would write a harsh, chiding letter to herself listing all her recent mistakes and commanding herself to make better choices in the future.

On his bedside table was a folded handkerchief with embroidery on the corner. Unable to keep her curiosity in check, she dared to unfold it to read the stitched words: *1 Peter 5*. She carefully refolded the handkerchief, making a mental note to look up the chapter.

She moved around the bed and tripped over the corner of the rug, dropping her writing supplies. She caught herself on the wall. As she bent to flip the rug corner back into place, she spotted something odd in the paneled wood. She ran her fingers along the minuscule crack.

What on earth? What are you hiding, Sebastian? Her fingers found purchase and, pressing one slipper against the wall, she tugged, falling onto her derriere as a small door creaked open.

"A priest hole?" She laughed in pleasure at the tiny door. She had only read about the hidden sanctuaries for men of the cloth in times of persecution. She tucked her supplies into her deep hidden pockets and crawled forward on her hands and knees, poking her head inside to have a better look. She met a spider's web at once. Vivienne muffled a shriek as she clawed away the webs from her hair and nose, sneezing and smacking her forehead on the makeshift panel.

At the tapping of boots approaching, she backed out of the hole, shut the hidden door, righted the carpet, smoothed her hair, and darted back toward his desk. The pins in her hair slipped out, and to her horror, her locks tumbled to her waist. She would look, for all the world to see, like a bride awaiting her husband. Her cheeks flamed as she desperately tried to right her hair to no avail.

"No." She would not be caught. It would be beyond humiliating to be seen so, especially if the boots belonged to Sir Sebastian. What could she say to him to explain away her abominable actions? Heaven help her if he thought she was attempting to ensnare him in a true marriage. *What else would he possibly think with my hair down in his chambers without my companion?*

She glanced at the priest hole and, without a second thought, launched herself at it. She clawed open the door and crawled inside, but her hips caught between the panels. Wiggling her body to fit, she slid herself through, reached to find the handle behind her, and jerked the door shut.

The boots paused at the doorway. Peering over her shoulder through the faintest crack, she spied Sebastian entering. His broad shoulders and muscular frame made the bedroom seem impossibly small and her far too close. If she sneezed, it would be over in an instant.

She studied him, with only a hint of guilt gnawing at her, as he moved to a trunk along the wall and withdrew a fresh linen shirt, tossing it upon the bed. He pulled at his neckcloth and yanked off his shirt, his broad back muscular and bronzed, as if he often trained without his shirt in an open field. She snapped her head forward and buried her face in her hands. What kind of proper lady hid in a gentleman's room and then proceeded to gawk at him? Would she never learn to keep her curiosity in check?

When the door shut and the room was at last still, she uncovered her eyes and reached back for the latch, fumbling a bit before pushing it open. On her hands and knees, she backed out. Her legs slipped through the opening easy enough, but somehow her hips caught in the opening. "What on earth?" She twisted her hips and tried backing out of the tiny door once more, but her hips wedged firmly this time. She groaned, but no amount of tugging would budge her hips. She was caught fast and true.

For a quarter of an hour, she wriggled every which way as panic consumed her. She begged the Lord to release her. Finally she hung her head. Consuming Muriel's baked goods had come to haunt her at last. This was perhaps a million times worse than being discovered with her hair down.

"Sir Sebastian?" Charlotte called to him, her skirts slapping her legs in her haste to cross the garden.

He shot to his feet. "Miss Vale? Whatever is amiss? Is it my grandmother?" He glanced up at Grandmother's first-floor window.

"Nay." She pressed a hand to her stomach, her breathing fast. "Forgive me for alarming you, but I have looked everywhere, and I cannot find Lady Larkby."

He started. *Has she run away? But why would she depart without her companion?*

"She would not leave me behind, Sir Sebastian," she said, as if reading his thoughts, and she wrung her hands. "I sent her to explore the manor during the day so she might familiarize herself, and that was two hours ago. I have not seen her since, and I am worried that she has either gotten lost in the grounds or some harm has befallen her."

He rested his hand on her arm. "Have no fear, Miss Vale. I know every inch of this estate. We shall find her."

She lifted her hand to her flushed cheek. "Thank you, sir. I should have come to you sooner, but I did not wish to cause a scene over naught. She sometimes gets caught away in her musings whence puzzling out her book in progress. However, she can always be found easily."

"Set your mind at ease. You did the right thing in coming to me. You search the grounds, and I shall start with the house before moving out of doors. I have not seen her exit the house, and I have been out of doors most of the afternoon, save for a few moments. We shall find her," he promised, more to himself than to the companion.

He raced inside. He searched the length of the house on the ground floor and checked each room, to no avail. He climbed the stairs to the first floor, checking every room. His door was at the end. *She wouldn't be in there though.* However, he could not leave any room unchecked. He flung open the door and cast a glance about, his gaze resting on muslin skirts hugging shapely hips that protruded from the panel in the wall. His jaw slackened. "Is that you, my lady?"

"Oh dear Lord, it is the end then," came her muffled reply.

He squatted beside her, averting his eyes from her posterior. Apparently, her hips were stuck in the narrow doorway. "Are you hurt, my lady?"

"In body? No. In spirit?" She whimpered. "There is no recovery."

He swiped his hand over his mouth and sat back on his heels, his laughter bubbling out.

"This is not a laughing matter, I assure you."

He threw his head back and laughed again. "I beg to differ, as I am heartily looking forward to your no doubt interesting explanation of your predicament."

"I suppose I couldn't ask you to simply trust me."

"And miss out on your rationalization? No."

She sighed. "Then would it be possible to keep this a secret between us?"

"I shall take it to the grave, my lady." He knelt, studying the panel. "I see the flaw that is keeping you wedged. I believe your hidden pockets under your gown have created an issue." He tugged at the bunch of skirt, but it barely moved. "What do you have stuffed in your pockets?"

"What I always carry when I have a leisure hour—a pocketbook of poetry and my small notebook and pencil."

"That would cause the issue. I am surprised they are not visible under your skirts while you stand."

"They are, but again, it is for my leisure hour." She grunted. "Could we possibly continue this conversation when I am unwedged and preferably face-to-face?"

"A knife should see you free in a matter of moments, but I think you would wish for an alternative solution, even if it takes a few moments longer."

"As I'm rather fond of this gown, let us try another means."

With a few tugs, he at last drew Evie through. She sank onto the floor, red-faced and hair askew, dirt marring her mottled cheeks.

He crossed his arms, sitting back on his heels as she dusted off her hands.

"I trust you are awaiting an explanation."

He grinned. "That would be good."

She cleared her throat and looked to her filthy skirts. "I have had some time to consider what I was going to say should you be the one to discover me."

"The truth would be a good place to start."

"Yes, well, the truth isn't always the easiest to convey, as you and I well know." She looked at him, her eyes filled with regret. "You should know that I was born with an extra dose of curiosity. It has never been kind to me, and no matter how hard I try to tame it, I fail when it matters most. I was exploring and wanted to be better acquainted with the whole of the house, a-and . . ."

"And when you came to my room, you decided to see what I was hiding behind closed doors?" *What excuse could she possibly have for going through my belongings?* He stifled a grin as she stiffened.

"Not necessarily. I wished to better acquaint myself with the man who is my pretend husband." She grimaced. "It may not have been my wisest means of doing so, but—"

"That is fair."

She sighed, relief flooding her smile. "I thought so too. It is not as if you wrote books for a living and I might read those to see what type of personality you possessed. It really isn't fair." She rushed onward. "As to how you found me, I tripped on the carpet." She pointed beside them. "Which led to me discovering the priest hole, and I've always wanted to see one in person. Once I managed to open it and examine it up close, I heard noises in the hall and decided the best course of action was to hide."

"You hid in the priest hole . . . while I was in the room?" His gaze skidded to the discarded linen shirt on the bed and back to her, sucking in his cheeks and raising his brows.

Her face turned red. "Yes. But once I saw you draw off your shirt, I turned away! I vow it."

"You saw me with my shirt off?" He crossed his arms, unable to resist puffing out his chest.

She buried her face in her hands. "Please, I assure you, I have learned my lesson against curiosity."

"That bad of a view, huh?"

"Oh no! You are very well sculpted—" She halted, narrowing her eyes at him. "You are teasing me."

His shoulders shook as he laughed again. This time Vivienne cracked a smile.

"I haven't laughed so much in many a year until I met you, my lady." Her gaze flickered at the name. He needed to quit calling her as he did when the highwayman. It was almost as bad as calling her Evie. He cleared his throat and held his hand out. "Now, let's return you to your quarters without the servants catching sight of you leaving my chambers looking so. I would hate to be caught by a pickthanks, even if we are pretending to be man and wife."

"You are aware that the maids put me in the bedroom with the shared dressing room," she blurted out.

"I am quite aware. Pardon the charade, my lady. On my word as a knight, I have not and shall *never* enter your chambers through our shared door." He held out his hand to her. "Do you trust me?"

She slowly grasped his hand. Her hand felt so right in his.

"I do not really have a choice."

She was right on that score. "I suppose the real question is if your curiosity will keep you from opening the shared door yourself when I am away from the house."

She lifted her hands. "My curiosity shall stay tucked away for the duration of my time at Lark Manor."

We will see about that. He led her to the door, peeked out, and seeing no one, pushed her out, grinning as she raced across the carpet to her door and darted inside. He would have his hands full with Evie Poppy under his roof.

Chapter Twelve

THE NEXT FEW DAYS, VIVIENNE was determined to be on her best behavior. She settled into a routine of taking her morning constitutionals along the river, followed by visiting with Grandmother Larkby over tea multiple times a day and spending the heat of the day in her room writing.

Charlotte, of course, noticed Vivienne's diligence of acting a lady and more than once pressed her to share everything that had occurred the day she'd disappeared. However, there was only so much humiliation Vivienne was willing to suffer, and the retelling of it would have been the end of her. Instead, she merely inferred that she had been stuck and Sir Sebastian had found her. No matter how much Charlotte pressed, Vivienne would take this one to her grave. And if she had her way, neither Muriel nor Tess would ever know.

With a flourish, she finished the final line of the chapter with the most romantic scene she had ever penned, thinking of her handsome highwayman for the whole of it. Between Bash's return of her funds, this novel, and the serialized story for the *Bath Chronicle*, she would have more than enough for the staff's wages and be able to indulge in adding a few new pieces to her wardrobe each season to avoid appearing dowdy once the brightness of Muriel's generous trunks of frocks faded.

"It has been three days since you have spent any time in Sir Sebastian's company. There are only so many meals you can take in your room due to 'the muse finding you.' The servants are talking," Charlotte said, embroidering a pillow upon the window seat. "I think you should forgo your hours of writing today and seek him out if you want to stanch the rumors downstairs of you two having a quarrel. It will surely reach Mrs. Larkby before the day is out if you do not see to it."

Vivienne blew on the fresh ink on the page, and when satisfied it would not run, she flapped the open notebook in the air for good measure. "You don't understand, Charlotte. I can't see him."

"I would understand if you would tell me, but as I will not press you again, you need to see to this on your own without any of my help." Charlotte stabbed the fabric, scowling and muttering.

Vivienne closed her book and rose. Charlotte was right, as always. If she didn't love the girl so much, she might consider it nice to have a companion who wasn't always in the right. She patted Charlotte's shoulder and headed into the hallway, checking first in the library to see if Sebastian was playing billiards.

A passing footman, holding a tray with a covered dish, noticed her searching and approached with a slight bow. "May I be of service, my lady?"

She forced confidence into her voice. "I was hoping to find my husband. I have an urgent matter to discuss with him."

The footman nodded, eyes flashing with concern. "An urgent matter? Allow me to take this to Mrs. Larkby's room, and then I will assist you and fetch him from the stables."

"Stables?"

"I believe he was going for a ride." He bowed again.

"No need to fetch him. You have a tray to deliver, and I would enjoy a turn out of doors. You have been most helpful." She nodded to the man and hurried around him, praying she did not look like the guilty houseguest that she was.

Bash was running the comb down Brigand's flank when he heard a feminine voice. He stiffened, realizing his mistake. He had brought his horse to the manor. Of course, he had never expected the woman he had abducted on Brigand to be a guest in his own home. And with her having been on the striking horse, she would no doubt recognize Brigand in an instant . . . and closely thereafter, *him*.

He chucked the comb into the wooden bucket, leaving his mount halfway groomed. Brigand shook his mane and stomped in protest.

"Sorry, boy. I've got to run. Noah will see to you." Bash raced out of the stall, shutting the door behind him to find Evie picking her way across the stables, lifting her skirts to avoid unsavory lumps on the pavers.

"Lady Larkby? What brings you to the stables?"

Her gaze met his, her cheeks blossoming at being caught with her hem revealing her pretty ankle. He hadn't seen this side of her when she was his captive—a shy maiden. The woman on the road had been fierce, bold, and fearless. This Vivienne *Larkby* was shy, uncertain. He needed to do his best to reassure her that he would follow through on his deal and encourage the fiery spirit he had seen in her to resurface once more. Her quick wit and ability to catch him off guard was addicting. It was not every day that Bash found someone who could surprise him.

"You, actually."

"What a lovely surprise. I have not seen you nor your companion for days."

"She has not left my side since that day, and I suppose our schedules did not align, as I have been breakfasting quite early."

He peered behind her.

"Well, Charlotte has to nap some time." She smiled. "Your grandmother and I have spent some lovely time together. I dare say that she seems much happier than just a few days ago."

"That is my prayer." He inclined his head. "Shall we walk beyond the stables? I can show you the grounds, as I believe you were too *caught* up to see them the last time you went exploring?"

"About that—"

"All is forgiven and do not think another moment on the situation."

He extended his arm, eager to distract her. "You'll need to know the ins and outs of the estate in order to entertain yourself whilst not in town."

"Very well." They walked in silence as she studied the fast-flowing river. "So what made you wish to become a Yeoman of the Guard?"

"My great-grandfather served the Crown, as well as my grandfather. My father died in service."

She pressed a hand to her heart. "I am so sorry. It is a terrible thing to lose a parent."

"I never knew him, but I felt compelled to follow in his steps. Our family has had a long legacy of knighthood, but there has not been a Larkby knight since my great-grandfather. I was granted the knighthood only two years ago for going above and beyond for the Crown."

She cleared her throat. "Sir Sebastian, please forgive my next question."

"Oh dear."

"What?"

"You have never shied away from uncomfortable questions, and now you approach one with an apology? I tremble at what you may ask." He grinned.

"This question is delicate in nature." She reached out and plucked a wildflower, but instead of the stem breaking, she brought up the entire root. She grimaced and knelt, patting it back into the earth. "Sorry! I thought the stem weak."

He knelt and unfolded his pocketknife, handing it to her. "'Tis only a wildflower. No need to try to plant it again."

"Thank you." She accepted the knife, her fingers grazing his. The blade sliced cleanly through the wildflower, and instead of handing the knife back to him, she proceeded to gather a bouquet. "What are we to do when your grandmother recovers?"

"You truly believe she is getting better?" Hope surged in his chest.

She nodded. "The doctor saw to her this morning, but as I left her chamber, I heard him exclaim over the color in her cheeks. I have reason to hope . . . which has me wondering what that means for us."

"I have hope too." He rested his hand over hers, and to his surprise, she did not pull away. "Let us not dwell upon what would happen if we must tell her the truth. That is tomorrow's worry."

"Even though I am concerned about our next step today?"

"The first step is to see she is well again." He bowed his head, whispering, "Lord, let it be so."

"And if she does recover, shall we only break her heart with the truth?" She voiced the very fear of his heart.

He exhaled. "I fear it is the only path, but she is a kind, reasonable woman and will see the logic behind our charade. She will be disappointed but will not give you away to society in any event. We shall uphold the deal. Until she is fully recovered, be the granddaughter she has always wished."

"That shall not be difficult, as I have come to care for her in these few days." She groaned. "This lie was to be one of mercy, Sebastian, and now it feels like anything but."

He kicked at a dead bloom on the path. "I never asked you . . ."

"Yes?"

"By this arrangement, are you sacrificing a hope of marriage to a gentleman of interest?"

Her cheeks bloomed. "There is no gentleman in my heart. I would be mad to release my independence for a man whom I do not hold in affection. No, our arrangement is not causing my marriage prospects harm."

He thought he caught a gentle inflection on the word *gentleman*. Did she have feelings for the highwayman? He longed to find out . . . but to do that, he would need to become the highwayman. Surely to court her in such a disguise was madness? But didn't she say madness was the only way she would be induced into matrimony? And what if she discovered it was him while he was in disguise? Would she despise him? Think he was playing her for the fool? He couldn't risk it—as much as he wished to.

They came to the arching stone bridge and strolled to the middle. She leaned over the railing, watching a mother duck and her ducklings swim beneath, smiling at the sight, and then they returned to the path on the manor's shore. They followed the river in silence as she studied their surroundings.

"It would be a pity not to learn something about each other's childhood." Bash cleared his throat. "I had thought we should better acquaint ourselves, seeing as we are thrown together for the fortnight."

"True." She nodded and was about to continue, when a low growl cut her off and sent her veering into his side.

Bash thrust himself in front of her, shielding her with his outstretched arm as a dog strode onto the path, hackles raised.

"Don't worry. I'm actually very good at calming dogs." He took a slow step forward, stretching out his hand. "There's a good boy," he said in a soothing tone. "No need to worry. We are friends."

"I don't think he's worried. He's mad."

"He's mad only because he thinks we will hurt him."

The dog lunged toward him, snapping his jaws, spittle clinging to his mouth.

"Sebastian?" Evie whispered. "Maybe we should just vacate the path and let him pass."

"He's only testing me." Bash grinned, not breaking eye contact with the beast, whose hackles were as high as ever as he growled. "That's a good boy." He took another step toward him, and the dog charged. Bash dodged as the dog snapped wildly, his claws spread.

Evie cried out, and Bash grasped her hand, running with her as the dog nipped at their heels.

"Can you swim?" Bash yelled, stripping off his coat.

"Yes, but—"

He wrapped his arms around her waist, plunging into the river's depths.

Sebastian kept a firm grip on her, and together they kicked to the surface, gasping. The beast stayed on the path, growling at them as the river swept them away from the imminent danger. Sebastian stroked with one arm toward the bank, keeping Vivienne firmly in his other arm as she kicked, despite her skirts tangling her legs, and paddled with her free hand.

"Can't risk climbing up on our side of the bank. The dog may follow," Sebastian managed between strokes.

She nodded, concentrating on not thinking of whatever was touching her limbs in the murky water and focusing on kicking to the shore opposite the manor. Sebastian gripped the stones of the riverbank, his fingers white with the effort.

His chest heaved beneath the plastered linen. "Can you manage to climb up?"

She peered at the rocks. "I wish I was confident in my skills . . ."

"Can you hold on to my back?"

She blinked at him. "Pardon?"

"Wrap your arms about my neck and shoulders, and I can climb us both out of here."

She eyed him. It wasn't necessarily that she doubted his ability, but her gown was soaked and the stones were slick.

He flicked the dripping water from his eyes, grinning. "I can do this."

"I know you can." She wrapped her arms about him, pressing her cheek to his shoulder. Satisfied she was not going to fall, she said, "Ready."

He braced his feet against the stone wall and reached for the first handhold, testing it before he trusted it as secure, slowly climbing up the bank, as if he had done it many times before. Her grip slipped and she faltered, tugging him with her back into the water. Water spurted up her nose, and she broke the surface, coughing.

His hand barely managed to wrap about her wrist as the current pulled them farther downriver. They kicked back to the wall once more. He anchored them with one hand and slid her in front of him, the river dragging her against him. "It might be easier if you are hanging on from the front of me. That way if you fall again, I have a chance to catch you before we are swept away."

Her cheeks burned at her clumsiness. "Sir Sebastian, I-I couldn't."

He gritted his teeth. "I'm afraid you must. I may be strong, but I am not certain how many more climbs I have in me, and I am not about to leave you in the water while I climb to the top and reach down for you." He didn't wait for her to agree and repositioned her before him. She kept her arms about his neck, face-to-face with him.

He seemed so familiar in his mannerisms and confidence. He grinned and began the climb again. When his arms stretched out, she was drawn even closer to him. Instead of having their noses nearly touch, she decided resting her head on his broad chest would be the better of the two. She attempted to keep still and hold her own weight. She had no idea how he was managing the feat with her clinging to him, but he did not seem to doubt his ability.

He reached the top, gripping the stones. "Do you think you can climb onto the shore yourself?"

She reached for the bank, crawling up as gracefully as she could with her skirts clinging to her drawers. He followed behind, then sprawled on his back beside her, panting.

"So you *are* human." She laughed.

"Just barely." He winked at her, still breathing heavy.

She shivered, cradling her arms over her soaked gown.

"We best get you back to the manor before Grandmother or your companion wonders what has become of you again."

He rolled himself to standing and lifted her to her feet. She shivered.

"I am sorry I cannot offer you a dry coat. I can, however, offer you my arm."

She accepted it. He nudged her closer to him as they hiked back toward the manor.

"I'm afraid it will be rather a long trek. The river took us at least three miles from where we fell."

"So many?"

He nodded. "We are on our neighbor's property now."

"We best hurry, because I would hate to be discovered in such a state." It was bad enough that Sir Sebastian had a view of her looking like a half-drowned bunny with her skirts and hair clinging to every curve. "Have you always had the ability to scale walls with a maiden on your back?"

"It is a requirement for becoming a knight—we must save at least one damsel in distress per annum."

"I'm happy I assisted you in meeting your required number twice over."

He laughed.

She had come to love making him laugh . . . and it was a dangerous thing, given it would all end soon. "Grandmother Larkby's heart has been pressing on me every moment, Sebastian."

He nodded. "As it has me."

"What do we do? I cannot parade here as your wife forever. Have you thought of how to break the news to her?"

"I'll admit that I haven't wanted to give much thought to it. I hardly dare to hope."

She nodded. She wouldn't press him, not when she knew the pain of hope unrealized.

"Sir Sebastian?" A grand lady holding her husband's arm appeared on the path that joined the riverwalk. "Whatever happened to you?" She eyed Vivienne, a question in her gaze.

"Greetings Mr. and Mrs. Waterbury. To avoid an aggressive dog, my wife and I were forced from the path."

"How terrifying!" She gasped.

"You left the dangerous beast alive?" Mr. Waterbury frowned.

Sebastian gestured to himself with open arms. "I had no weapons on my person."

"I'll see to it the dog is captured." Mr. Waterbury nodded as sharply as his tone.

"But not harmed," Vivienne cried, thinking of Tess's dog. He had been aggressive at first too—but that was because he had been forced to fight in gambling dens. Tess had spent months building trust and working with him, and now he was devoted to her.

Mr. Waterbury shook his head. "It needs to be put down."

She gripped Sebastian's arm. "Please, you must not let the dog be harmed. Mayhap he is afraid of humans. You said you were good with dogs."

Sebastian nodded. "If you do manage to have him captured, Mr. Waterbury, bring him to Lark Manor. We shall see if he can learn to trust."

Mr. Waterbury narrowed his brows, his disagreement evident. "Very well, but if a dog caused my wife to leap into the Avon, he would be dead by nightfall."

"Then it is good that he happened upon us instead," Vivienne murmured to Sebastian.

Sebastian bowed to the couple. "If you'll excuse us, Mr. and Mrs. Waterbury, we need to return home to change."

"We can fetch a servant to drive you."

"It would be faster to walk." He nodded to them.

"We shall send around an invitation. Mrs. Larkby sent us a note telling us all about your new bride, and we must get to know her ourselves." Mrs. Waterbury called after them.

The walk back to the manor was faster than she would have liked, even if she was soaked through. The thought plagued her. She should not be allowing herself to grow attached to a man whom she would hardly ever see after her part of the bargain was complete.

Bash panted as he slammed the crate door closed behind the starving hound that was tearing into the slab of beef inside. It was an old trick, but a good one. He wiped the sweat from his brow and grinned at Noah, who flopped on the grassy bank beside the wooden crate, breathing heavy.

"And that, my friend, is how you capture a wild dog." Bash rested his hands on his knees, drawing in a full breath after the chase the hound had caused them. He hoped Evie would be pleased with his efforts, and that he'd managed to capture the hound without harm to themselves or the animal.

"Now comes the hard part. We must see if the dog is diseased or merely distrustful of humans. If it is a matter of trust, there is hope—" He paused at the sight of a rider astride a beautiful black mare cresting the far hill, in the unmistakable blue coat of the Royal Horse Guard and glinting helmet with its regal plume.

He squinted at the rider and back to Noah. Whoever he was, Bash would need to hold the conversation in private. "Noah, do you think you could manage to get the crate back to the kennels and then fetch Farmer Stone? His land is adjacent to ours, and he examines any of our animals who have taken ill."

Noah eyed the dog inside that now lay on his belly, using his paws to hold the T-bone in place as he gnawed it. "If I got the cart from the stable, I could manage it with one of the hands and then fetch Farmer Stone."

"Have Ladd pay him for his troubles." He nodded, and Noah darted up, racing toward the stables. The boy was eager to prove himself every day to Bash, it seemed. He would have to reassure Noah that there was no need to be anxious, as he would not be easily fired from his position. While his last employer ruled through fear and an iron fist, Bash and his family chose kindness.

The rider approached the stone bridge, and at the flash of a bright smile and dark hair under his helmet, Bash grinned at Wynn Paxton, his closest friend in the Royal Horse Guard.

"Wynn! What brings you to Bath?" he called as Wynn crossed the bridge.

Wynn reined in his horse, hopped down with a groan, and stretched his back. "Prisoner transfer to Bathwick."

"And they assigned you to see to that?" Bash frowned. "You are a mounted guard for the Prince Regent's household."

"They had their reasons, and my captain agreed."

"The prisoner is a threat to the Crown?"

"To the Prince Regent's very life, which is why they assigned only the best of the best." Wynn gestured to himself and to Bash before fishing out a sealed letter from the inside of his coat, handing it to Bash. "Present this to the warden of Bathwick. You are to bring the prisoner to Bristol to the Barley Pine Tavern."

Bash sighed. It would take the remainder of the day, and he would not see Evie's grateful reaction to his finding the dog, for which he hoped to receive a kiss on the cheek in thanks. He'd be lucky to return by midnight, but he could not refuse a direct order, and the idea of traveling to Bristol had crossed his mind since his grandmother's friend Bishop Clairmont resided there. If Bash had to go to Bristol, he could easily secure a special license from the bishop in case they had need of one in the coming weeks. He grinned at the idea of actually being wed to Evie.

"Why are you smiling? This isn't exactly your type of adventure." Wynn lifted a single brow in reference to Bash's alternate identity as the highwayman.

"An adventure is an adventure—great or small. Do you want my cook to prepare you a meal before you depart?"

Wynn shook his head, the plume fluttering in the gentle breeze. "I have orders to return to London at once after delivering the prisoner to Bathwick Gaol."

"They thought him likely to attempt escape and wanted him removed from the coast nearest France?"

Wynn nodded. "He's a valuable informant to Napoleon. Apparently, the Organization is endeavoring to reform him and turn him into a spy for England, but that is all I know. You know how they like to break their information into fragments to avoid any one man knowing the whole of the plan."

"I will see to it at once. I'm assuming that my yeoman uniform is not required now that you have delivered him to a prison and I am transferring him to a covert group?"

"Unless you want to parade the mission in front of hundreds, no." Wynn stretched his arms over his head and sighed. "It would be wonderful to rest at Lark Manor after all your stories about your childhood home, but I suppose that will have to wait for another day. Godspeed."

Within the hour, Bash was on the road to Bathwick with a spare horse in tow for the prisoner's use. The collection of the prisoner was easy enough, as the warden was expecting the handoff. Bash kept an eye on the man as he mounted. Despite the haunted circles under his eyes, the man was striking in his appearance, with his blond hair and broad shoulders. Bash would have thought the Organization, which was what he and his friends called the covert group that trained spies, would have chosen someone who'd blend in more with the crowd . . . unless they thought his looks a boon to loosen lips of the French aristocratic ladies in future missions.

The way the prisoner commanded the mount with ease spoke of fine horsemanship. If he spoke, Bash was certain the prisoner would have the cadence of a gentleman, which made Bash wonder what led the man to risk forfeiting his lands and title, if he had one, to aid Napoleon's cause. But as protocol demanded, he did not engage the man in conversation during the hour-and-a-half ride to the Barley Pine.

Bash had no idea whom he was meeting, but the man would be required to provide proof. He halted Brigand in the dusty yard of the tavern, the prisoner halting at his side.

Within moments Telford strode out onto the yard, his layered cape fluttering behind him, his bicorne lending an air of governance.

Bash shook his head, grinning. "So much for becoming a barrister and enjoying the quiet life." He dismounted and clasped his friend's hand, clapping him on the shoulder. "I should have known that you could not stand life away from serving the Crown."

Telford shrugged. "I tried, but when I was approached with taking over the Organization last year, I could not resist." He nodded to the prisoner. "Osmund Deverell, are you ready to redeem yourself in the eyes of England?"

Deverell. Bash squinted at the man, trying to reconcile the name with the memory of the newssheet headline that eluded him.

"I'll do whatever it takes to get my land, ships, and title back."

"Good. Because everything will be demanded of you in return. If you are deemed unfit, Deverell, you will be sent back to prison for the rest of your days for your crimes against the Crown." Telford gripped the horse's reins and motioned for the prisoner to dismount.

"As I said, I am highly motivated." Deverell pressed his lips into a grim line as he stood before them.

Telford signaled a man standing in the shadows of the tavern. The man gripped Deverell on the shoulder and guided him away.

Bash released a whistle. "Quite the motivational speech."

"And every word true. The man is dangerous, but valuable."

The headline came flooding back. "Osmund Deverell was that baron and successful merchant turned spy for France, yes?"

Telford nodded. "He lost everything attempting to secure a better title and wealth in France by using his ships as runners for Napoleon."

Bash clenched his fists at the thought of the men Deverell placed in danger by smuggling for Napoleon. "How do you plan to redeem a rogue like him?"

"By using my army of resources, a vicar, and a healthy dose of fear." Telford glanced at his pocket watch. "I wish I had time to visit longer than the span of a quick meal—"

"It's the nature of what we do—we serve." He slapped him on the back. "Now, tell me what you can in front of your latest recruit."

Chapter Thirteen

SEBASTIAN HAD RETURNED TOO LATE last night for Vivienne to speak with him about his chase to capture the dog. She longed to know what had happened to the beast. But Sebastian hadn't appeared for breakfast . . . even though she had been sitting here in hopes of seeing him, sipping on tea that had long grown cold. She even went so far as to take the morning's ironed newssheets from his place, pleasantly surprised to find the first installment of her serialized story in the *Bath Chronicle*. She could only pray the public looked favorably on the story, as the *Chronicle* had yet to print serialized stories before this one. She returned the newssheets beside his place setting with a sigh.

Perhaps it was best to be away from Sebastian. Her emotions grew cloudy when she was around him. She had never felt such things, except with the highwayman. He was a completely unavailable man, which was most likely why she felt drawn to him. Was it ludicrous to consider the dangerous man safe and the knight dangerous when it came to her heart?

She shook the question from her head and surrendered the breakfast room to the maid, who was no doubt pacing outside the door, waiting for her to leave. Vivienne trotted up the steps to Grandmother Larkby's room. She needed to find a way out of this mess she had created while keeping Grandmother Larkby's heart intact. She slipped into the room, smiling her greeting.

"I would love to see anything other than these walls." Grandmother clasped the doctor's hand. "Bartholomew, do say I can go out of doors?" She gestured to Vivienne. "I would love to show my new granddaughter the gardens."

The doctor looked out the window, nodding. "I do not see why not. A day in the sun might help bring the bloom of youth back to your cheeks."

"It will take a great deal more than a day in the sun to do all that." Her eyes sparked. "How about Vivienne takes me on a jaunt in the pony cart?"

The doctor released a long-suffering sigh. "Fiona, that is quite a deal more than taking in fresh air in the gardens outside your window."

She smiled up at him, batting her lashes. "Come, Bartholomew. I have been dreaming of all I could do once more if I had the chance."

He looked to Vivienne over the rim of his wire-rimmed spectacles. "Are you able to drive?"

"A pony cart? Of course." She hadn't driven one since her childhood days, but Father had trusted her with an ancient pony.

Grandmother clapped her hands. "Tell the groom to prepare Fluffy," she said to the nearest maid as a second moved to Grandmother's closet, fetching clothing for the journey. "Vivienne, I shall meet you downstairs."

Vivienne grabbed her mint pelisse, not worrying about dressing for the occasion, as they would only be about the estate. She did not even bother to tie on her bonnet. It was so much more refreshing to have the sun on her cheeks. She stood just outside the front door and studied her temporary home. It was far enough from Bath to feel as if she were in the country again, but it was nice to know that all the amenities she could ever wish for were a short drive, or invigorating stroll, away.

At last the footman carried out Grandmother Larkby, who was so wrapped up that only her face peeked out of her shawl. The groom led a gray-and-black Shetland pony pulling a black cart trimmed in gold, with burgundy seats. Fluffy was aptly named.

"May the Lord bless us and His face shine upon us!" Grandmother

Larkby paraphrased the verse, lifting a smile upward with her eyes closed, basking in the rays. "I did not think I would have the chance to see the grounds once more, much less take a drive."

The footman gently set her in the seat. He then turned to assist Vivienne into the cart, which could have easily fit four children. With Grandmother being so frail, they had room to spare even with her abundance of wraps and blankets.

Vivienne settled her skirts, and at Grandmother Larkby's nod, Vivienne snapped the reins and Fluffy pranced forward. Vivienne guided the horse down the tree-lined avenue that led to the river and the hillside of Lark Manor. She slowed Fluffy as they crested the stone bridge, continuing the pace on the other side of the River Avon.

"Faster!" Grandmother laughed.

Vivienne snapped the ribbons, setting the pony's clopping hooves to beating against the packed earth as the wind pulled Vivienne's hair from its coiffure. Grandmother giggled, and Vivienne could not keep from joining in her infectious, unbridled glee.

Grandmother removed the shawl from her head and allowed the wind to flow over her hair as well. She lifted her arms above her head, her aged hands reaching for the sky. "This reminds me of my girlhood in Scotland. My da would let me ride my pony as much as I wished, and I did, until I met Darren Larkby one day on the highlands. He cut such a handsome figure atop his mount."

Unable to keep herself from ferreting out every love story she encountered, Vivienne asked, "And it was love at first sight?"

"Not for me." Grandmother Larkby grinned. "He had to convince me of his love for nearly a year before I agreed to marry him and leave my life behind." She swallowed. "It was so hard to leave my family, even though I loved Darren. The hillside here reminds me of my old home, and it was because of these hills that Darren purchased this estate for me and planted the roses from my home in Scotland, as if I were the Queen of Babylon and he wished to create a wonder of the world to bring a smile to my face. We were quite happy raising our twin boys here. I did manage to return to Scotland every summer until Darren passed and I was no longer able to travel alone."

"How long has he been gone?"

"Two decades. I had young Sebastian to look after by then, and his presence helped with my grief over the loss of my husband . . . and son." She rested her gnarled hand on Vivienne's arm. "I cannot tell you the peace it gives me to know that Sebastian has found the love of his life at last—to know that the Larkby name might continue through him and not just his horrid cousin who is content to ruin the family name by his gambling and endless line of ladybirds."

Even though Vivienne wished to know more about this cousin, she needed to avoid a conversation involving heirs, as babies would no doubt be next in the elderly woman's thoughts. Vivienne unnecessarily snapped the reins. Fluffy took the encouragement to bolt, sending the pony cart bouncing wildly about and Grandmother squealing in delight.

Bash stretched his aching back and brushed the hay from his breeches. He had fallen asleep beside the dog's kennel, attempting to calm the animal. He had wanted to get the dog to trust him by spending time with him, but the hound was positively feral. It would take more than a night and morning spent outside the dog's kennel for the beast to shed his wariness of humans. Bash should have gone back to his feather bed, but Vivienne had been so devastated at the thought of the animal being destroyed, he'd felt compelled to personally see to the dog's well-being.

He massaged the knot in his shoulder. He knew the real reason he'd stayed had little to do with a dog that would have bitten off his hand and more to do with the lady behind the request. He was in trouble—deep trouble. He strode into the breakfast room, but the buffet had been cleared. He swiveled to the grandfather clock on the wall. He had slept far longer than he had anticipated. He hurried up the stairs and changed into a fresh ensemble before peering into Grandmother's room as he tied his cravat.

The bed was empty. His heart staggered for a moment, but a maid appeared from around the corner with a fresh pile of linens.

"Excuse me, Bridget? Have you seen Mrs. Larkby and Lady Larkby this morning?"

She bobbed in a shallow curtsy. "They went for a drive in the pony cart, Sir Sebastian."

"They what?"

Charlotte popped her head out from Vivienne's bedroom. "Sir Sebastian?" She hurried over. "I'm so glad I caught you. Lady Larkby wished for me to tell you that she is driving with your grandmother, as per the doctor's permission."

"Grandmother is so well then?" He nearly laughed in relief, but it was squelched by the idea of his ladies about the property without him for protection, given the news from Telford. He trusted his neighbors, but Bath drew all sorts, including men traveling through who tended to cross Lark Manor's estate to save time. "Do you know where they went?"

She shrugged. "They only said they would be about the estate."

He sprinted down the stairs and almost went to Brigand's stall, then sighed and claimed a far inferior horse, a dapple-gray mare. He did not wait for Noah to assist him and made quick work readying the horse before leaping into the saddle and riding for the back edge of the property.

They were not along the path by the river. Did they go beyond the tree line? He directed his horse over the bridge and galloped across the hills, when he heard a scream. His heart thudded in his chest, and he pressed his heels to his mount.

At the top of the hill, Bash spied the pony cart racing to a cluster of trees. If the horse did not stop, he did not wish to think what might happen to them. Why did Grandmother not take the reins? She had been a superior horsewoman in her day, but perhaps she was too weak to do so?

He bolted down to them, waving his arm and shouting. "Pull back! Pull back on the reins!"

Evie continued to struggle with the horse as Grandmother, at last, broke from her laughter and took the reins from Evie, clucking to the animal and halting him mere feet from the trees.

Bash closed the distance, stretching his limbs to gallop faster than he had in years, bringing the horse to a halt that had her rearing and tossing her head in protest. "What were you thinking, Vivienne? You might have been injured."

She gaped at him, hurt flashing in her eyes. "Do you think I intended for the horse to run away with us?"

"That is neither here nor there." Grandmother chided him, her cheeks a pretty pink. "We both know I could've stopped the horse at any time, but where is the fun in that?"

"Grandmother Larkby!" Evie gasped. "I thought I was about to kill us both!"

"But you didn't, my dear."

Grandmother held the reins in one hand, but he knew the action had strained her weakened limbs. He remembered a day when she would race him across the hill country and win. He scrubbed a hand around his neck. How could he fault her for behaving as he would in his twilight years? "Allow me to hold Fluffy's bridle and walk you back."

"Walk? It would take an hour to return at that pace." Grandmother motioned him into the cart, her eyes sparking with mischief. "Join us."

His brows lifted at the tiny cart. "There is precious little room."

"Nonsense. Draw your bride onto your lap, and there shall be room aplenty. Fluffy is more than capable of carrying the three of us. He needs the exercise, apparently."

"Grandmother . . . ," he scolded, but she did have a point in how long it would take to return to the manor. He wished to have her indoors before too long.

She crossed her arms. "You two hardly act like a couple who were so in love that they eloped in secret. No kissing that I can see, or hand-holding, and now you are reluctant to hold her even if it means bringing me to the comfort of my own manor that much sooner. What is going on with you two? Did you quarrel? Because I can think of a few ways to settle the matter quickly, beginning with Vivienne sitting upon your lap."

Bash met Evie's gaze, silently asking her if this was too far to take their pretense of marriage.

To her credit, she did not blush this time. "Grandmother needs to be put to bed after such a fright."

"I was not frightened." Grandmother sighed. "But I must admit that I am weak with exhaustion."

Evie's eyes flashed with alarm, and she at once motioned Bash inside. "It will be faster. I shall not protest to you holding me on your lap if it means that she can be in her bed that much sooner."

He dismounted, eyeing the cart again. He could have sworn Grandmother was laughing at how he slowly affixed the horse to the back of the cart, but she pressed a fist to her lips and coughed forcefully. Evie stood and struggled to maintain her position, balancing with her arms out as he climbed into her vacated seat. He grasped her elbow, and she reclined in his lap, keeping her eyes on Grandmother, who smirked in satisfaction.

He wrapped his arms around Evie to snap the reins, sending the pony into a trot. Having her in his arms again felt right, and he was beginning to wonder how he might keep her there. He'd already procured a license from the bishop in case of an emergency. *If only I could manage to convince her to stay.* The traitorous thought sent a stab of guilt through his back. He had promised that he would not force her into a marriage—that she was right in trusting him.

As if feeling his gaze on her, she turned to him, their lips nearly brushing. If he leaned forward, he might taste her sweet lips once more. How simple it had been when he had been the highwayman. But he was and always would be a knight. He cleared his throat and snapped the reins as Grandmother cackled with laughter, having caught their almost kiss.

"I've never met two people so in love who were so opposed to kissing in front of an elderly relation. Would it help if I pretended to look the other way or snored a bit as I fell into a convenient sleep?"

Evie stiffened in his lap, but she winked at Grandmother. "To kiss a knight is not something I take lightly."

Chapter Fourteen

VIVIENNE TAPPED HER NIB TO the inkwell, watching the ink dribble back into the bottle. Anything was preferable to allowing her thoughts to run away . . . even if it was part of her writing process. It had become too dangerous to do so after Sebastian's impressive climb out of the Avon.

Another week at Grandmother Larkby's side saw vast improvements in her complexion and in their blossoming friendship. Vivienne almost wished her union with Sebastian were true, if only to please the dear lady. Then, there was the pile of invitations on her desk, distracting her from her writing, as they were addressed to the knight and his bride. The lying had to end. Vivienne flipped the invitations over, hiding the address, and allowed the next scene in her story to take her away until her head hurt and fingers ached. It was better than dwelling on the upcoming heartbreaking conversation with Grandmother Larkby, but if she did not speak the truth this very day, her heart might burst from the weight of the deceit—well intended though it may have been.

Perhaps it had become so painful because Vivienne wished the union to be true for her own sake as well. She pressed her hand to her lips. The knight had almost kissed her a second time. What would it be like to have one so honorable to call her own? To have someone who was always for her, shielding her from the cruel arrows of her stepbrother and his wife? To have Sebastian Larkby at her side for the rest of her days would be a prize indeed. Her cheeks heated at her weakness.

But he is not yours. And never will be. She leapt up from her chair as if the truth were burning her petticoats. A stroll in the garden to pick some roses for Grandmother Larkby would be just the thing to clear her mind before the confession. She hurried down the hall, keeping her head down lest she catch sight of *him* in the library. She snatched up the pocketknife that Sebastian had begun leaving in the foyer for her use, reached the garden undetected, and sliced long stems to aid in arranging the blooms, smiling over the kind husband who'd planted them for his wife so many years ago. Her thoughts once more turned to how kind a husband Sebastian would make.

Stop this madness! He is not yours. Besides, what about the plan to remain in control of her future? If she allowed herself to fall in love with the knight, that control was in danger. But Sebastian was nothing like Sir Josiah Montgomery. To be loved by a knight so true could change everything. Disgusted with herself, she gripped the roses too sharply and hissed against the bite of thorns as barking shifted her attention to the stables and the kennel attached to its side.

Sebastian squatted down, peering through the rail of the fenced paddock with a treat in hand, speaking to the dog inside. The dog nipped at the wire separating the two. She approached quietly so as not to catch Sebastian's attention. The dog focused on the treat and leapt, nearly snapping Sebastian's fingers.

"Good boy, Cerberus." He tossed a treat.

"You are training him yourself?"

He whipped about and grinned when he saw her, rising and brushing his hands on his biscuit-colored pantaloons. "I told you I was good with animals. The kennel keeper used to have me help him train the hunting hounds that we sold."

"Lark Manor sells hunting hounds?"

"We used to." He dug his hands into his pockets and lifted another treat. "Cerberus is reluctant to trust me, but I hope to win him over."

Vivienne shook her head. "If that is the case, you might want to reconsider naming him after a three-headed hellhound."

"He deserved it after chasing us into the river, and it will warn off anyone who tries to pet him in the future." He whistled to the dog and called him back to the fence, tossing him the treat when he did not immediately start growling.

"When did Lark Manor cease training dogs?"

"When I moved to London to serve the Crown, I sold off the prized sires and mothers. Grandmother did not care for the kennel but had allowed me my pastime as it helped aid the estate." He tapped his finger against the fence, speaking softly to the dog as he finished his treat.

"Speaking of Grandmother Larkby . . ."

He reached for her hand, his touch feeling almost familiar. "It's time we discuss what to do. I have an idea—"

"Lady Larkby?" Grandmother Larkby's maid, Helen, paused behind them, hands folded before her skirts. "Mrs. Larkby is asking to see you."

"We will continue this conversation tonight?" She smiled her apologies to Sebastian.

He nodded. "It cannot wait any longer."

"I agree." Relieved to know he had a plan, she followed the maid to the first floor and knocked lightly on the ajar door, bouquet in hand.

"Enter," answered a crackling voice.

As per Vivienne's instructions, the maids had flung the curtains back and left the windows wide open, allowing fresh air into the chamber that had been so dingy. Fresh blooms always graced the desk, the mantel, and the bedside table, brightening the room a good deal.

"What an angel you are. My grandson has fortune indeed to have found you."

Vivienne dipped her head. "It is I who am blessed by having you in my life." And she meant it. It would crush her to lose their friendship, but with the elderly woman's obvious recovery, there was no way out of their lie that had been so well intended. Would the truth send Grandmother Larkby back to death's door? The idea made Vivienne's stomach turn. She could not allow this woman to suffer.

Lord, I'm sorry I got myself into this situation by not trusting in Your provision, but, Lord, what am I to do? I cannot hurt this dear woman. How do we amend this situation of our own making? Should I wait for

Sebastian's plan, or is it Your will I speak the truth with only the greatest love for this dear woman? At this moment, only truth seemed right. She emptied the second vase of the roses dipping their heads and began arranging the fresh ones. "Grandmother Larkby, I have something to confess, and it will not be easy to—"

"I thought you were away from my rooms because you were bathing!"

"Pardon me, Mrs. Larkby?"

"Don't you have a ball to attend this night at the Sydney Hotel?" Grandmother Larkby interjected.

Vivienne turned from fiddling with the blooms. "Yes, but it is of little consequence."

"Little consequence? You mentioned Lady Jennings invited you ages ago. It would be horribly rude to refuse to attend after accepting so long ago. And I well know the temptation of dancing. I lived for balls when I was in my youth. No, you cannot spend all your time by my side. You are a bride, and Sebastian needs to show you off for me." She huffed, straightening her cuff. "If I were not imprisoned by this failing body and shackled to this beautiful estate by the orders of the good doctor, I would be dancing the night away with said doctor and boasting to anyone near that my granddaughter-in-law is a rare beauty and accomplished."

Vivienne adjusted the rose at the center of the vase, and after turning the vase just right, she dusted off her hands and sat beside the woman. "I hardly think it is proper to leave your side at this time."

She snorted and patted Vivienne's hand. "I was merely tired from our adventure and have since recovered. It is *highly* proper. You cannot stay beside me forever, and I would not wish it of you. The best medicine you can give me is to attend the ball and be merry on my behalf, while wearing this." Grandmother lifted a wooden box, lifting the lid to reveal a lovely set of diamond hair pins.

Viviene traced the pins with her fingertip. "I've never worn anything so splendid in my hair."

"With locks such as yours, they should be adorned. These were from my darling husband. Wear them for me tonight and when you return, bring me some forbidden sweet, along with all the details. And being a writer, I have no doubt in your ability to account for the evening to me in style."

How could she refuse this last request? Sebastian had said he had an idea. Maybe it was wise to wait to hear it from him before blurting out the painful truth. One more evening parading as his bride—she would do this for Grandmother Larkby. "Thank you. It will be an honor to wear something your husband gave you. But, upon my return, we have much to discuss."

She waved her away, impatiently. "Yes. Yes. Our grave discussion can wait until then. You need to get dressed for the evening ahead. Parties at the Sydney Hotel usually begin at five of the clock. You do not wish to miss having dinner in the gardens. The invitation mentioned a hot-air balloon for guests to ride inside. Imagine. When I saw the first one take flight over a decade ago, I about fainted, but they continued to practice to the point where I quite enjoyed seeing the balloons above, adding to the lovely tapestry of the sunset. Who knows—maybe I will recover enough to ride one this season?" She motioned Vivienne out the door. "Before you depart, be sure to stop by and show me how lovely you look, my dear."

With a kiss to the woman's cheek, Vivienne joined Charlotte in their suite and began the process of dressing for the ball. Having selected the gown and inspected it for wrinkles, they laid it on the bed while Charlotte saw to Vivienne's hair, sewing tiny pearls that had been taken from an old necklace Mrs. Hart had given Vivienne long ago into her coiffure to make her locks shimmer. It would take a long time to remove each pearl, but the effect was splendid.

Charlotte dabbed her nose with a handkerchief and finished setting the final pearl into place. "Are you certain you wish for him to escort you without me? This cold is dreadful—otherwise I would leap at the chance to attend with you."

"You need your rest, and yet you insist on doing my hair."

"No one can manage your hair as well as I." Charlotte patted the plait. "But if you make an appearance with him, there will not be the ability for you to retrench in the future. All will know you tried to deceive them. Your name will be tainted."

"That is only if we are found out. And I, for one, will never tell this secret to anyone besides Grandmother Larkby, who will not give me away."

Charlotte fetched the citrines. "Are you certain?"

Vivienne nodded, setting the citrine eardrops in place, admiring them in the dressing table's mirror. "It will be my grand adventure that I shall look back upon in my golden years . . ."

"Like the highwayman?" Charlotte grinned. "You haven't mentioned him in a while."

"I knew I shouldn't have gushed so about him when you first arrived. I was only dying to tell someone in person what had occurred. I should have known that you would've seen through my story to my attraction." Vivienne sighed and fixed the necklace in place. "Yes, I had my doubts that any man could take Bash's place . . . but I have to admit that Sir Sebastian's character is outshining the appeal of a thief."

"Oh good. You are at last seeing that bit of reason." Charlotte laughed, handing Vivienne her gloves. "It is time you and your knight see what you are made of."

"Pardon?"

"If he is what you imagine a husband should be, let your guard down and see if this is what God has planned for you. If not, it's time for this ruse to come to light and for you both to take the consequences, whatever they may be."

What had been intended as a charade of mercy for his grandmother was quickly swelling out of control, and attending this evening's party at the Sydney Hotel as Sir Sebastian and Lady Larkby was evidence of that fact. But as usual, he could never refuse his grandmother, and she was well aware of his weakness to please her.

Bash felt as if every eye was upon them as he entered the hotel gardens with the ravishing beauty on his arm and looked about for a free dining booth. Such a gamble he had never taken before, lying to the whole of society as a knight. If they were caught, he had the license and would marry her in an instant to save her reputation. It would hardly be a burden to wed her—but their futures would change forever.

Thankfully, the grounds were packed with hundreds of guests, and he prayed that numbers would aid them with hiding in plain sight. "I'm afraid there are not any booths available, but I will fetch us some cold ham and rolls with our drinks."

"I'm not hungry yet, but feel free to fetch yourself something if you would like a repast." She rested a hand over her stomach. "Sebastian, I fear we are reaching the point of no return. We cannot continue on like this—the lying to your grandmother is keeping me awake at night and stealing into my thoughts every time I sit down to write. I do not think it is God's will for us to deceive her for the sake of her health when she has made such a miraculous recovery." She shook her head. "I doubt He would have blessed the idea if we had stopped long enough to ask Him. Lord knows my vicar would have an opinion on the matter. It is one thing to lie during a war to save lives, but it is another to actively deceive a whole town."

He reached for two glasses of apricot-strawberry punch and handed one to her. "I agree. However, I wish to honor our agreement."

"I would never wish to entrap you."

Was that his imagination, or did a flash of longing cross her expression that matched his heart? It was why he had conveniently forgotten to speak of the plan when they were alone in the carriage, wishing to hold on to the farce for a few moments longer so that he would have an excuse to be near her all evening—to dance with her under the stars. "Then we are in unity, for I do not wish to entrap you either." He bowed over her hand.

"Excuse me, Lady Larkby?" A footman approached in an emerald-and-black livery. "Lady Jennings conveyed to me that you and Sir Sebastian were to be the first to enjoy tonight's balloon as her honored guests."

So much for staying hidden in the numbers. Bash tamped down his rising anxiety. He had found that when thrust into such situations while undercover, a cool head was the best way to avoid being found out in a lie.

"The balloon?" Her voice piqued with interest.

"Yes, my lady. The marchioness has provided only the best of entertainment for tonight's party."

She turned to Bash, her hands clasped to her throat. "Do you think we could? I know we should probably keep to ourselves, but as we are already the guests of honor, this would be a chance in a lifetime, and think of how much fun it will be to tell Grandmother Larkby before . . . before . . ." She dipped her head.

He leaned into her, whispering, "One last bit of fun before we confess all to Grandmother. I am confident she would want us to do this for her." He motioned the footman forward and trailed him into the gardens, where a bright balloon of crimson and gold stood above a large wicker basket anchored by four staked ropes and guarded by four men in the same emerald-and-black livery.

He led her to the steps at the back of the basket. When her fingertips brushed his, her eyes met his and a spark traveled up his arm and settled into his heart. "Shall we, my lady?"

She climbed inside, modestly guarding the hem of her gown. He joined her, and the balloon's engineer signaled to the footmen to release the anchors as he turned up the flame.

She gasped at the rocking of the basket and threw her arms about his waist as they rose. She lifted her lashes to him and started to draw back, but he stopped her. At the question in her mien, he grinned. "I've never been in a balloon before either. Perhaps I am frightened as well and require a bit of courage."

She leaned into him as the balloon lifted into the sky. The crowd beneath them pointed and waved to them, and Evie smiled and waved back. The higher they rose into the sky, the more the merriment in the gardens dampened and the more she tightened her grip about him. She rested her head on his chest and released a sigh of contentment.

He loved her. Of that he was certain. He had not ceased thinking of their days on the road together. But if he confessed such duplicity, would she reject him, no matter what society would say over the scandal of her turning him away? Besides, he had made vows to the Crown. No matter the pain it caused him, he could not—would not—confess his mission for the Crown, even if meant that he could never share this part of himself with the woman he loved. It was ridiculous, really, that he was so close to having this new dream and so far away.

She caught him staring down at her and offered him a sad smile as she whispered, "I am quite determined to make the most of these final moments alone with you. For whatever happens, I want you to know that I am glad to have known you, Sir Sebastian."

Whatever happens . . . He knew what he wanted to happen. He glanced over his shoulder to the aeronaut and decided that to hold Evie would be enough for now.

Chapter Fifteen

As soon as the guards anchored the balloon, Bash scooped Evie into his arms and hopped out of the basket, smiling to the next couple in line.

Evie laughed softly and pushed against his chest. "Set me down, good sir."

"If I must."

She smiled up at him shyly. "I'm afraid you must."

He did so, and her breath caught.

He grasped her elbow, drawing her toward him. She had not trembled once in the balloon. "Vivienne? Whatever is the matter? You are as pale as a candle."

"I should have known better." She gripped his hand and hauled him toward the trees. "Why oh why did I let my curiosity win again!"

He peered out from the trunk, but Evie yanked him back by his coat. She groaned into her hands. "This is a disaster."

He grasped her hands, gently tugging them from her face. "If you do not tell me this instant what has you so upset, I will go mad."

She stared across the gardens. He followed her gaze toward the man in a canary waistcoat who was downing a glass of flip. She ground her teeth.

"Vivienne." He fairly groaned. "Tell me who and what someone has done so I can remedy whatever is bringing you such distress."

"Sir Josiah Montgomery is in attendance tonight. H-he is the man my stepbrother wishes me to wed."

His gut twisted. *So, this is the fellow that she was forced to flee.* He could not risk revealing how much he knew about her past—things only the highwayman knew. "I see. Is he the fellow in the canary waistcoat and matching cravat by the refreshment table near the dining booths? You are certain?"

She sighed. "He has lost a stone or two since I've last seen him, but I am certain. He looks harder, as if he has been training. It's strange. The man enjoys his food and the company of his ladybird too much to be found in the fencing hall." She shook her head. "Perhaps my flight pushed him to work his anger out with a rapier." She plastered her hands to her cheeks, groaning. "What am I going to do?"

His ladybird. He gritted his teeth against the urge to break the fellow's nose for forcing Vivienne to flee her home to avoid a match with him. Bash rested his hand on hers. "You are not alone anymore."

She looked up at him, her eyes impossibly wide. "No?"

"As your husband, I offer you my protection—my name."

A haunting whisper of a smile was her answer. "If only you could, Sebastian, but without us actually being bound together, there is little you can do."

He frowned. "You doubt my ability to protect you?" All of England was ablaze with talk of the golden-haired highwayman who had robbed Sir Thomas. Would she feel safer in his company if she knew she was with her Bash once more?

"It is not that. With the banns being read and the news of my union to Sir Josiah, and *our* timeline being off, Sir Josiah will not be assuaged until he speaks with the clergyman who bound us in matrimony and sees the certificate of marriage. And if there is no proof and Sir Josiah decides to take me to Gretna Green against my will . . . all this will have been for naught."

Heat exploded in his chest at the thought of any man touching *his* Evie. "If he so much as dares to look at you, I'll show him what a man really is." His fists curled.

She rested her hands on his fist, uncurling it and lifting his knuckles to her lips in an unexpected gentling gesture. "And risk your position beside the Prince Regent? I will not ask you to sacrifice so much for me."

He could not pause to think of the tenderness with which she spoke to him—as if she were bidding him farewell forever. "It would not come to blows. My word as a nobleman should suffice for a gentleman of his standing."

"He may be one in title, but a gentleman he is not." She shook her head. "He has gambling debts and has been desperate for a marriage ever since Muriel threw him over."

"He was *engaged* to the friend you mentioned?"

She nodded. "Even if you and I proposed we had a secret marriage these three years, nothing could convince him or my stepbrother. Our lie is about to become public. We should have never let it go so far."

Her hand actually quaked in his. This woman had ridden in a hot-air balloon, been captured by a highwayman, faced down rogues, and raced into the night without fear, but she was brought to trembling before this weasel? How she must have suffered under her family to be brought to such a state. He turned her to him, echoing her tenderness in lifting her hands to his lips. He would not see this woman he loved taken down by a man such as Sir Josiah. Not while he had breath in his lungs. "Listen well. I will not see you married to him."

She laughed. "You have no power, Sir Sebastian. Sir Josiah will see my reputation ruined and send word to my stepbrother, who will force me into a marriage with Sir Josiah to redeem this disgrace that I have brought upon the family."

"I have the power of my name and, should that fail, my fists." *And if you allow it, a marriage and all that I own—though it is not much.*

"Some things cannot be cured by fists."

"Well, it's worth a shot to his jaw to see if it can be." He grasped her shoulders, desperate to see the fear in her eyes banished. "But if it comes down to it, I will marry you in an instant."

"Sebastian," she whispered, her voice trembling.

What had he said? Was she so against the idea of having him as her husband? Even if she didn't love him as he loved her, he would do anything to see her protected. "I know you want your freedom, but lawfully having my name is the way for you to possess that freedom."

"And it would spare Grandmother Larkby's heart. We would have to tell her all though." She pressed her hand to her cheek once more. "But what of the dates of the certificate? People will know."

He sighed. "That is where the truth will have to be revealed if questioned by your stepbrother—after the certificate of marriage is in hand to make an honorable match out of us both. Society will talk." He lifted her chin in his hand. "However, they will eventually forget, especially when the Prince Regent takes the throne with me standing behind him. No one will dare to speak ill of you when we have the ear of the king."

"You would do this for me?"

"This and more."

"Why?"

He bowed, his forehead meeting hers. He closed his eyes, breathing in her delicate scent of lavender. *I love you and your harebrained ways— the way your beautiful mind spins the most obscure phrase into a story all its own. How you love with all your heart—loving a woman who has been my world and going so far as to consider wedding me to spare her heartache.*

But he did not dare voice his heart, not yet anyway, when she might misconstrue his words as those coming from a knight in shining armor with only the thought of rescuing a damsel. She was no damsel in distress, but he wanted more than anything to be her knight. "You know why, my lady."

Her lashes fluttered, her lips parting with an answer, when Sir Josiah loomed. She started, wrapping her hand tighter about Bash's arm.

The smug lift of the man's lips sent a jolt of agitation through Bash. "My dear Vivienne, I have found you at last. Imagine my surprise when I discovered that you were proclaiming yourself to be married when I know our banns were read only weeks ago."

"Gretna Green has saved many a reluctant bride from a poor union." Bash bowed his head.

As Bash's rank dictated, Sir Josiah bowed from his waist, albeit reluctantly.

"And I am called Lady Larkby now."

"Yes, but you see, my dear Vivienne, the word is that Lady Larkby has been writing for years and, therefore, has been married to Sir Sebastian for years. You have only been with this man for a short while and, therefore, I must assume he has only pretended to wed you to get you into his bed."

Evie's jaw slackened.

"I know this must come as the gravest of shocks to you, but your marriage is counterfeit, as he is married to the authoress," Sir Josiah interjected. "However, I will forgive your haste and wed you at once, for I am most eager to become your husband and make an honorable woman out of you."

Bash had never been one to be shoved about. He gently tucked Evie closer to him. "You are mistaken. There is no other Lady Larkby but Vivienne." That much was true. "They are one and the same."

Sir Josiah's brows rose. He crossed his arms, appraising him. "Indeed? Then you do not mind giving me the name of the vicar who wed you, along with the certificate that I shall have authenticated before I can consider the matter closed."

"How dare you. Might I remind you that I am a knight to the Prince Regent himself? He takes me at my word, and it is more than sufficient for the likes of you."

"The likes of me?" He snorted. "I am a nobleman and a wronged fiancé with excellent swordsmanship."

Evie, at last, recovered her voice. "Are you challenging a Yeoman of the Guard to a duel? Such an unwise move. But what else should I expect from a man with a considerable gambling debt to a dangerous man? It has made you desperate, and it shows."

His cheeks puffed, reddening along with his neck. "Muriel had no right to disclose such a matter to you, and you certainly should've had the wits to keep it to yourself." He returned his attention to Bash. "If you do not produce the certificate, I shall have you sued, Sir Sebastian, for damaging my fiancée's good name."

Bash narrowed his gaze. "Then by all means, I shall send for the certificate."

"You do not have it with you?" He grinned, looping his thumbs in his waistcoat and rocking back on his heels. "I suspected as much."

"I serve the Prince Regent. I must leave places at a moment's notice. No, I do not have the signed certificate with me," Bash spat back. "Shall you check with the marquess and the marchioness to see if they carried their certificate of marriage with them this night? Or perhaps another newlywed couple?"

"It is a reasonable enough request. She will return with me to Chilham to live under her stepbrother's protection until the certificate is here." He extended his arm to Evie. "Come, my dear."

"You have overstepped yourself for the last time this night. I will depart before I consider it necessary to beat you." Bash turned on his heel, Evie clinging to him as they wove through the crowded gardens. Bash ordered their wraps from the hotel.

Evie leaned into him as they waited for their cloaks in the foyer. "He will not cease his pursuit of proof, Sebastian."

"He should accept my word as a knight." He sighed. *Even if my word is less than truthful at the moment. But tonight that changes. Tonight truth will be had.* He patted his waistcoat, thankful he had brought the license with him on a whim.

As close guard of the Prince Regent, doors opened for him. He'd never thought he would be using his position to gain a marriage license from his grandmother's friend within a moment's notice though. As he looked down at Evie, he was not upset about the turn of events. While it did seem the most logical step, he still hesitated to take away the freedom she had so fought for. But in reading her expression, he didn't see any sorrow in her eyes. He saw resilience and acceptance. Had she accepted her fate of wedding Sir Josiah or him?

He handed her into the gig. With the certificate signed and witnessed, they would be all aboveboard. However, should her stepbrother ever inquire of the date, that was another battle entirely. People forgot. But this one would be a difficult one to overlook. However, with his connections to the Prince Regent, if he ever needed to call in a favor to see that Evie was accepted into society, he would. As the idea formed in his mind, he knew he could save her. He simply had to bring her to court with him in London and introduce her properly as Lady Larkby to silence the gossips in the ton.

Evie drew in a sharp, short series of breaths, and he found her sinking onto the seat, bravado gone and raw terror in its place.

She rested her face in her hands as her breathing spiraled out of control. She closed her eyes. *Not again. Please, Lord, not now.* Her breathing came in gasps now, and she slid to her side on the carriage bench, attempting to still her racing heart by focusing on the tufted leather, the stitchwork of the gloves clutched in her hands—anything other than her fear of being found out by Sir Josiah and forced into a marriage with him. But by his snide grin and the way he'd claimed her hand, she had little hope of escaping him forever. He was like a dog on the hunt, and she the fox.

Sebastian's voice rumbled, sounding as if it were coming from above water. The gig rocked for a few moments before it halted, and at the gentle touch on her shoulder, her breathing slowed as she caught the scent of leather and peppermint. He drew her into his arms, cradling her until the shaking in her limbs lessened, and she discovered they were parked in a private grove of trees on the opposite side of the hotel, far away from the prying eyes of guests. He was so thoughtful.

"Did I ever tell you that I suffered from anxiety as a boy?" he whispered into her hair.

She stilled, not trusting her voice yet. She turned her head slightly to glimpse up at him. "You? A yeoman?"

He nodded, brushing her hair from her cheeks. "It took me years to conquer it, and even now I have to recall the verses Grandmother shared with me every night before I went to bed."

She thought of the embroidered verses on the handkerchief on his bedside table. "The ones from First Peter that are on your handkerchief?"

He smiled down at her. "Yes. Your excursion into my bedroom is paying off."

"I was unforgivably nosy, wasn't I?" She shivered, and he held her tighter, as if he knew that he was the only thing grounding her from an attack of anxiety. "But it speaks well of your character that you forgave my forwardness. Can you quote the verses from chapter five for me? I read them afterward and found comfort in them."

"Of course." He cleared his throat. "'Casting all your care upon him; for he careth for you. Be sober, be vigilant; because your adversary the devil, as a roaring lion, walketh about, seeking whom he may devour.'"

If that isn't the truth, I do not know what is. Sir Josiah is a lion, and I am his prey.

"'Whom resist stedfast in the faith, knowing that the same afflictions are accomplished in your brethren that are in the world. But the God of all grace, who hath called us unto his eternal glory by Christ Jesus, after that ye have suffered a while, make you perfect, stablish, strengthen, settle you.'"

She nodded, soaking in the verses.

"I know my words may sound all well and good, but I've been through such attacks as these. For me, the lion stalking me is fear. It is only in Christ's strength that I have found my way through the battle of anxiety and fear." He stroked her hair again. "I know this attack of fear is partly my own fault."

"You have been a source of peace for me. The fault lies with Sir Josiah."

"So you have not had attacks before your betrothal?"

"My first attack came after my father's death when my stepbrother mentioned marrying me off the moment I turned sixteen." She rubbed a fist under her eyes. "I suppose that since then, I associate any arranged marriage with that feeling. I pushed aside mentions of a match by being useful to my stepbrother. I-I usually can ignore my anxiety when he and Sir Josiah are out of my thoughts. My writing helps me forget the fears that torment me, but seeing him, a man who is the culmination of all my fears, there is nothing to hide behind." She shook her head.

He nodded. "Distraction is all well and good. I've done it myself. However, when the distraction is not on hand when a spell comes—"

"It fails," she whispered.

"Yes. These verses helped me in ways that I cannot even explain, and it would be my honor to share them with you." He reached into his pocket and withdrew a handkerchief. "My grandmother made this for me. I keep it whenever I am away from home." He pressed it into her hand.

She ran her finger over the stitching, something blooming in her chest over this knight's thoughtfulness. "I can't take this."

"You are merely holding on to it for me." He lifted her hand to his and kissed it lightly.

The touch sent her heart lifting, and the fears melted away at this man's selfless act and humility at admitting that he was not fearless, as she had assumed. "I shall treasure it and use it well."

"I only ask that you do not use it well for your nose though." He shuddered.

"You should have thought of that before you gave it to me." She lifted it to her face.

He halted her from dabbing it to her nose and helped her to sit upright while still keeping an arm about her. She hoped he would continue to sit beside her, continue to keep her at his side. She hadn't felt this safe in so long . . . not since the moment Bash had saved her from those drunkards.

He withdrew a second handkerchief, dabbing her cheeks before folding her hands about the cloth. "This does help explain your determination not to wed. I am curious though. Does your anxiety apply only to arranged marriages?"

She tucked both handkerchiefs into her pocket and rolled her shoulders back. *No more tears. It's time to take charge.* "I have never had an attack when thinking of a match made of kindness and friendship, if that's what you are asking. I am a romance writer, after all."

"Kindness and friendship." The corner of his mouth tipped up. "That is very promising news for me. Shall we go on a twilight ride before we return to Grandmother's? I do not know about you, but this charade is beginning to wear on me."

Any intimacy she felt between them faded at his comment. She had indeed felt the strain of the conversation to come. "A drive is just the thing I need, but it is hardly proper."

"I concur, which is why I have a proposal for you."

"A proposal, sir?" She clutched the neck of her fan, waiting for her heart to race once more, her breaths to turn short and ineffective. But instead of panic surging through her blood, she felt . . . hope?

"I know you associate an arranged marriage with that memory of powerlessness, but I swear to be a good husband, a loving husband in name only, if you are in agreement. If this plan causes you distress, I will see you on a boat to the Americas to avoid a match with Sir Josiah."

"A-are you asking me to elope with you to Gretna Green?" Excitement at the idea of marriage over the anvil brewed. It sounded *very* much like a love match.

"I was granted a special license." He reached into his coat and withdrew a folded document. "I requested the license in the likely event our union might be questioned and there was no way to salvage the fabrications we'd made, merciful though our intentions were at the time."

She unfolded the document, reading it and running her finger over the seal. He had thought of everything. Her heart sped at his kindness. He was all goodness. "Are you certain you wish to do this for me?"

"I would do anything for you." He took the paper and folded it, returning it to his pocket. "Never fear—it will be in name only, but it will be the proof we need to keep your reputation safe. The deal shall continue on as we had planned—this is only a formality to aid in the legitimacy of our claim."

So much for a romance blossoming. "A formality—what every future bride wishes to hear. I suppose we did fly too close to the sun." She could continue on with her dream, but with his protection and name. She would never lose it. In her heart she had feared that while he'd claimed he would not marry in the future, he would come to change his mind once his duties became less demanding, and when such a time came, she would be out of a job once more.

"I have thought this through, and I see no other course but forward, tearing the tangled web of lies with a sword of truth in the form of a holy ceremony with a certificate to prove the match." He grasped her hand in his. "Vivienne Poppy, will you do me the honor of becoming my wife? I would never go back on my word—we would be bound by name only."

She grasped his hand, sealing their deal. "Very well, but you should know that I sleep with a weapon on my nightstand and Charlotte near."

He grinned. "I would expect nothing less, my lady."

"Let us get this business over with and return to Grandmother Larkby."

He snapped the reins, directing the horse in the opposite direction of Lark Manor. "Hold on—it is rather a long drive to Bristol. I do not dare have us married in Bath, where anyone might see us."

Chapter Sixteen

SEBASTIAN KNOCKED ON THE DOOR, hat in hand. Vivienne smoothed down her pink sarsenet evening gown. They would not be shamed in their dress at least, even if their marriage was hasty. She still could not quite believe Sebastian had made a contingency plan if they were caught. If she were an heiress, she would think his plan came from a place of greed, but she had precious little to offer besides her good name and her terrace home in Bath. No, he stood to lose far more than he gained from their union. She watched him as they waited for what felt like an age. His shoulders remained straight and his brow devoid of perspiration, reassurance in his gentle touch upon her lower back. He was a good man, and those were hard to find.

The door wrenched open. The maid eyed them with open curiosity. "Vicar Brown is having dinner at the moment. I do not think he is open to visitors."

"Tell him that Sir Sebastian Larkby is here to see him about a marriage—I have brought a special license."

Her pursed lips softened, and she smiled as she motioned them into the parlor. "I will see to it that he receives your message at once, Sir Sebastian."

He reached behind him and grasped Vivienne's hand in his, tucking her into his side as he led her into the small parlor. She looked about the room, which was so sparsely decorated that there was not much to distract her and occupy her mind. She would not dwell on the fact that she was about to marry. For even if she was gladdened at the prospect of not losing Sebastian after this adventure, it was sudden, and she had already had one attack of nerves tonight. She could not have a second.

She picked at a woven blanket that graced the back of a worn wooden chair before the fireplace. Granted, she would not be sacrificing much. *Other than a love match with Bash.* She shook that thought from her mind. The highwayman was never a choice. *He is a cad, a thief, and devastatingly handsome beneath that mask, I'm sure.* She looked to Sebastian, who had his hands behind his back and paced the room. Sebastian was striking, and it seemed his hair was growing in, but she could not be certain of what the color would be yet. She smiled at her musings. Trivial matters such as one's hair mattered little. Sir Josiah had plenty. *Lord, is this what you wish? For me to marry this knight? It seems too good to be true—an answer for so many of my secret prayers.*

Sebastian's pacing did not cease, and as he seemed deep in thought, she crossed to the window, staring up at the moon, following the trail of moonlight to the vegetable patch. "Do you regret making our plan, Sebastian?"

His features softened as he joined her in looking out the window, his hand resting on the sill. "I wholeheartedly believe that you were sent by God Himself to Grandmother's side to breathe new life into her." He took her hand in his. "We went about things in haste and made a choice in fear, but this is the perfect solution."

"How? You are giving up so much."

"I wish you would stop saying that." He rested his hands on her shoulders. "Don't you know that I have become fond of you?" He chuckled. "Why else would I see to the safety of a dog that tried to bite you?"

"Because you raised them at one time and hounds hold a soft spot in your heart?"

He shrugged. "Partly, but sleeping beside the kennels was extreme, even for me. No, my intention was to please a lady."

"A noble endeavor." She looked up at him and smiled. "It would certainly count toward your number of chivalrous acts per annum."

"Absolutely. Because of this fondness and your habit to attract trouble wherever you go, I am reluctant to leave you without protection.

When I am called away to serve the Crown, I wish to protect you from afar. With this certificate of marriage, Sir Josiah will have no claim on you. You will be safe. You will have a family. You will be loved by Grandmother. Your future is secure."

Was this how Muriel had felt when marrying her privateer? A mixture of fear and hope? Muriel and Erik were quite happy, and he was a kind duke who not only accepted his wife's antics but had bought her a bakery in their village so she could continue the baking that made her happy. And now Sebastian Larkby was willing to promise himself to Vivienne, that she might have protection, the career of her dreams, and a family in Grandmother Larkby. *He, too, is a good man.*

"I have come to love your grandmother. I am pleased our marriage will no longer be a lie, for her sake."

Vicar Brown appeared in the doorway, a napkin tucked into his neckcloth, his fingers pinching a roll that appeared to have been dipped in the drippings of his dinner. "Sir Sebastian Larkby, my maid says you have a special license?" He popped the roll into his mouth, his lips smacking as he sucked his fingers clean before wiping the residue on the napkin at his chest. "Are you certain you do not wish for the banns to be read in each of your churches? It would lessen the wagging tongues."

Sebastian produced it, laying it on the man's desk. "We have waited long enough."

"Very well then." He wiped his fingers on his napkin once more and reached for his Bible, flipping it open with ease to a piece of paper in the middle. "Jill! Come in here and act as witness!"

The maid scuttled inside and stood in the corner with her hands folded before her, offering Vivienne a small smile before staring at her feet.

"Do you take this woman as your wife?"

Sebastian and Vivienne looked at each other.

"Aren't you forgetting something, Vicar Brown?" Vivienne interrupted. "A reading, perhaps? Shouldn't we be joining hands?"

"My dinner is waiting. You have obtained a special license, and therefore I shall give a special, abbreviated vow exchange. Hold hands if you want."

Sebastian's hands reached for hers, turning her toward him as the vicar raced through the vows, running his finger down the piece of paper tucked in the Bible. Sebastian bound himself to her and she to him. He dipped his forehead to touch hers, smiling as the vicar unceremoniously declared them husband and wife.

Vivienne breathlessly signed her name beside Sebastian Larkby's on the certificate, the vicar and maid witnessing the marriage. She was a married and titled woman now. Her stepbrother could not force her into a marriage with Sir Josiah. She smiled up at her husband, and he gathered her hand in his strong one, gently kissing the top of it. She was safe at last.

He assisted his bride into the gig. His *bride*. Even if their marriage was in name only, the responsibility of her protection and happiness was real and of vital importance to him. They had an easy friendship. This would prove a boon. He climbed in beside her and snapped the reins.

As they rode back to the manor, the burden of the lie lifted, and Bash was grateful that he'd supplied his grandmother with the granddaughter she had always wished to have. Evie needed his grandmother as much as she needed Evie. He only wished that she might come to need him one day . . . beyond protection from her stepbrother. He tamped down the thought. He had years left to serve the Prince Regent. It was only a matter of time before George took the throne. Bash had worked diligently to see to it that he stood behind his friend, offering him support even if the people found him wanting as their king.

"You've been quiet." Evie broke the silence. "What are you thinking about?"

"Returning to London."

"Oh." Her voice dipped. "So soon?"

"Soon enough."

"Very well." She yawned behind her gloved hand. "If you do not mind, I am quite tired after tonight's unexpected events. I will close my eyes."

It was just as well. His mind was likely spinning as much as his bride's. It did not take long to reach the manor, what with his thoughts completely overtaken by what they had done. The wheels rolled to a halt, and his bride was truly asleep. *So she had not been merely avoiding conversation with me.* He moved to shake her shoulder, but with the moonlight cascading down her golden locks and thick lashes, she seemed so at peace, and he was loath to wake her after the attack of nerves she had endured. When he was a boy, nothing had helped to retune his own body after an attack quite as much as sleep.

He scooped her into his arms, cradling her to his chest as he stepped down from the gig, which took some doing, given the height. Her head lolled against his shoulder, but her soft snoring was steady. He nodded to Noah, who'd stumbled out from the stables, hair askew. He looked twice at the sight of Bash holding the lovely woman and blinked away his astonishment.

The servants must have heard them arrive, as the butler opened the door at once. Ladd's eyes widened at the sight of Lady Larkby.

"Have no fear. She is merely exhausted. We shouldn't have attended tonight, but I did so wish to show off my bride." He took the stairs slowly, knowing that with every step she was that much closer to never being in his arms again. He paused at her door and gently knocked it with the toe of his boot.

Charlotte appeared in the crack of the door, her jaw dropping.

"She fell asleep after a fright."

She held the door open, standing to the side. Concern etched her features. "What happened?"

"Sir Josiah was at the Sydney Hotel."

"La! Say it isn't so? He is here to spirit her away, isn't he?" She twisted her hands. "Did she have an attack of nerves?"

"Yes, but we have seen to the issue."

"What do you mean?" She snatched up a crocheted throw, motioning for him to set Evie on the bed. "You did not challenge him to a duel, did you?"

"I'll admit, the thought did cross my mind." He laid Evie on the bed, admiring her hair on the silk pillow. She must've been truly exhausted to sleep so soundly. "We decided to marry instead."

She dropped the blanket.

"As in *legally* marry." He opened his coat and withdrew the certificate of marriage.

She grasped it, her lips parting. "This is real."

"It is."

"She married you?" She pressed her hand to her mouth, smiling.

"That's what the paper says."

"Praise the Lord." She handed back the certificate. "I am tempted to wake her to obtain more details than a few grunts from you, but knowing how exhausted she is after one of her spells, I will stay my questions until the morning."

Chapter Seventeen

A PRESENCE CLOSE TO HER face had Vivienne's eyes flying open to Charlotte standing over her with her arms crossed, scowling at her.

"Seems someone had a busy night. Would you care to enlighten me, Lady Larkby?"

Vivienne moaned as she swung her feet from the bed, her head hammering. It always did so after a spell. "What time is it?"

"It's nearing ten in the morning. I couldn't sleep, so I've been keeping myself busy embroidering one of your reticules. Sir Sebastian tells me you are wed. I want to hear it from you. Tell me what is going on this instant. Employer or not, so help me, I will throw you in a carriage myself and take you back to Draycott Castle if you two have another fabrication in the works. Though, I do not know how one forges a wedding certificate. So that leads me to believe that you have finally fallen in love with him, or he pressed you into a marriage. But what would he get out of it if he did?"

It took Vivienne nearly an hour to convince Charlotte that she was of a sound mind and hadn't been forced into a marriage, while skirting the topic of love. But after their very lengthy conversation, Charlotte was satisfied and finished dressing Vivienne.

Charlotte added a lace shawl over Vivienne's shoulders. "If you want any chance of a deep relationship with Mrs. Larkby, I suggest you confess everything this very morning, or this will be the worst decision of your life."

"I had much the same thought." She ran her hands over her hair, ensuring each pin was in place. A conversation of this magnitude required her to be as put together as possible. "I'll do some writing while I await her in the parlor." Vivienne grasped her notebook and pencil.

"Not her bedroom?"

"Yesterday, she mentioned wishing for a change of scenery to the maids, who told me, and I think the environment will be more conducive to my confessing all. If I see her lying in bed, looking pale, I may rethink the truth."

Charlotte gave her an encouraging smile. "You can do this, my lady. Truth is best."

Vivienne trudged down the stairs and spied a maid. She paused in the parlor doorway and requested tea to be brought once she pulled the cord. "Have you seen Sir Sebastian this morning, Bridget?"

The maid bobbed her head. "He's training Cerberus near the kennel, my lady."

She nodded her thanks, curled into the window seat, and flipped open her book to the scene that had been giving her no end of trouble, but that she needed to conquer before the end of the week if she was to meet her publisher's timeline. She attempted to write while she waited for Grandmother to appear, but no sentences came across as she intended. Her mind was too muddled with the conversation to come.

Grandmother's voice floated down the stairs. Vivienne shot to her feet. She readied Grandmother's seat with her current embroidery project and pulled the bell cord, summoning the tea. It was time to confess. Even if the charade was no longer a charade, the lie between them was causing her breathing to be painful, and she hated the idea of keeping such a secret from the kind woman.

The footman slowly lowered Grandmother at the threshold. She leaned heavily on her cane, her smile faltering when she saw Vivienne's pained expression. "I see we are to have that talk now." She sighed. "And I hear the rattle of the tea cart. Perhaps a bracing cup would be best to hold on to, to steady us both for what is sure to be ill news, given your state."

"I'm afraid it is as you fear." Vivienne assisted Grandmother onto the settee as the footman rolled in the cart and placed the tea tray on the side table.

Pouring the drink and handing out treats that would turn to dust in her mouth if she endeavored to eat them now, Vivienne wrapped her hands about her teacup and looked straight at Grandmother. "Our marriage is not what it seems."

Grandmother lifted her gnarled hand. "I know, my dear. You do not have to explain."

Her lips parted. "Y-you . . . know? What do you know about the marriage?"

"Everything." She smiled, patting her on the arm. "I may be old, but I am not a fool. Sebastian has never mentioned you before. I well remember our conversations of me asking him to marry and his stout refusal. I know the only thing that would move him to marry would be a great love." She chuckled, popping a biscuit into her mouth. "I never thought that great love would be me."

Shame filled Vivienne's belly. "I am so sorry I deceived you." She dipped her head. "We both love you. It nearly destroyed us both to be harboring such a lie for so long. We didn't wish for you to become ill again whenever we did tell you, so we kept delaying on the hope that you would make a complete recovery. And when you did, there was no other excuse left to hide behind."

"While I do not condone lying, I can see how you had both chosen to do so in the name of mercy and love. I forgave you both long ago." She rested her hand on Vivienne's scalding cheek before brushing an errant curl from her forehead. "I only wish that you were my granddaughter by marriage."

Vivienne caught the dear woman's hand and kissed the top of it. "On that account I may give you peace. We are indeed married now."

Grandmother gasped, her hands flying to her lips, her teacup rattling in its saucer and then tumbling to the floor as she scrambled to standing. She wobbled without her cane as she cried out, "You are? I have a granddaughter?"

"Indeed!" Vivienne caught the woman's arms, balancing her as Grandmother bobbled a little jig.

"My prayers have been answered. Hallelujah!" She lifted her hand heavenward before clasping it over her heart. "I should have known the Lord would have answered my dearest prayer before I went home. He always waits until the last minute to answer a God-given desire of mine. I believe He enjoys the drama of it all—making certain that all know it was brought about by His hand alone." She pressed her forehead to Vivienne's. "You *do* love each other, don't you?"

"I am fonder of him than of any man I have ever met." Vivienne helped her return to her seat. "Sebastian is kind. He married me to keep me safe from my stepbrother and an unwanted betrothal to a cruel, twisted man. As a result, I am your granddaughter by law."

Grandmother wrapped her in her arms. "I was so fearful that I would lose you after only just finding you, my dear. And as for your husband, love will soon follow. I've seen the way Sebastian treats you. He has never shown such deference to a woman before. But tell me, how did this come about?"

Vivienne quickly explained all, beginning with her poor research to claim a forgotten title as her pen name years ago and ending with Sebastian's foresight in requesting a special license.

The door opened, and the butler bowed. "My lady. Mrs. Larkby. There is a caller here for Lady Larkby. He claims to be Lady Larkby's—" He looked askance and shook his head. "He claims to be her betrothed."

The joy from moments before fell aside as her vision swam. She gripped the decorative pillow at her side.

"I explained that it was impossible for you to be betrothed, as you are wed to Sir Sebastian, but he would not be deterred from his preposterous claim. As a result of his impudence, I left him on the porch. Shall I show Sir Josiah Montgomery inside?"

Grandmother clutched Vivienne's hand. "No. He must be mad to make such a claim."

A scuffle sounded at the door, and Sir Josiah pushed past the butler, shouting, "I will not be kept from my intended! You have no right to leave me, a titled lord, on the front steps as if I am an errand boy at the wrong entrance."

Grandmother rose, standing before Vivienne, shielding her. "How dare you enter my house uninvited. Ladd, fetch Sir Sebastian at once."

"I mean no harm." Sir Josiah bowed to her. "Forgive me, Mrs. Larkby, but I am overcome with the pressing need to speak with my future bride."

"I am not your future bride. I am wed." Vivienne rose, placing her hand on Grandmother Larkby's elbow, guiding her to sit once more.

Sir Josiah plucked a biscuit from the tray. "As I stated at the Sydney Hotel last night, there are facts that do not align with your tale, and I doubt you are truly married to the man and your marriage certificate is forged. I will take you back to your stepbrother's house now." He smirked. "Take comfort in the fact that I will not hold your naivete against you. But if you require a show of my devotion, I shall be taking part in Mr. Waterbury's annual tournament for charity tomorrow and will wear your colors as I attempt to claim the generous prize money for our wedding trip." He bowed, extending his hand. "Might I have your lace shawl for a token?"

She crossed her arms and frowned at him. "My husband shall be wearing my colors and no one else."

"He is to take part?" Sir Josiah's eyes sparked.

"He is now," Grandmother interjected.

"I would enjoy taking the knight down a peg and maiming him in the process." The fool man had the gall to laugh.

Vivienne lifted her chin and narrowed her eyes. "He is not merely going to take part. He is going to win. And if you have the desire to remain able-bodied before the tournament, I suggest you take your departure before my husband returns and takes leave of his manners as he shows you to the door."

Chapter Eighteen

BASH STRODE OUT ONTO MR. Waterbury's field, already brimming with contestants, with Evie on his arm and Grandmother safely seated under the white tents, surrounded by her friends and her maid to see to any needs that she might have. After hearing of Sir Josiah's visit while he was preoccupied in the kennel training Cerberus, Bash had struggled with his desire to challenge his wife's former fiancé to a duel. However, it would not be a good reflection on the Crown.

But he agreed with the ladies. Using his skill to humiliate the pompous man by besting him at the tournament and securing the purse was an excellent display that the Prince Regent would approve of, as it spoke well of all yeomen. In years past, Bash had been in service during the tournaments, but even when visiting home, he had refused to enter, as others needed the purse more than he. Now that he had a wife to care for, the prize money would see to her while he was away.

"It looks like the targets grow more and more difficult toward the end of the fields." Evie pointed in the direction of the first roped off area for the sharpshooters.

Lord Waterbury had a target set up that even the most excellent of shooters might find challenging to hit, along with a knife-throwing contest with stuffed targets, and a fencing contest with ten pistes marked and ready for the contestants. Whoever bested all three matches was to be granted an absurd purse of one hundred pounds.

"Good. It will make it that much easier for me to win."

"I know I haven't told you much about Sir Josiah, but he was trained by the best masters in marksmanship and fencing . . . I know naught about his knife-throwing skills."

"As was I." He grinned. "And my knife skills are top-notch."

"Honestly, Sebastian, don't you think this has gone too far?" She rested her hand on his arm. "After all"—she lowered her voice—"he was right about us."

"That's not what you said yesterday." While he enjoyed seeing the bloom of anger in her cheeks once more, he was furious with the cause. It had secretly thrilled him to hear Grandmother's account of Evie's belief in his ability to best the man. "But to admit it now, there would be severe consequences. I will not allow your reputation to be tarnished by the cad. Even if he was correct, it was highly offensive when he barged into our home to bully you when I was not there. I will not stand for you being affronted thus."

"I am used to his ways." She shook her head. "And I should not have allowed him to goad me. He will be severely offended when you best him publicly."

"It is a friendly game." *Far better than the duel I was tempted to challenge him to.*

"Not anymore. When we set Grandmother in the tent, Mrs. Zander caught my arm and said that Sir Josiah spread the rumor of our suspicious marriage circumstances at the party after we left."

He grunted. *Confound that vindictive woman.* "And why would Mrs. Zander divulge this to you? I thought she was angry with you over the jewelry still."

"She is. If it is the truth, she may wish to hurt me. If it is false, it has done its work in harming my peace." She sighed, playing with the citrine ring on her finger and holding it up in the afternoon light. "However, I do not regret you purchasing the citrines."

"I'd do it again." He grasped her hand, his voice gruff with emotion. "I will protect your name and virtue, my lady."

Something flickered in her eyes. Recognition?

Surely she doesn't know I'm Bash? He cleared his throat. "Now, I best win the match as you said I would." He bowed over her hand and trod up to the first game—shooting.

He grasped the forestock of his flintlock rifle, nodding his thanks to Noah, who had eagerly agreed to be his assistant for the day. Bash strode out onto the green, taking his place in line. Ten men fired at a time at their targets. Only the top three shooters would move on to the second round. Bash was in the second group. His aim was true, and from his position he heard Evie cheering. He lifted his rifle over his head, smiling as he caught sight of her waving her handkerchief in the air. The third group strode forward and fired.

His aim was true throughout each round, and he and Sir Josiah were the last ones standing, along with a man from a neighboring village whom Bash did not know.

Bash positioned the butt of his rifle against his shoulder and planted his feet. He drew in a deep breath, keeping his left eye trained on the target and, with his competitors, fired. The crowd cheered as the judges strode to the targets, making note of each before whispering to the runner, who trotted to Mr. Waterbury.

Mr. Waterbury lifted his hands to silence the crowd. "For the first time," he called out, "there is a tie. Sir Sebastian and Sir Josiah! Therefore, there is a change in the rules. The prize will be given to the winner of two out of three contests."

Sir Josiah leaned on his muzzle and smirked before kicking the butt of the rifle and striding to the next roped off area.

As per tradition, the contestants were offered drinks as they strolled with the crowd to the next event, fencing. While Bash was proficient with a rifle, the rapier was what he had trained with the most. He drank as the first round of contestants fenced on the row of pistes. Many were not skilled, but what they lacked in finesse, they made up for in daring strikes, making for an entertaining match for the onlookers.

Bash was called to take his place against Sir Josiah, as they had tied in the rifle event. The man stood, rapier in hand, a grin already overtaking his features as if he was confident in his ability to best Bash. The man strode onto the piste, positioning his feet as he found Evie in the crowd and sent her a wink.

Anger flashed hot and bright in Bash's chest. He no longer cared about this man's ruffled feelings and barely veiled hatred. He wished to best Sir Josiah and humiliate him into the ground in front of all for the unkind words he had spoken against the woman whom he had planned to marry—and whom he continued to mock. Bash might not be able to duel, but he could fence with all his considerable skill. He struck true again and again, his opponent seeming to awaken to Bash's talent. The man was quick and light on his feet, proving to be a master with the rapier. A trickle of worry entered Bash's heart.

Vivienne grasped the handle of her parasol, wishing she was allowed on the piste to face Sir Josiah to put him in his place, but even if she possessed the talent, she would have never been allowed to do so unless disguised as a man.

The men batted each other's strike, and as the match progressed, Sir Josiah became more aggressive in his attacks, trying tactics unbefitting a gentleman. He whipped his rapier across Sebastian's neck, drawing blood as Sebastian leaned back, barely preventing the blade from doing further damage.

The scorekeeper shouted his disapproval of Sir Josiah's lack of sportsmanship, along with the crowd.

She sucked in a breath, leaning down to Grandmother's chair to hiss, "How dare he? This is supposed to be a friendly match. Sir Josiah seems to be determined to win even if it means setting aside etiquette. Should we stop the match? I know the man to be ruthless."

"My grandson did not become a Yeoman of the Guard by developing the trait of mercy. He will meet the man's bluster and will never surrender." Grandmother nodded beneath her parasol. "Wait and see. He will put the upstart in his place."

She nodded. Sebastian had gained nobility by his courage and not by retrenching. To surrender the match to Sir Josiah would cast dishonor as a yeoman. The emotion she felt as Sebastian was sliced a second time, atop his hand, surprised her. This man was kind and good and true. He did not deserve this. "To the victory hasten, Sir Sebastian!" She cried out above the crowd, not caring at the stares she received for such a display of affection.

Sebastian sent her a grin and saluted her with his rapier, sending her heart to skipping.

Sir Josiah took the opportunity to send her a leer. She wondered why he wouldn't simply let her go if he disrespected her so much. Why was he intent on destroying her reputation? Wouldn't it be easier to believe that she had actually married a knight?

Sebastian seemed to rally at her encouragement, until the break was called and he sank on his stool, gulping his glass of water. She pushed through the crowd and hurried to his side. "Sebastian, there's something that you must know about Sir Josiah."

He shook his head, panting. "I will not step down."

"I know. I thought you would like to know that he has a bad ankle from a fall off his horse last summer. Strike him there and he will crumple like ash." She slapped her palms to emphasize her words.

He grinned at her, taking her hand in his. "While I do not condone cheating, I appreciate your concern and information." He bowed over her hand. "I will guard myself better now that I know I am dealing with a cheat and not a gentleman."

"Kiss her for luck, my boy!" Grandmother Larkby called across the row of pistes from her place in the tent.

Grandmother's request was picked up by the crowd, and soon all were chanting for him to claim a kiss from the authoress. She felt her cheeks flame, and Sebastian quirked a brow. He rose, towering over her as he bent his head to her.

"I will not please the crowd. But should you feel inclined to bestow a token in the form of a kiss, I believe I shall find the strength I need to be the victor."

Her gaze rested on his full lips. *What is the harm of a single kiss? Perhaps it will bring us to a place beyond friendship.* The chanting of the crowd grew, and seeing no other way than to comply lest she cause people to suspect their ruse, she gave him a short nod. "To kiss a knight such as you and bestow a burst of strength would be my honor."

With her parasol shielding them from view, his lips met hers, sweet and chaste. The fullness of his lips beckoned her to deepen the kiss when it sparked a buried memory within her heart. She gasped and wrenched back—seeing not her husband but the roguish grin of Bash the highwayman.

Chapter Nineteen

HE KNEW SHE'D FIGURED OUT who he was as he grasped her shoulders, desperation lining his piercing eyes. "My lady."

"You." She strained against his hold on her shoulders. "Don't you dare 'my lady' me."

He leaned down and whispered in her ear. "Don't struggle. People will see. I promise that I will explain all soon. In detail."

"Yes. You will." She hardly refrained from clenching her fist and marching away that instant. The moment she turned, the crowd would spot her fury. That would not do. "They will know I'm angry the moment they see my face." She dipped her head, drawing a breath.

"I can fix that." He wrapped his hand about her waist, bent, and stole a second kiss, making the crowd roar in delight.

She whirled away, her cheeks burning, but the crowd would only think it was her maidenly sensibilities and not ire causing the blush. She had to keep her tears at bay. She had been an utter fool. *Is the man even Sir Larkby?* She shook her head. There was no way everyone in the countryside of Bath would address him as a knight and him not truly be a knight. But what was a knight doing parading as a highwayman one moment and supposedly serving as the Prince Regent's right-hand guard the next? It made no sense.

She joined the crowd lining the pistes, her mind whirling. Muriel's husband was no stranger to subterfuge. And in a time of war, appearances were not always true. And then, there was Baron Deverell, Muriel's former gentleman of affection, who was aiding Napoleon! *Sir*

Sebastian the highwayman could be into all sorts of traitorous deeds. She wrung her hands around the neck of her parasol. How could she stand here in the crowd and act like her world had not been upended once more? *Here I have been romancing that I have been rescued by a true knight in shining armor, only to discover that he is a wolf, a rogue, a-a common highwayman.* She pressed a hand to her churning belly. No matter his faults, there was nothing common about Bash Larkby. She turned from the fenced-off area and sought out the tents.

"Are you quite well, my dear?" Grandmother clasped Vivienne's hand as soon as she reached her side. "With a kiss like that, I suppose it does make a girl lightheaded," she teased.

Vivienne shook her head, dreading what she needed to do. She might have lied about being a titled authoress, but she did not cause anyone true harm. But if a man lied about something so dire as being a highwayman who held up people at gunpoint, she could not trust him . . . no matter how much she needed him. "I need to return home."

"But the match is about to begin again! Don't you want to see the defeat?" Grandmother whispered, her eyes sparking with concern. "Did you eat something spoiled by the hot sun?" Her eyes widened. "I hope not. Soon, the nobility will be running every which way, seeking privacy to cast up their accounts. Shall I attend you home?"

Vivienne laughed weakly. "Oh no, I do not want to give anyone cause to gossip, and we are so near to home that the walk might do me good. I am simply overwhelmed." She patted Grandmother's arm. "Please express my thanks to the hostess. I shall take my leave of you, Grandmother." She bent and kissed her on the cheek. "Goodbye."

Grandmother pressed her lips into a thin line and nodded. "Very well. I hope you feel better soon, my dear."

Vivienne took care not to race as she headed toward the edge of the property, where a copse of trees would offer her shelter from prying eyes as she lengthened her walk to a run. Five miles was nothing for a country lass. As she crested the hill, she glanced behind her to see the contestants begin the final match on the pistes. For someone who could leap so fearlessly from a racing horse onto a moving carriage, he should win with his eyes closed. At least Sir Josiah would be put in his place. She marched past the trees and down the hill toward the stone bridge to Lark Manor, intent on packing her bags the moment she returned to the manor. The thought of what he could yet be hiding sent her into a dead run. If Baron Deverell, a man who'd proclaimed to love Muriel, could poison her and attempt to abduct her, what could Bash do to her now that she knew of his part in the robbery, when he was supposed to be an honorable yeoman?

In her days in Chilham, the run would be nothing—but she had not run in too long, and the ever-growing stitch in her side begged her to slow her pace. She ignored it. A stitch would disappear, but Bash catching her alone could cause irreversible damage. If he was a highwayman, she had stumbled into something far bigger than she had thought. She pumped her arms, readying herself to leap over the short stone wall that separated the Waterburys' land and the Larkbys'. The top of her foot struck the stones, and she tumbled forward, catching herself with her hands as she rolled boots over bonnet.

She lay in the grass, nearly giggling at her foolishness. What if the servants saw her sprawled out and laughing? They would think she was in need of a trip to Bedlam. She rolled to her side and brushed off her skirts as she stood. She removed the bonnet she had refinished with the express intent to make Sebastian admire her eyes. The bonnet was crushed, and it would take a great deal to repair it. She tossed it into the tall grass and raced down the hill and crossed the bridge.

Had he been laughing at her? Had he known how much she thought of the highwayman? Or of how her hopes had changed from the highwayman to having a fond relationship with her husband to . . . a hope for love? She brushed a fist over her eyes. She should never have fantasized over the highwayman returning to her—things never turned out in real life how she would have written them. She should have never agreed to this insane scheme. The time for trust was over. Despite how much it would pain her to leave Grandmother Larkby, she would have to change her name again to avoid the scandal and run from him. She would have to sell her terrace home to fund her escape. She strode through the tree-lined path to the gardens to the side entrance of the parlor and raced up the stairs to her room.

Charlotte sat up in bed, her hair mussed from her nap. "My lady? Whatever happened? Why is your hem—"

"Sir Sebastian Larkby is not who he says he is." Her voice broke as she sank into a heap before the fireplace. "And I fear he is part of something that we can never recover from."

Charlotte hurried to her side, grasping her hands. "What happened? Did he harm you?"

"You are going to laugh at this." She giggled through her fear, noting Charlotte's growing concern. "He's the highwayman."

"No." Charlotte gasped, sinking back on her heels. "No! How on earth do you know that?"

She sighed. "He kissed me."

"And how did a kiss reveal he was . . ." Charlotte's lips parted in realization. "You *kissed* the highwayman, Vivienne Poppy? What were you thinking? You cannot go around kissing men."

"I didn't mean to, but he had just rescued me from two horrid men, and I was near hysterical from relief at his saving me, and I-I kissed him in my thanks."

Charlotte rested her face in her hands, groaning. "Vivienne! What am I going to do with you? How am I to possibly protect your reputation when you do such things? Imagine. Kissing your captor?"

"I know! It was reckless and foolish." She lifted her fingers to her lips. And entirely the thing of dreams . . . or nightmares now. She slapped her cheeks, desperate to spur herself into action. "And with this knowledge, I have but one course. I need to escape and seek an annulment."

"B-but wouldn't him being the highwayman be a dream come true?" Charlotte shook her head. "I thought you were fond of him? So why this sudden need to run?"

"We are in a time of war, Charlotte. If a man who is supposed to be head and shoulders above all others in character and honor is *robbing* nobility, there is something traitorous afoot. I doubt the Prince Regent would look kindly on Bash's alternative identity. I hardly need to re-mind you of Baron Deverell and his obsession with Muriel."

"That is a good point." Charlotte shuddered, spurring into action. "I will pack at once. How much time do we have?"

"Mayhap an hour before their return? The tournament should be ending then."

"I shall send for the carriage while you pack. We shall leave in a quarter of an hour." Charlotte pulled the bell cord.

The women rushed about the room, tossing clothes into the satchel. The trunks would have to wait until she and Charlotte were safely away in her townhouse, where Vivienne could fortify herself until she made a plan of escape. They could not stay there for longer than absolutely necessary—not with Bash knowing her whereabouts. She would have to send her trunks to a friend's estate to keep him from following her. She'd move to the other side of England if needed, mayhap even the Scottish Isles. Tess was forever recounting her long holidays there with her father in their cottage. Vivienne hated to sell her darling home, but if she needed funds to start over, she had to do what she must.

A grating twenty minutes had passed by the time they fled the manor, a bag in each hand, and into the awaiting carriage as a fine mist coated their pelisses.

"Wonderful. At least now I know what I put my heroine through whenever I make her trudge through the countryside in the rain before the hero saves her." She shivered, settling back onto the tufted seat.

"Let us pray that Sir Sebastian does not find us thus," Charlotte mut-tered, pulling the plaid over their laps.

"Sir Sebastian is no hero," Vivienne whispered, so as not to be over-heard by the driver.

"Surely there is an explanation, but I am struggling to think of one at the moment. I shall hail a hired carriage the moment we return to your townhome. Though I do not know where we shall flee from there."

"We shall return to Draycott Castle and seek the duke and duchess's counsel. There, we will be protected, and his grace can reach out to the Prince Regent to discuss Sir Sebastian's activities."

She grasped Charlotte's hand and stared out the window as they approached Bath, taking the road to her terrace home in the Circus. Haste was of the essence if they were to leave Bath before Sebastian Larkby, or whoever he was, showed up to claim his wife.

Chapter Twenty

RAIN PELTED HIM AS HE raced across the meadow to Lark Manor, not daring to borrow a horse lest word circulate that his bride had left him and Grandmother behind . . . but then the rain had begun, and he was certain some were leaving the tournament in lieu of waiting out the rain under the tents. In any event, he had lost precious time. When he had bested Sir Josiah and discovered her nowhere to be found, he sought Grandmother, who turned out to be blissfully enjoying her goblet of vanilla ice under the tent, watching the rain pelt the nobility who were too far from the tents to seek shelter in time. She had confirmed that Evie had returned home, which had him thinking she had run. Grandmother sensed his need to find his bride and assured him that the good doctor would escort her home in the gig and sent him on his way.

He leapt over the hedge of the garden, the gravel skittering underfoot as he raced through the gardens to the back door, leaving it wide open as he ran inside. He didn't bother with propriety as he shouted, "Lady Larkby? Evie! Where are you?"

The butler appeared, pale. "Sir Sebastian? The lady said she had some unexpected business in town and departed in the carriage less than a half hour ago."

He grunted. They had made so much progress, and she *had* trusted the highwayman before. And yet she must have suspected him of something dastardly to run away from Grandmother and risk her career. "Order Brigand to be saddled at once and inform my grandmother that I shall be at my wife's townhouse for the night." He charged up the stairs and drew on his dark clothing and heavy cloak for the rain. He paused, staring at his desk. He would need proof that he was not a criminal nobleman. She had believed his word one too many times without proof. He removed a key from a hallowed-out book on the shelf, unlocked his desk, and withdrew a letter with the seal of the Crown on the bottom-right corner. He tucked it into his waistcoat, beside his heart.

The journey to her townhouse was short, but as the rain thickened, darkness enveloped the city and made riding difficult with the blasts of wind whipping between the buildings. He reined in his mount as he watched the women run into the terrace apartment, ducking under a plaid blanket to shield them from the rain and the wind that plastered their skirts to their limbs. He directed his horse to the servants' entrance. He patted his horse at the rear of the home. "Stay here, friend. You shall be taken care of in a moment." He eyed the door. It would be too obvious, though perhaps the servants were busy, but he would not take the risk of alerting anyone to his presence. He climbed on the saddle, leapt for the ledge over the doorway as he had done once before. He jerked open the window and climbed inside. He raced down the hall as voices on the ground floor floated up to him. From what he heard, the footman was instructed to keep the doors barred from anyone else while they packed the home.

He slipped into her room. He kept his hood drawn and leaned against the window frame with his arms crossed, waiting to speak with his wife. It probably was not fair to consider her his wife after only standing before the vicar and signing their names hastily to a certificate that bound them by law, but he could not bear for her to think ill of him . . . even though he deserved it after robbing her and stealing across the countryside with her in the saddle before him and then marrying her without confessing all first. It was abominable. And entirely unknightly.

But that first kiss.

It had sparked an interest that he had never felt before, and by the ardor in her kiss, he felt, if only for a moment, a mirroring of his desire in the sweet maiden. It had taken everything in him not to kiss her for the weeks they had been together and again when they'd stood before the vicar—in truth, he supposed he might never be allowed to kiss her lips again, even if he had hoped it and thought of it every time he beheld her in the morning light . . . and afternoon light and evening light. All the lights. He ran a hand over his face. He was a sop.

The latch sounded, and she hurried inside with her taper, firmly shutting the door behind her. She set the taper on the dressing table, the mirror reflecting the light so that the room danced in its soft glow, highlighting her pleasant form. He had no right to gaze upon her as if she were truly his bride, nor could he afford to dwell on how pretty and brave she was—a combination that nearly strangled his resolve to keep her at arm's length. *Perhaps when this is all over, I can visit her enough to keep the gossips at bay?* But the mere idea of only seeing her briefly while on holiday plagued him. Now that he knew her, he was not certain how to continue in a world without her.

She looked into the mirror and caught sight of him in the reflection. She gripped something on the table and, turning, flung it straight at him.

He ducked as a book fell short at his feet. "Where do you think you're going, my lady?"

"As far away from you as I can manage," she spat, reaching for a painted porcelain vase.

"I thought you required my protection." He tossed back his hood and lifted up his hands. "Am I not holding up our part of the deal?"

"Deal? Deal!" Her voice rose. She pinched the bridge of her nose, as if to gather herself. "Our deal was off the moment I discovered your duplicity. You are the highwayman." She nodded to his hair. "If you had not shorn your hair, I would've recognized you in an instant, but you are so cunning, you thought of that on your own. How long did you know that I was Lady Larkby? Did you plan it the moment you found my diary? Did you know before I entered the stagecoach? Did you think me a fool and laugh at me behind my back?"

"Certainly not. And I am not so cunning as all that. After I left you the first time in your terrace home, I had an unfortunate encounter with head lice, which in the end was most providential." He took a step toward her.

She darted a step back. "Stay where you are."

"I have, of course, since then gotten rid of them, by the most extreme means." He grinned.

"That is not why I retreat." She clenched her fists. "Are you even a knight of the Prince Regent? Or have you duped your grandmother as well as the whole of Bath into thinking that you were someone honorable? A knight of the Crown? Such a crime is unforgivable by the law—worthy of execution, I believe."

"I am a knight. I have not lied on that score. In fact, I have only lied to you once."

"Once is enough. A knight who is also a highwayman is not to be trusted in a time of war. If you are not a spy, then you are a thief *without* honor." She shook her head. "I have gotten in too deep with you. We may be connected by law now, but it won't be for long. I never wish to see you again."

"That does not suit me in the least. Besides"—he slowly crossed the room, stopping short before her and removing the porcelain from her hand, setting it in the basin—"everything is not as it seems. I am not in actuality a highwayman by trade."

She snorted. "Pray tell that to my ruined pelisse and gown and Sir Thomas."

He ground his teeth and ran his hands over his bristly hair. "I felt terrible about abducting and robbing you, but it was necessary to preserve my cover. But I returned your funds with interest. Did you not wonder why I did so?"

"Your cover? Then you *are* a spy."

"Of course not. I serve the Crown."

"How is nearly ruining my reputation in the process of your robbing the coach serving the Crown? Was that part of your cover as well?

You should think over your lies carefully, as a true gentleman would never compromise a lady thus."

"I do not become a highwayman for my own amusement, Evie. Sometimes there is a greater mission than preserving a nicety."

"Nicety? You are no buffoon. A reputation is everything—you nearly brought my character into question, no matter how inadvertently. I hope it was worth it. If it is true that you were acting on orders, did you at least find whatever you were looking for that day?"

He swallowed back an explanation. "I am not at liberty to divulge my mission."

She crossed her arms, her eyes narrowing. "What did the Prince Regent require you to take from my carriage?"

He crossed his own arms, mirroring her. "Again, I am not at liberty—"

"There was no other passenger on that coach besides Sir Thomas and me. Judging from the pile of stolen goods and funds that you dumped from the saddlebags, you robbed the coachman and us but did not go through the trunks, so you must have found what you were looking for. And as the Prince Regent does not want for money or jewels . . . I'm guessing your objective was obtaining . . . Sir Thomas's letters? But why would you want those?"

Perceptive. He turned to the vacant fireplace, setting his boot on the grate. He mulled over how much he dared to tell her. He feared if he looked at her, she would know the answer.

"You weren't going to return the letters for a ransom. There was something in there that the Prince Regent wanted contained, wasn't there? Why else would a Yeoman of the Guard dare such an act?" She moved beside him, picking up a framed miniature of a gentleman from the fireplace mantel, stroking the painting with a thoughtful expression before setting it back. "If it was for the Prince Regent, it must have been something grave indeed to cause you to take such drastic measures and potentially ruin your family's good name, your career, and your family's legacy, which I know is everything to you, given the measures you took to see your grandmother happy."

He sighed. "It was difficult but worth the chance I took. My allegiance is not to titles but to the royal family. If I can serve the Crown with honor, even if no one else knows but me, it is enough."

She studied him, the weighted silence stretching between them. "I suppose if the Prince Regent puts such trust in you, I should as well if you can provide proof of your allegiance to him."

"I thought you might ask." He reached into his waistcoat pocket and extended the folded letter to her. "You will see the Prince Regent's seal on the bottom, declaring me a knight. I have brought a second letter, where he calls me his closest knight—his most trusted man. I cannot provide proof of his request that I act the highwayman. He asked in person, and if he should've provided anything written regarding it, I would've promptly burned it."

She crossed the room and lifted the papers to the taper, studying them. As she read, the lines in her forehead smoothed, and then she returned them. "I see. It appears that truth is at long last on your side. You can at least answer me this."

"Anything—as long as I keep the Prince Regent out of our conversation. Agreed?"

She nodded, folding her hands before her skirts. "Do you care for me at all? Why did you offer your name?"

"You know the answer to both of those questions."

"Do I?" she whispered. "I thought I did, until this afternoon."

He closed the distance between them and took her hand in both of his, caressing it. He wished to take her in his arms. *My lady, do you not know that I have been thinking of you since the moment I met you?* How could he tell her that now when she'd looked at him with mistrust only moments before? It would take time to heal the wound of his misdirection. He should have told her his identity before, but his vow to protect George bound him to silence. "You do know, my lady. Would I have married you if I did not care?"

"We both care for Grandmother Larkby. It was enough to marry to please her."

He lifted his hand to her cheek, brushing back a curl. "A man would do most anything to please a lady—but actual marriage?" He smiled. "That is far indeed."

She took a step back from him and crossed her arms over her stomach, as if protecting herself from him. He fought back a wince.

"What do you wish to do from here, Sir Sebastian?"

"Please, call me Bash as you once did. Will you return to the manor house?" At her hesitation, he added, "I know you probably weren't expecting to stay beyond a fortnight. I cannot express my gratitude. You single-handedly have brought my grandmother back to life, Evie."

Her mien softened at the name. "That power lies in Christ's hands alone, sir."

"Yes, but He often sends His angels to do His will, and I have no doubt that He sent you." He wished to tell her how she affected him. How since she'd come into his life, he'd been thinking of a life beyond the Yeoman of the Guard, but he had a long road to travel yet. And he knew her. She wanted nothing to do with a true marriage. Why else would she risk everything to pretend to be his bride?

And here, he had entrapped her. No, she would be much better off without him. She had waited too long for her freedom to surrender it now. No matter what it cost him, he would see that her best laid plans were realized—even if it meant that he was to stay away from the women he loved and Lark Manor for the rest of his days. "Tell me what you wish and it is done, my lady. You have only to command me."

Command him? Vivienne's heart stirred under his gaze as glimmers of their time on the road made her body relax now that she was certain he was telling the truth. She did know this man. He was kind and courageous and yet possessed that hint of danger that she could not help finding appealing. *If only I could command him to court me—to treasure me as I have begun to hold him in affection.* "What I wish for is impossible, I fear," she whispered.

He dropped his hands. "Because I have taken your choice of whom to marry away."

It was a statement, not a question. Before she corrected him, the door flew open and Charlotte hurried in, her eyes wide. She gasped at the sight of him. She dropped a letter and snatched the porcelain vase from the basin and held it aloft.

"You both think a porcelain vase is a good weapon?" Bash chuckled, which brought a shadow of confusion to Charlotte's expression.

Vivienne lifted her hands. "It is fine. There was a misunderstanding."

"He is not the highwayman?" She matched Vivienne's breathless whisper, keeping the porcelain aloft.

"He is, but he is, for certain, also a Yeoman of the Guard. I'll explain all later." She motioned to the letter on the floor. "Did you receive some news?"

Charlotte eyed Bash once more, then slowly lowered the vase and scooped up the letter. Weariness filled her eyes, her shoulders sagging under the weight of the news. "My mother is ill. I need to attend her."

"Charlotte! Please go at once. I shall be fine on my own."

"That is the other thing. You won't have to be alone. The letter was brought by Miss Tess Hale. She is in the parlor with her dog."

"Tess?" Vivienne tossed on her shawl and, leaving Bash behind, raced down the stairs, where Brexton was bringing a tray of tea into the parlor with his wig askew, betraying the fastidious servant's exhaustion in running the entire household in a moment's notice.

Tess Hale rose from the fire she had been stoking, her mottled pointer lying before the hearth. She flew to Vivienne's side, her cape billowing out and her gaze roving over Vivienne. "You are here. Thank goodness."

She grasped Vivienne's wrist and pulled her to the settee, calling over her shoulder to Brexton. "Do send some hot biscuits. I am half-frozen and famished." She crossed her arms, staring at Vivienne.

Tess had always been the most sensible of the three friends. Vivienne worried her bottom lip under Tess's scrutiny.

"I am happy to see you, Tess, but I am wondering why you are here."

"I received your letter, and I hardly believe the contents. In truth, Muriel and I had half decided that it was a novel plot you were working through and had forgotten to include that part in your letter, as you regularly seek our input. We both recalled the time you had one character stabbed in the hand and wrote to Dr. Madden asking how to best mend the wound and forgot to include that it was for a novel—and he went racing along the countryside, despite his towering years, to make certain you were not bleeding to death. You sent the village doctor into early retirement."

That had not been a good day. Her secret had nearly come to light, but the doctor had kept her confidence and was most helpful in providing information for her to write the scene with accuracy. "What I wrote was not for a novel."

"I was afraid of that." Tess groaned. "Vivienne! You cannot be in seriousness? You are parading about as Lady Larkby, the *wife* of some knight? This is ten times worse than Muriel's faux pas. In fact, you are making her seem quite saintly in comparison—falling for your abductor, breaking *every* rule of propriety, and *lying* to a dying woman?"

The door creaked open to reveal Bash. He had left his cloak in her room. He wore the dark clothes of the highwayman and cut a dangerous figure. Gazing, he assessed the situation.

Tess threw off her cape and reached for the dagger in her boot, sending Wolfie to his paws with a growl in his throat and his hackles raising. "You better have a good reason for being here, Sir Sebastian. If that even is your title." She scowled as her eyes roved over his highwayman's attire.

"It is and I do." He lifted his palms out, a smile playing at his lips.

"Tess. Please." Vivienne rested her hand on her friend's shoulder, her eye on Wolfie. As an animal rescued from a fighting den, he was not to be crossed. "Call off your hound and allow Bash to explain."

Tess snapped her fingers at her dog and motioned for him to stand down. She sank beside Vivienne, twirling the dagger through her fingers from hand to hand. "Talk."

Bash lowered his hands, marked respect in his gaze. "Evie and I had a mutual need. I am only disclosing this to you as Vivienne trusts you. My position as Yeoman of the Guard is unique, as I carry out clandestine missions for the Crown while disguised as a highwayman."

Tess's brow twitched. "And you have proof of this?"

Vivienne nodded. "He does. And if anyone was selfish in their need, it was I, but Bash's request was that I make his dying grandmother happy by pretending to be his bride," Vivienne rushed to add, explaining how she met Bash as the highwayman, how he took her funds and left her with precious little before returning the money *with* interest, his finding her at the masquerade, their mutual need, Bash's position, and the fix they found themselves in. She refrained from mentioning all the kissing though.

Tess pinched the space between her brows, grunting. "And did no one think of the consequences of bringing the truth to light regarding such a lie to an already weakened elderly woman?"

"Not until it was too late," Vivienne admitted and twisted her hands. "In the short time I have spent with Grandmother Larkby, I have come to respect and love her. And the very thought of paining her rent my heart in two."

"If you, Sir Sebastian, are as honorable as all that, then why not marry my friend and repair this foolishness?" Tess snorted. "It seems by far the simplest solution."

"It is." Bash nodded. "We were about to mention that part of the story. We have wed."

"What?" Tess whirled to Vivienne. "Is this true?"

"Sir Josiah found us out at the Sydney Hotel. We had little choice but to marry."

Tess's gaze flitted to each of them before a satisfied smirk settled into place. "So you wed the knight and still managed to secure the hand of the dreamy rogue? I underestimated your attraction for the man."

Vivienne gaped at her friend's betrayal of her confidence. "Tess!"

Tess's smirk fell. "You have not professed your love to each other?"

"No!" they said at the same time.

"Such an ardent refusal. Interesting." She twirled the knife again. "I think that someone here is still telling a falsehood, given that you each have surrendered much for the sake of the other. If such selfless sacrifice is not love, I know not what is."

Vivienne refused to look at Bash. He could not know of her heart. It was one thing for him to offer for her hand out of duty, but it was another matter entirely for him to think she had any sort of marital love for him. It complicated their understanding. In truth, she had never felt such passion toward any man, but Bash had single-handedly destroyed every barrier she had set up around her heart. Before him, no gentleman had caught her attention enough to consider marriage. They had always fallen short of the memory of her father—a picture of what a gentleman ought to be.

He grasped her hand, and she looked up to him to find a question in his gaze. She had not dared to imagine that he might come to feel affection toward her. His kisses certainly sent her head to spinning. Of course, she had never actually been kissed by anyone other than him, so she did not know if the act of kissing caused such flappings and flutterings in her heart or if it was Bash doing the kissing that led to such feelings.

In any case, she would need to do more research to determine that fact if she was to continue writing romantic scenes with accuracy. But the very idea of kissing someone other than Bash made all the swirling feelings fall flat. It was Bash and Bash alone who made her heart stir. *I love him.* She lifted her eyes, studying him. She loved Sir Sebastian Larkby.

Tess clapped her hands together. "As touching as all these fabrications being brought to light have been, I am exhausted from traveling without resting in a posthouse and need to retire, and since Charlotte's dear mother is gravely ill, I shall be attending you tonight, *Lady Larkby.* As you are married, I have no qualms in allowing Sir Sebastian the room adjoining yours, Vivienne, while Wolfie and I take the guest room. You mentioned in your letter that it was on the second floor, yes?"

"Indeed. The sheets should be clean enough."

Tess pressed a hand to Vivienne's lower back, moving her to the door as her dog followed close to her skirts. "Lead the way, Lady Larkby, but for payment of my services, I'm going to have all the hot biscuits sent to my room and eat them under the covers. Tomorrow, I'd like to do a bit of shopping before we return to your new manor, where I'd like to be introduced to the woman who unknowingly set this all in motion."

Vivienne cast a glance over her shoulder to Bash. To her delight, his smile mirrored what was in her heart—hope.

Chapter Twenty-One

VIVIENNE STRODE ARM IN ARM with Tess about the city, holding a small wrapped box of writing supplies procured from a luxurious shop on Bond Street. Vivienne was incandescently happy. She could live her life away from the control of her stepbrother and his wife. Her plans, though perhaps not best laid, were actually working. Sir Sebastian had given her assumed title credence, she was making just enough for her living expenses, she had a new family, and best of all, she loved Bash and had hope that one day her husband would love her in return.

They dashed across Green Street, weaving around vendors' carts and a hack and nearly colliding with a pair of gentlemen on Milsom Street. She righted herself, her apology fading on her tongue at the sight of Sir Josiah Montgomery and another gentleman who looked familiar, but whom she could not place. Sir Josiah's buttery lips pursed as he looked her up and down. His subtle grin told her that he found her as comely as always. She did her best not to shrink backward, but it was difficult with him leering at her.

"How providential. See, Alden? I told you that *the* Lady Larkby would be in Bath today. I know her so well. My future bride has been up to no good." He chuckled. "But as a man who understands such inclinations, I can respect that she wishes to have a little dalliance before she settles down to be my wife."

"How dare you. I am *nothing* like you." She reeled back as he took another step closer. "In case my actions were not clear, Sir Josiah, I have no desire to become your wife and am wed to another, as you very well know."

"Yes, your so-called title has been bandied about parlors for years. However, I did a little research, and it came to light that the resurfacing knighthood of the Larkby name is recent. I know for a fact that the man who holds the title has only been knighted in the last two years for services to the Crown, while Lady Larkby has been writing for quite some time, as a few acquaintances of mine tend to enjoy such trite, trivial novels as you put out every year."

Her stomach churned. No one had put that together yet, and as soon as word circulated, she would be ruined.

"I can only deduce that you have been using his title for your own benefit for your novels. I can only wonder how it came to be that you two became acquainted—it borders on contrived coincidence."

Or destiny. But she didn't dare voice it.

"I am afraid that such a practice, as using his title for yourself, must end when you become my bride," he finished.

"Something which will never happen, as Sir Sebastian and Lady Larkby's marriage is legal," Tess said, speaking up at last.

Vivienne nodded. She was shocked her friend had remained silent this long.

"Proof of which has not been shared. Even then I would not believe a paltry certificate. Only the vicar himself who bound them will do to convince me of their union." He reached to Vivienne. "If you are not conducive to such an arrangement, there are other, less desirable measures I shall take to claim what I was promised."

Tess audibly growled. "If I had my dog with me, I'd set him on you for that."

"I spoke only of hiring a barrister to claim what should rightfully belong to me." His eyes widened with feigned innocence, and he motioned to the man beside him. "I have long thought I should have a terrace home in the Circus, and it was promised to me *in writing*."

Her knees weakened, but she forced steel into her voice. "You would take my home from me, would you? You have no need of it, and my father willed it to me. It cannot be taken, nor promised by my stepbrother. He has no claim on it, and I am a woman of four and twenty. I can do as I please."

The barrister shrugged. "Wills have been broken before, and a breach of promise is a grave offense that must be offered restitution."

She felt a hand on her elbow. Tess pulled Vivienne around the gentlemen. "Enough. You call yourself a gentleman and yet you accost ladies on the street? I shall inform Sir Sebastian that you are plaguing his bride."

"We will see. There has been more than one young lady led into a bed thinking she had a true marriage certificate, only to be abandoned with a brood in hand for the man's legal family."

Vivienne gasped, and Tess's grip tightened on her arm. "If I were a man, I would challenge you to a duel." She tugged on Vivienne's arm once more. "Come, we must be returning home."

Vivienne matched Tess's clipped pace. "Thank you."

"You two have been living in a fairy tale. If you do not control Sir Josiah's curiosity, this is brewing to be a scandal of epic proportions. You thought Muriel's faux pas of proposing to a baron was scandalous?" She snorted. "Not to be harsh, but Sir Sebastian is *only* a knight. If he were a duke, you would be excused, but the way your chronicle is heading, you won't be able to set foot in polite society again, Vivienne. I know you've had Charlotte as your companion, chaperoning you the entire time, but this will only end poorly now that a barrister is involved. Consider this the church bell ringing your fate."

Vivienne sighed. "Bash wishes to continue serving the Crown. He cannot keep rescuing me from Sir Josiah, especially with all that has happened."

"Which he can still do while serving the Crown, but I think it might be best if you revise your plan and follow him to London—a childless bride should not be separate from her husband." She nodded to the front parlor window of Vivienne's home, where Bash was reading a paper.

Vivienne studied her handsome husband. He was devoted to the

Crown and kept busy, so maybe he would not mind having a bride along with him. They might live their lives, grow their careers, and simply have a match in name only, as they had planned, while showing society that they were happy. They were good friends, in any event. "I suppose you are right in that it would help the validity of our marriage."

"Of course I'm right." Tess pulled her inside and pushed her into the parlor.

Bash lowered the newssheet. He must have read the concern in Vivienne's features, because he shot to his feet and crossed the room at once. "What happened?"

"Sir Josiah hired a barrister. He is attempting to steal my home on the grounds of a breach of promise unless I admit our ruse."

"He had the gall to seek you out in the street? He is aiming for a duel." He clenched his fists. "And I am beginning to think that the only way to end his pursuit is to give it to him."

"Nay." She rested her hand on his arm. "We *were* in the wrong, and even if I didn't promise myself to him, he feels entitled to compensation to the point of hiring a barrister and threatening our peace."

"And the moral of this little story is that lying is never a good idea." Tess tsked, crossing her arms.

Vivienne and Bash rolled their eyes at her.

"Very helpful, Tess. Thank you." Vivienne scowled.

"There is only one thing left to do." Tess looked to Sir Sebastian. "You must not leave her in Bath alone with your grandmother. Make plans to take her with you to London. Prove your romance to all of London. Make them believe you, and then maybe *you* will believe you."

Vivienne's cheeks warmed at the idea of what that would entail. *Kisses? Most certainly. Dancing in his arms? Required. Strolls in Hyde Park? A must.* She nearly groaned. How on earth was she to keep her distance from him if he was wooing her in all the ways she had ever written about?

Bash nodded slowly. "I am beginning to think you are right. I know that this was not what we agreed upon though. What do you think, Evie? Would you consider taking our match of convenience to another height? I can lease us a home all our own. It won't be as grand as your terrace home here, but it will suffice, and I shall provide you a writing room and a small library. I'll even add a rolling ladder, which is completely unnecessary, but as you have mentioned it on several occasions, I know it is important to you."

"A library with a rolling ladder? How can a lady refuse such a gallant proposal?" Vivienne fanned her cheeks with her hand.

"You have retained some of your senses, I see. Time to make you a list." Tess harrumphed, shoving off the parlor's doorway and aiming for the writing desk. She removed a pen and paper. "Bash, do you think you can secure a house by the end of the week?"

Vivienne pulled up short. "That soon?"

"We are so beyond what is seen as proper that you two have lost all chance to have an opinion. Yes, that soon." Tess jotted down something on the paper. "You need to prove your affections once and for all, or I am taking Vivienne to my father's cottage in the Scottish Isles, where there is no shopping, no dining, and no lending libraries."

Vivienne gasped.

"The lending libraries were what did it?" Bash chuckled.

"Food I can sacrifice. The company of most I can forgo—but books?" She shook her head. "Such a banishment would be more than I could bear." She craned her neck to see what Tess was jotting down. "Whatever does *Serpentine* kisses mean?"

"Kissing by the Serpentine waters in Hyde Park," she answered, dipping her pen in the inkwell. "The two of you need as much help as you can get. I'm composing a list of things that I recommend you both do and where they should happen in order to get your romance in the forefront of everyone's minds. And since you are married, it makes it much easier to think of things."

"Who knew you were such a romantic?"

"I read." Tess snorted. "Unlike you and Muriel, I don't believe in all that nonsense in romance books, but the ton gobbles it up, and therefore I know our plan will work."

"I shall leave first thing in the morning then." Bash bowed over

Vivienne's hand. "Move with me to London, and you shall have your subscription to all the books your heart desires, Evie."

"I never thought I would have to leave my home again, but such a proposal cannot be refused." She placed her hand in his. "To London we go, my knight in shining armor."

Tess broke the tender moment with a clap. "Fresh tea, anyone? We've got some planning to do."

For the remainder of the evening, they discussed the best course of action and even selected parts of London where Vivienne would like to live. By the end of the day, she was exhausted and all decided to stay one more night in the townhouse before the ladies eagerly took to their beds by ten of the clock.

But now that she was in bed, she could not sleep. She propped herself up on her elbow, staring at the crack in the curtains where moonlight splayed in her bedroom. It had been nice to be in her own townhome again with the comfort of her things about her, if only for two evenings. Her gaze rested on the adjoining door. Her husband was just beyond it. They had all concluded on the first night that the footman might suspect if she placed Bash on the second floor, where the guest rooms were located. It was more than proper now, but the idea of Bash on the other side of the door in her home made her heart pound. Tess had kept to her room on the second floor, as she was well aware of Vivienne's snoring.

She was finally drifting to sleep when a pounding at the front door brought her scrambling to her feet. She reached for her dressing robe and drew it about her thin nightgown, slipping out of her room as Bash did the same. In the moonlight streaming through the hall window, his broad shoulders were illuminated beneath the thin linen shirt untucked from his black breeches. His calves and feet were bare. She shifted her gaze as his grin spread. He'd obviously noted her approving appraisal.

The front door jerked open, and at the noise, Bash enfolded her hand in his as they hurried down the steps. The footman stood with a letter in hand, his brows knit. "It bears the royal seal, my lady."

Bash snatched the missive with a nod of thanks. He strode to the parlor, paused by the window, and broke the seal. "It is from the Prince Regent."

"How on earth did he know where you were? What does he say?" she whispered, adding, "If you can tell me, that is."

"I informed the staff where I was going and a footman delivered a change of clothes for me while you were still asleep this morning." He tucked the letter into the top of his breeches, flashing his muscular midriff for a moment. Her cheeks burned again. He poked his head out the door and called to Brexton, "Hire a swift mount for me, and have him ready to leave in a quarter of an hour."

"You must leave?" Vivienne looked up to him, disappointment filling her that their plans were once again being changed.

He gently took her hands in his. It felt intimate given their state of undress. "I am being called back to London for a task. I will not be taking my horse so I can trade mounts at posthouses along the way, so I shall leave Brigand in your care."

"I would promise to take him riding, but he has proven most loyal to you."

"I'll instruct him to allow you to ride him. He is most intelligent." He winked and ran his thumb over her knuckles. "While I am there, I shall find us a home with room enough for your library."

"And perhaps a room for Grandmother in case she wishes to stay with us?" She glanced at their surroundings. "I doubt she will wish to leave Lark Manor, but I would be loath to leave her behind. I know we would have a jolly time together in London."

"It makes my heart light knowing that you love her as I do." He lifted her hand to his lips.

Pretending to be in love with him would not prove a difficult task. "You shall be missed, but Grandmother Larkby and I have much to discuss, and I to do, to prepare for our move to our new home."

"I know we did not start our relationship as most married couples, but I do hope that we can continue to become even greater friends."

Friends. She would take what she could get if it meant that she stayed by Bash's side. *Lord, I know he desires us to only have a match of friendship. Guard my heart from falling completely in love with him.* She bit her lip. *Who am I kidding? You and I both know that I am irrevocably in love with Bash Larkby.*

Chapter Twenty-Two

BASH SLOWED HIS HORSE AS he entered the outskirts of London. He had ridden through the night before, but it was harder when he was on a mount other than Brigand, who knew his every command almost before he gave it. But as one horse could not travel the distance at such a pace without resting, he didn't dare use Brigand this night. He needed to be able to change mounts, as time was of the essence according to the note sent by courier. He had burned the missive in the servant's hall fireplace before he departed Bath. However, its contents stayed with him. *A sheet from letter missing. Return for further instruction. G.*

He thought he'd retrieved all the letters from Sir Thomas . . . Did the Prince Regent only now find out a page was missing? If George was being blackmailed, and Sir Thomas was the fiend behind it, the man had either great courage or power to protect him.

He directed the mount to the posthouse stables and waited as the man drew up the receipt. Taking shank's mare toward his nondescript flat to change into his uniform, he glanced at the townhouses along the way, picturing his Evie on the threshold. She was too gentle for this part of town. He didn't have enough saved to purchase a fine home, but he could set up Evie well if they leased—many of the ton did so to keep up the appearance of wealth without having the expense of owning a vast estate.

Reaching his home, he made quick work of changing into his guard's uniform, his eyes burning. In the past, he had stayed up far longer than a mere twenty-four hours, and the Prince Regent would not see sleeping as an excuse not to come directly when summoned to Carlton House.

Now too tired to walk, Bash hired a hackney coach and tried to stay awake for the five-minute drive. He tossed a coin to the driver and passed through the gates, nodding to the guards there who knew him. He straightened his crimson coat and hurried through the portico and the first and second halls to the grand staircase. Not for the first time was he grateful that his position allowed him to bypass the servants' entrance and staircases. He crossed to the Prince Regent's private rooms to the left of the staircase gallery and grinned when he saw who was on duty. He nodded to the first night sentry guard and relieved him of his position outside the Prince Regent's chambers, claiming his pike before addressing the second guard.

"Wynn Paxton, whatever are you doing acting as a sentry?"

"I lost a bet with the sentry who was on duty, and as the captain of the King's Guards holds a grudge against my family, he heartily approved it. So here I stand in a borrowed crimson uniform. This hat is extremely cumbersome, but I have to admit, I am beyond dashing in it—too bad there are no debutantes nearby to swoon over me." Wynn tugged at the strap pinching his chin, which held the massive black bearskin piece in place, and lingered as Bash took his position before the prince's chambers. "How was your time in Bath? Is your grandmother in good health?"

"The best of health. She made a remarkable recovery against all expectations."

They both straightened and quieted as a lord and lady entered the gallery and then disappeared down the stairs.

"Praise the Lord. Was it your presence that revived her?" Wynn continued after the couple had disappeared, and he relaxed his stance.

"I wish I could take the credit, but that lies with Evie."

"Evie? Who is she?" He grinned. "A comely nursemaid?"

Bash cleared his throat. "My wife."

His friend's pike lowered, along with his jaw. "Your what?"

Bash swallowed back his laughter. "I was married while in Bath."

"For someone who never takes leave, you get a lot accomplished when you do." He shook his head. "Even if I am not in your yeoman's club, I thought we were friends."

"We are. This marriage took us all by surprise."

"Yes, but I didn't even know you were paying a young lady call. I didn't even know that you wished to get married, a fact you failed to mention the last we spoke—"

"All this is true. To be fair, I didn't have much time during the prisoner transfer." He scratched his jaw. "And this marriage came out of nowhere."

"Forgive me if I do not believe you are a secret romantic. You never wanted to get married. What happened?" He scowled. "Did the woman entrap you?"

Bash gritted his teeth. "More like I entrapped her." He sighed. Wynn would not let this go until he heard the whole story, and as the Prince Regent liked to sleep in, he most likely had time. "The idea of marriage all began when I went to the Pump Room for a curative drink."

It was marvelous to be back with Grandmother at Lark Manor and its majestic rain-drenched green hills. Vivienne and Tess strode alongside the road to Bath as Wolfie chased after the Blackface sheep emerging from their shelter for a snack. She admired the picturesque landscape and wondered for the hundredth time what Bash was about for the past three days in London. Perhaps he had completed his mission and was already looking for their new home? *Our home.* She lifted her left hand and admired the oval citrine set in gold filigree. What a dream to belong to a man such as Sir Sebastian Larkby.

Tess released a short shrill whistle, summoning her dog to their side and sending Vivienne to tucking her hand behind her skirts lest her friend begin teasing her again for admiring the ring from Bash.

Tess scratched the dog between the ears. "So, Lady Larkby, is Sir

Bash's absence pressing upon your heart as you picture him riding as the golden-haired highwayman once more?"

She laughed under her breath. "Mayhap. I must admit that I miss Bash terribly. I have grown accustomed to running into him about the manor and taking a repast with him."

Tess tossed a stick, her dog racing off to fetch it. "Then you have no regrets? I did feel slightly guilty for forcing the issue of moving to London the other night, but someone had to speak up and save you from yourselves."

"You were right though. We were living in a fairy tale, thinking we could get away with our subterfuge." *And now I do not have to fear saying goodbye to him.* "I have no regrets."

"Indeed, if I had not pressed you two into a move, I am beginning to think you may have come up with the idea on your own." She grinned as she took the slobbery stick from the dog, flung it again, and wiped her hand along her skirt. "That man is smitten with you."

Vivienne bent and picked a flower, pulling out petals one at a time and watching them float to the ground. "Do you really think so?"

Tess snorted, planting her hands at her waist. "Do you think he would have married you to continue the ruse if he did not care for you?"

"Mayhap not the ruse, but to save my reputation."

Her brows lifted. "He cares enough for you to care for your reputation."

"He is a knight and a gentleman."

"And you are defending him quite passionately." Tess giggled as Wolfie pranced toward them with the stick. "Which tells me that you are in love, and if the both of you are in love, whatever is keeping you two apart? If it is pride, it is not worth your unhappiness."

A carriage rumbling toward the manor kept Vivienne from answering. "Who can be calling right before dinner? Grandmother did not mention any guests."

Tess shielded her eyes from the sun. "It must be family. No friends would do such a thing."

"Family." Her heart skipped. She had gone so long without true family that the idea of perhaps finding another dear person who belonged to Bash made her grasp Tess's hand as they gathered their skirts and raced down the hill. This marriage was proving a blessing indeed.

Pausing in the side garden, the two righted themselves as she caught sight of a gentleman, in the first rate of fashion, descending the carriage. The two friends darted through the kitchen entrance, nodding to the staff as they hurried past to the parlor, where their embroidery lay in wait with the pot of tea Grandmother had so thoughtfully sent for when she must have spotted them from the window.

They quickly took their places on either side of the fireplace as the door flung open and the butler announced, "Mr. Larkby."

Grandmother groaned under her breath and rose with Vivienne and Tess. The young women exchanged a look at Grandmother's reaction and missed the entry of the man, who was now already bowing. Vivienne curtsied, staring at the carpet as her cheeks heated. *Another Larkby? Grandmother did mention Bash had a cousin.* How had she ever thought the title to be retired enough for her to use? What had the family thought of an authoress using their name? Mayhap they were not great readers of novels.

The gentleman straightened, and she nearly gasped—the barrister? *He* was a Larkby? *Why did he not say something when Sir Josiah cornered us on the road?* She pressed a hand to her stays as a familiar sense of condescension filled the room. What news did he bear that kept him from divulging his connection to Lark Manor in the shopping quarter and setting aside all rules of etiquette to call so late? She glanced at Tess. Her concern amplified when she saw Tess's chewing of her lip—an action she only did when she was on the verge of saying something she shouldn't.

The butler departed, mumbling about fetching a cup, and Vivienne moved to the teapot and began pouring and passing the tea.

"Grandmother, how wonderful to see you looking so well." Mr. Larkby strode into the room, pausing between them and leaning against the fireplace mantel.

"Is it, Alden?" Grandmother accepted the cup from Tess and set it aside on the table without interest.

Vivienne drew in a sharp breath at her candor and laid her hand on Grandmother's shoulder. "You mentioned a second grandson, but not that he is a barrister."

Alden smirked. "And I was not told of my cousin's marriage until a friend from my university days wrote to me saying his fiancée had supposedly wed Sebastian."

"A small world." Tess chomped down on her Shrewsbury biscuit, affixing her glare at him. "And what a welcoming picture you have presented to Vivienne by threatening to take *her* family home in Bath as recompense for a breach of promise that she never made."

"Alden Francis Larkby. You did not!" Grandmother's voice shook.

He lifted his hand. "I promised to look into it for Sir Josiah as a special favor, but I came to discover that he has no intention of selling it to repay his vast gambling debts to me, so I took my revenge by telling him that he has no claim on the building. His pockets are too empty to hire a second opinion. He will not be bothering you again in regard to the townhouse."

Vivienne nearly sagged with relief, her thanks frozen on her lips when the butler appeared with the cup, setting it on the tray and backing out of the room.

"Consider my duplicity as my wedding gift to you and Sebastian," Alden finished.

"*Sir* Sebastian," Grandmother interjected. "Do not pretend to forget his rank, Alden."

What on earth has passed between the two to cause such animosity?

"Yes, well, seeing as he is my cousin, I may be forgiven my liberty of neglecting his title in my grandmother's home." He helped himself to the tea, giving Vivienne a pointed look for her neglect as he did so. "It was a swift union indeed, as I did not hear of his attachment until after the marriage, which I discovered was done by a special license. With his departure to London, I did not expect his bride here, nor visitors." His gaze rested on Tess for a moment. He flicked his attention to Grandmother. "I was hoping to have a moment alone with you, but I suppose my visit may still have the required outcome."

"As you did not announce your visit, I do not think you should be holding any sort of expectations." Grandmother picked up her cup and blew on it.

The butler appeared in the doorway. "Mrs. Larkby, dinner is served."

She rose with her cup in hand. "You are here abnormally late, Alden. Will you be joining us for dinner?"

Tess rested a hand on her stomach, whispering to Vivienne, "Make my excuses?"

She eyed Tess's hand on her stomach and grasped her arm. "Shall I ask the maid for some peppermint tea for you?"

She cast a glance between the three of them, her brows raised. "I'm well enough, but this is a family matter. Do you really want me here? He may have looser lips if I am gone."

"Good point. I shall inform you of all later." Vivienne motioned her out the door as the rest of the party crossed the hall to the dining room, and Vivienne whispered a request to the footman to send a tray up to Tess's room.

Dining with Alden Larkby was far from pleasant. With every passing minute, she fought from squirming in her chair. This barrister did not settle well with her. Something was different about him. He seemed like a ton mother awaiting a new eligible bachelor to arrive at the ball—anxious and wholly too friendly, to the point of leaving genuineness behind. She felt his eagerness focused on dear Grandmother Larkby.

"What brings you to my home, Alden? Surely you are not here only to welcome our dear Vivienne into the family with your roundabout gift?"

"She was an added boon to the trip." Alden's voice dripped with honey as the butler placed a bowl of steaming tomato soup before him. "I, however, came as soon as I heard that you were ill, dearest Grandmother."

"I was ill a month ago, Alden." She blinked at him as she bit into a scone. "But I suppose you were disappointed in my recovery, seeing as you have been waiting for my death to claim your inheritance."

Vivienne choked on her water.

Grandmother smiled at Vivienne. "My recovery is mostly due to this girl. She has brought new life into Lark Manor and our Bash." She chuckled. "We never thought he would marry in my lifetime, did we?"

"No." He did not seem pleased by it, judging by the press of his lips. "Her arrival is quite unexpected."

"Which made the surprise all the sweeter." Grandmother leaned over her teacup and clasped Vivienne's hand.

"And because of this fact, you inquired after amending your will?" He scraped his butter across his bun. "Grandfather would not have approved of your vacillation."

Vivienne stiffened. "Why would my arrival have anything to do with her will?"

"Finally. We reach the real reason behind your visit." Grandmother narrowed her eyes at Alden, daring him to contradict her. "Lark Manor is in my name. I may do with it as I wish. Your grandfather saw to that long before he died."

"Interesting that you would think so." Alden met her glare.

So much for proper conversation. Vivienne needed to steer the conversation away from money. "How long have you been a barrister, Mr. Larkby?"

"That is of little consequence in this conversation." He dismissed her question with a flick of his wrist. "I have some unsettling news for you, Grandmother. I am not planning on staying in town long."

Grandmother saluted him with her teacup. "How on earth could that be disappointing, especially since I did not know you were coming this evening?"

"Grandmother!" Vivienne dropped her soup spoon and sent the elderly woman a chastising scowl. This had crossed from civility to barely veiled enmity. "I have never seen nor heard you act thus."

Grandmother sighed. "I'm sorry. You are right. No matter my issues with Alden, I should at least attempt to treat him as I would a stranger."

"Anything would be better," Vivienne muttered.

"Your lawyer reached out to me, given your request that Lark Manor be passed to this woman, who is not even your blood relation. I presented a counter request that you be lawfully removed from Lark Manor."

Grandmother laughed, clapping her hands. "Oh my, Alden. Of all the things you have ever done, this is by far the most ridiculous. I will not abandon my family's home in my dotage."

"Exactly. This is the *family's* home, which *will* be passed on to me in the event of your death, as I am the oldest male relative."

"Correction. It *was* going to be yours before Vivienne joined the family. I did not want to cause any more strife between you and your cousin by leaving him my money *and* the manor, but given your unwillingness to abandon your sordid lifestyle, I did not wish to see my home sold off when Vivienne and Sebastian could fill it with my great-grandbabies. The money will see to its upkeep."

He gritted his teeth. "And you thought this would cause less strife—to write me out of the will and give it to an outsider? I am the firstborn male. I am a barrister, and as such, I have many friends in the law. I will not be bested so easily."

"Is that a threat, Alden?"

"It is fact. I agree that your wealth should be left to maintain the house."

"Good."

"For me, very good. For you, not so much." He steepled his fingers, drumming his fingers together. "I brought your new will before the magistrate."

"You actually went that far?" The mirth in Grandmother's eyes faded.

Vivienne dropped her cup into the saucer, breaking the handle. "Of all the brazen—how would you even be allowed to contest Grandmother's right of ownership?"

His lips curled at her interruption. "My petition was granted, with the adjustment of a generous allotment per annum to care for you in your twilight years. And given your propensity to change your mind in your old age, I have brought help along with me to take care of you in these last days to make you more comfortable." He rose and rapped on the windowpane.

"What an earth are you talking about? I'm as healthy as I ever was." Grandmother tossed down her napkin.

Vivienne rose. "We will object to your petition, and you will not win once Sebastian speaks to the Prince Regent on Grandmother's behalf."

He downed his coffee and leaned over the table to claim the last scone from Grandmother's plate. "The thought that you have any fight left in you is heartening, Grandmother."

"Grandmother is well recovered, and I hope to spend many more years with this dear woman. We do not need whatever help you are suggesting." Vivienne stood behind Grandmother's chair. "She has me."

"Yes, but given the fact that no one has yet seen your marriage certificate nor been able to locate the vicar who married you, I don't think you have much room to speak on her behalf, especially since you are no relation."

She stiffened. "Perhaps not by blood, but my marriage to Sir Sebastian is valid. I'll take it to Grandmother's lawyer this very hour to verify its authenticity, if need be. You will not take everything from her, not while she has us."

"As you have claimed over and over. The validity of your marriage is neither here nor there. The law is on my side, and she is elderly. She needs protection, and the law is clear that the familial duty and responsibility fall upon my shoulders, as the oldest male relative, to decide when she can no longer think for herself. She will do as I say is best, and I have the law to back my claim, unlike you." He rapped thrice atop the mahogany table and a tall, thin man in a drab greatcoat and oversized hat appeared in the doorway.

The man's gaze rested on Grandmother and his mottled smile chilled Vivienne to the core.

Vivienne stood tall, forcing strength into her voice. "Who are you?"

The butler sputtered as he followed the man. "He would not remove his hat, Mrs. Larkby! He would not take the back entrance."

Grandmother rose, clutching Vivienne's arm. "What is the meaning of this? Alden, explain yourself at once."

"But you see, I already did. This is a perfect example of why I must do your thinking for you. You have already forgotten the conversation from moments before." He gestured the man further inside. "This man will see you to your new place of residence."

Grandmother's hand on Vivienne's arm was strong and without fear. "I have no desire to leave my home, nor will I."

The thin man grinned, approaching the grand lady. "You come along with us, my lady. Don't make no fuss now, or this will become much less pleasant."

Vivienne stepped in front of Grandmother, spreading her arms wide to ward off the man's approach. "What on earth are you talking about?"

Alden finished off his scone, dusting his fingers on the tablecloth. "Come tomorrow, she will find herself in a London asylum."

Vivienne gasped. "No!"

Grandmother sank to her chair, chuckling. "Is that all? Vivienne, calm yourself, my dear." She patted Vivienne's hand. "He is merely bluffing. He has been threatening to send me there since he was a boy. Ever since I wouldn't give him whatever he wished for. What was it the first time? I said no to a confection that I knew would turn your stomach sour?" She snorted. "I am as safe as I was in my mother's arms. He merely hired a man to play the part of an orderly. Though, I must say, he did a fair job in the ruse and much better than one would expect of an amateur."

"However, this time I have brought Grandfather's will, as well as yours, before the courts, along with my petition. And with you being past your eightieth year, it comes with a benefit for me, as I am allowed not only to be in charge of your welfare, but it is up to me should I decide to place you in an asylum and claim your fortune for myself."

"Alden," Grandmother whispered, the bravado in her eyes fading. "You wouldn't."

"It is already done." He removed a folded piece of paper from his coat and slapped it on the table.

Vivienne snatched it up. She perused the contents of the legal document. She pressed her hand to her mouth, holding in a whimper. *This is really happening. He is taking her away.* She cast a glance to Grandmother, her blood growing cold.

"Vivienne? What does it say?"

"It is as Mr. Larkby says." Vivienne knelt beside her, resting her hand on Grandmother's. "But Bash will never stand for this. He will protect you from this man's greed."

"Bash does not know. He is in London, and you are at my mercy." He nodded to the thin man. "Go with Mr. Hennessy, Grandmother."

Mr. Hennessy reached for Grandmother, his hands calloused and filthy against her fine sleeve. "Come, ma'am."

"Unhand her." Vivienne tugged at his arm.

The man's face hardened as he blocked Vivienne's attempts, and she stumbled onto her backside. The elderly lady cried out as Hennessy flung Grandmother over his shoulder even as the butler raced to aid his lady. Alden stepped in front of the butler. He was as broad as Bash, and there was little chance the ancient butler would reach his lady.

"Sir Sebastian will never forgive you for this." Vivienne hauled herself to her feet, glaring at Alden. "How dare you treat her thus!"

"Yes, and you are without a home. Get your friend and your things out of here at once." He shoved the butler back. "And take Ladd, as he is out of a job for crossing me."

Vivienne caught the butler's elbow and wrapped her arm about his waist to steady the elderly man, calling after the men. "How could you do this, Mr. Larkby? Leave Grandmother here until Bash can return home, and you can both decide what is best. Come to your senses. Have you no care for her?" The men did not heed her as she stumbled out of the manor after them, screaming and begging them to cease this merciless, cruel act.

"Whatever is going on?" Tess raced out of the front door, her eyes widening at the scene before her.

"Alden is taking Grandmother to the asylum." Vivienne's breathing became rapid, spots blooming on the outskirts of her vision. *Lord! Let me be strong for Grandmother! Save her, Lord. Save us.* She drew in a full breath, releasing the butler as Tess surged past.

Tess blocked the entrance of the barred carriage, which looked to be better designed for transporting murderers than innocent elderly women.

Alden laughed at Tess's attempts to block them, but Tess broadened her stance, lifting her fists. "Unhand the lady."

"A gallant effort to save your hostess, but it is unnecessary." Alden lifted a hand to guide her away.

She dug her foot into the ground and smashed her fist into his nose, drawing blood. With a grunt, Alden wrapped his arm about her waist and bodily lifted her from the ground, tearing her delicate sleeve as she kicked and flailed.

"How many women have entered the asylum because of family members who are eager to get their money? How many women are doomed to die alone in an asylum because of people like you?" Tess railed at him. "Let her go!"

That fate would not befall this woman. Not while there was a breath in Vivienne's lungs. She screamed and screamed for the staff, drawing the groom and tiger from the stable.

"Mrs. Larkby!" The fellows raced forward to aid their lady. Noah charged and appeared ready to ram Mr. Hennessy.

Alden held Tess in one arm and drew a pistol from his coat, halting any physical altercation. "I do not wish to use force, but I will if necessary."

The elderly cook cried softly into the butler's shoulder as Mr. Hennessy set Grandmother before the step of the carriage. Her shoulders sagged, the fight in her visibly fading—a sense of hopelessness permeating the air. The bloom that had been growing in Grandmother's cheeks vanished as she stood facing the iron bars. She lifted her head and folded her hands in prayer.

"Have a heart, Mr. Larkby." Vivienne slowly stepped forward. "She is a gentlewoman who has never harmed anyone. If you must insist on taking her wealth and home, leave her to my care. I have a townhouse of my own. I can see to her."

"A noble offer, but it is my *legal* duty as the heir to see to her comfort. If you should decide to change your mind, the duty would once again fall to me, and I intend to take a wife and do not wish to be bothered by relatives." He waved her forward with the barrel of his pistol. "However, I am not without a heart. You shall embrace her one last time."

She darted forward and clutched Grandmother in her arms as a chilling mist coated their shoulders and Grandmother's lace cap. "Can you do nothing to stop him, Grandmother? No argument you can make to entice him to change his mind?"

She rested her hand on Vivienne's cheek. "If he is determined, Alden will have his way."

"I will not allow you to perish in an asylum." Vivienne's throat tightened.

"You know as well as I that I will not last long at my age." The woman placed a hand atop Vivienne's head. "May God grant you a long life full of love and family. Be happy and blessed, my dear. Love Sebastian well. It is my greatest wish to see you both happy."

"I cannot allow you to go alone." She gripped her hands. "I will come with you!"

At this Grandmother's eyes flashed, and Vivienne caught a glimpse of the feisty woman she knew. Grandmother gripped her shoulder, pulling her into an embrace with surprising strength, lowering her voice. "You must not. If you come with me, you may never escape. If you wish to save me, you must get word to Sebastian. He is our only hope for my escape. He is close with the Prince Regent. Sebastian will plead my case and see that justice is brought on my behalf."

"Justice? Was this justice to see your fortune stripped away from you and your home taken without your knowledge because of your age?"

"Have faith, my dear. There are many good men in the world. You have been a strong woman for many years. It is not a sign of weakness to place your trust and hand in the care of a good man, and Sebastian is the best of men. He will know what to do."

Vivienne nodded, a plan formulating. She needed someone who did not need to wait for the law to decide to do what was right. She needed someone who was not afraid to break a few rules—someone like the highwayman.

Chapter Twenty-Three

HOW MANY TIMES HAVE I come and gone from this manor?

Vivienne raced about the room, making short work of packing with Tess due to practice and a healthy dose of fear. Alden's staff was flooding the manor. It was odd that the place of refuge turned so quickly into one of oppression. Everywhere she looked, she was reminded of the reason for Grandmother's absence.

"What are we going to do?" Tess whispered as she followed Vivienne down the hall.

Vivienne shifted the small trunk in her arms. "I'm going to pack some of Grandmother's things. I would hate for them to dispose of her gowns. We can leave her things at my townhouse and then alert Bash and see Grandmother freed from the asylum." She shot into Grandmother's room and flung open the closet. She tossed gowns back to Tess, who rolled them up and placed them in the small trunk so as not to raise Alden's suspicious ire.

"I know she has a pearl ring and an amber cross necklace from Grandfather Larkby." She lifted the jewelry lid. She wished to take all the pieces for Grandmother, but if Alden noticed, she doubted they would be able to leave with even the few. First, they had to save her. Then they would reclaim her jewels and anything else in the home she wished. Vivienne tucked two necklaces, a bracelet, and three rings into the pocket of Grandmother's favorite morning gown and rolled it up, tucking it into the trunk.

"I need to inspect Bash's original room to ensure he has left nothing behind he would not wish to fall into Alden's hands." She raced across the hall and into his room as Tess finished in Grandmother's. It looked as before, nearly untouched. She checked the priest's hole first before opening the drawers and finding nothing of consequence. She flipped open the book on his nightstand and found a gold necklace with a small blue jewel. It was hardly worth much, but it meant something enough to keep it. Her stomach twisted at the thought that it perhaps belonged to an old sweetheart of his. She shoved it into her reticule and moved for the closet doors to search his pockets.

"Find anything?" Tess asked as she joined her in searching the clothing.

"Just a necklace, but I am going to be thorough." Her fingertips grazed a small leather pouch. She fished it out and peeked inside. Inside appeared to be a piece of paper that was folded over and over until it was the size of a shilling. She stuffed it into her reticule too. "I need to find Bash. You need to stay at my townhouse in the event he might be on his way back to Bath. I doubt he is, but if he is, Alden will send him on a goose chase. You must circumvent that possibility."

"And if you do not find Bash in London?" Tess replied.

"We shall meet at my townhouse in a fortnight."

"So long? Anything could happen in that time." Tess groaned. "Are you certain you can travel alone again? If I come with you, you will be better protected, and it will give me some peace of mind."

Vivienne ran her fingers over a black sleeve, an idea forming as she caught sight of a second black highwayman's hat tucked in the corner of the wardrobe. She lifted Bash's shirt out and held it against herself. It would be entirely scandalous, but there were yards of fabric to work with. "What if I do not travel in a coach? What if—"

Tess eyed the clothing in Vivienne's hands and shook her head. "Surely you jest?"

"No one will think to look twice at a man traveling on horseback. Bash left Brigand to my care. I will take him, and Alden will dare not refuse. With Brigand, I will seem more imposing."

"I don't know, Vivienne. It's so risky, and not to bruise your feelings, but you are hardly strong enough for such a journey, and you are entirely too feminine to pull off that look."

She shoved back her shoulders. "I have to try. Are you going to help me or not?"

Tess sighed. "Of course I will. Pack the costume, and I will have you outfitted for your journey this evening. I doubt you will wish to stay in any taverns, and traveling by moonlight will be far safer for you if you are armed with a rapier and pistol. Travelers will give you wide berth." Tess removed the decorative rapier from the wall, along with the pistol that had been in the drawer and sprinted upstairs to hide it inside her large trunk of clothes while Vivienne finished searching the room.

Tess returned panting. "Unless Alden goes through my pile of underthings and spare stays, he won't find the weapons."

"Ladies?" Alden called from the foot of the stairs.

The women started and quickly tossed what they could from Bash's wardrobe to form the highwayman ensemble into a satchel. She gripped Bash's highwayman's hat in her hand and cast one glance back at his room. She and Tess rushed down the stairs, carrying the small trunk between them and the satchel in Tess's hand, while the footmen Alden had brought fetched their two trunks.

He eyed the hat in her hand but motioned them through the door without protesting. It had begun misting again. They stood on the steps, gaping at a horrid wagon before them as the footmen unceremoniously dropped their trunks in the bed.

"Where's the carriage?" Tess murmured.

"I suppose we are looking at it. Alden has graciously lent us a wagon for our exile." She smiled to Noah. "Tie Brigand to the back please."

He trotted off to do her bidding, and when he led out the black horse, she narrowed her gaze at Alden, daring him to steal Bash's mount, but to his credit, he said not a word. *I suppose he knows his limits after all.* She sent the lad another smile and whispered, "Wait for Ladd and come with him to my home in the Circus, along with any of the other staff who are unwilling to stay. Ladd will know the address. And if possible, bring Cerberus."

"God bless you, my lady. I'll see to it." The boy nodded eagerly and helped her climb into the wagon bed beside Tess.

She held her head high as it rolled down the gravel drive and through the iron gates.

The journey to the townhouse was short, but to keep her mind busy, Vivienne focused on the next step in her plan rather than what Grandmother must be enduring every moment they were apart. From the jarring of the wheels, she imagined how the prison wagon would be nearly unbearable to Grandmother's frail bones.

Brexton had already returned to Draycott Castle, so Vivienne turned the key to her front entry, keeping the door wide while the driver dropped the trunks inside and departed without a word. She locked the door, and Tess lit a lamp, turning the wick high. They rummaged through the first trunk to find the weapons, grabbed the satchel, and then crept upstairs, Tess gripping Vivienne's sewing basket in her arm.

Vivienne stripped off her gown until she was in her stays, shift, and scandalous underdrawers. She drew on Bash's shirt and discreetly inhaled the highwayman's scent of woodsmoke and leather. Tess adjusted the hem, which fell to Vivienne's knees.

"If we tuck this into the pantaloons, it should billow out enough to hide any of your curves, so you could still wear your stays." Tess tossed the breeches to her, which Vivienne caught with her face before they fell to her feet. She had been too heady from smelling Bash's shirt to be aware of flying breeches.

She retrieved them from the floor and tugged them on. They swallowed her, but between stuffing the shirt in and Tess wrapping the pants into place with a black shawl, the effect was satisfactory. Vivienne shrugged on the waistcoat, which Tess tightened with a few darts at the back. For the final piece, Vivienne slung the weapons' leather harness across her shoulders and over her hips. Tess shoved the pistol into the holster at Vivienne's chest and the rapier at her waist.

"Lord help you if you must draw your weapon." Tess scrubbed her hand over her neck. "If you are approached, first make eye contact with the person. Then use your *manliest* voice, and if they still do not back away, draw your weapon and be prepared to use it as a last resort. If a weapon is drawn, be ready to defend yourself." She shook her head as she adjusted the ebony knee breeches and lifted the coat for Vivienne to slip inside. Tess shoved and tucked here and there, but the sleeves were impossibly long. In the end, Tess took her scissors, whispered an apology to Bash, and chopped off the elegantly embroidered cuffs.

"Much better." Vivienne lifted her arms to demonstrate her movement. "I can hardly believe how heavy these clothes are. I will never again complain about having to wear stays, which are hardly a burden when compared to the neckcloth and the excessive weight."

"I know it is bulkier than you are used to. Do not get confronted then, or you will be in more danger than Mrs. Larkby." She stood back and admired her work. "What a well-tailored highwayman you turned out to be. And with your golden hair and riding Bash's horse, people might just think you are the legendary highwayman from the newssheets . . . albeit much thinner."

Vivienne stepped before the looking glass. Tess had drawn Vivienne's hair into a queue that she had stuffed into the high black collar, making her hair appear shorter. The coat was large enough to hide her shapely form. "Indeed. Dare I say swashbuckling?"

"Almost." Tess nodded to the vacant hearth. "Your hands are entirely too well kept. Dirty your nails as much as you can."

Vivienne ran her hands under the lip of the chimney, the ash coating her perfectly manicured nails. "Good thing I keep them shorter than is fashionable."

Tess ran her hand in the ash as well, lightly brushing it along Vivienne's ears and down her jawline. "That should help disguise the set of your jaw and lack of facial hair long enough to dissuade any travelers. Just take care not to brush it away." Tess rested her hand on Vivienne's shoulder. "As Brexton, I shall fetch Brigand. You get to the kitchen and pack whatever you can find."

She trotted down the stairs, the freedom her breeches offered feeling odd, as well as the heavy clomp of the boots Tess had discreetly purchased from Noah before leaving Lark Manor. They were still too big, but they would do the job. She crossed the kitchen to the dry larder and rummaged. The cook and Brexton had not left much, most likely thinking it would mold, but there were some fig preserves tucked away in the larder as well as a round of cheese. She looked about for a cleaver, but there were too many drawers and too little time. Drawing her rapier, she lifted it above her head and whacked the cheese, slicing off a good-sized hunk. *How satisfying.* She grinned.

She wrapped the wedge in cheesecloth and tucked the preserves under her arm. She wouldn't starve, but her breath would aid as well as her weapons in fighting off anyone. By sheer luck, she spied a leather canteen hanging in the larder. With a squeal of glee, she snatched it and filled it at the pump, drinking heavily before filling it again and slinging it across her chest to lay opposite the rapier. The added weight would be tiresome, but she could store the rest of her goods in the saddlebags. She gave the kitchen one last sweeping glance for any hidden goodies and spied the sugar pot. She grabbed three lumps of sugar and darted out the back door, where Tess stood with Brigand.

Tess rubbed Brigand's nose. She gritted her teeth and eyed Vivienne as she stuffed her findings into the saddlebags. "I know you are decent riding sidesaddle, but do you know how to ride astride?"

"If a lady can perch upon a sidesaddle wearing stays, it shall be nothing to conquer astride in breeches." She tilted her chin, pushing confidence into her voice and stance as she reached forward, the sugar in her open hand.

Tess pulled Vivienne's hand back and flattened her palm and fingers. "Lay your hand flat, or he will chomp off your fingers. Are you certain you do not wish to take the stagecoach dressed as a man?"

"I do not avoid riding because I am not adept. I just don't necessarily enjoy it. I always preferred running or driving the pony cart."

Tess pinched the bridge of her nose. "I should have talked you into allowing me to take your place. My da taught me everything he knows about horses."

"You know I can see this through faster, Tess." She moved to the horse's side and took the mounting block. "Now, are you going to help me up onto the horse or not?"

Tess grunted.

That was as close to agreement as Vivienne would get. She swung her leg over but promptly kept sliding to the right toward the pavers. She scrambled to catch hold of the horse's mane, her legs splaying as she jerked herself upward. Brigand tossed his mane in annoyance as she righted herself, losing Bash's hat in the ordeal.

Tess nodded and scooped up the hat, tossing it to her. "Off to a promising start."

"At least I didn't fall." Vivienne patted Brigand in thanks for being patient with her and not prancing to the side.

"There's that." Tess checked the saddle, walking around the horse. "It's a little over a hundred miles to London. Brigand is a magnificent animal built for endurance. He can trot up to forty miles without a break."

Vivienne shifted in the saddle, hoping for a more comfortable position. "Wouldn't cantering be faster?"

Tess shrugged and returned to petting Brigand's nose. "Momentarily, but he will tire sooner and need to rest. Slower and steadier is ideal. If you need to canter, he can last about seven miles. But if you are trying to outstride danger, he can gallop full speed for about two and a half miles before he tires. You'll need to hide before he is fatigued."

"Very good. No galloping unless an absolute emergency then."

"I know it will be hard to see any mile markers at night, but be in tune with your horse. He will let you know when he needs a break."

Vivienne's stomach roiled. There was much more to riding long distances than she had ever thought of before. She might seriously injure Bash's precious Brigand.

Tess reached up and clasped Vivienne's hand. "I know I have my doubts, but I take comfort that you are not alone. God be with you, Vivienne. You are going to need all the help you can get."

Vivienne pressed her fingers to her lips and waved farewell to her dear friend. There was something to be said about testing one's cour-

TO KISS A KNIGHT

age. It was all well and good to be brave in a parlor with friends and servants about or outside one's childhood home, with the lanterns always flickering, offering comfort in their familiar glow, or when one was usually cloistered in bed curtains with a ready taper nearby—along with a bellpull to summon servants. But when one set off into the unknown at the night hours, it was entirely a different thing.

Thankfully, the moon was full, or full enough to not die by one's horse tripping in a hole in the street. Brigand's stride was true and strong. And with her weapons glittering in the moonlight, any loiterers on the sidewalk avoided eye contact. When she was beyond the city, she kicked Brigand into a trot, praying for favor in the long journey ahead.

Chapter Twenty-Four

BASH SANK DOWN ONTO THE tavern bench at the end of another shift, a thick stew in front of him. With Sir Thomas out of London for a day or two yet, Bash had decided it was best to continue his duties to the Crown instead of chasing after the man. If he left his post the moment he had supposedly returned for duty, it would surely rouse suspicion. It wasn't his preference to let the matter rest, but he needed to keep to his shifts lest people put together that the absences of Bash always aligned with the appearance of the highwayman who was beginning to grace the newssheets of England. *And then, of course, there is the small matter of Brigand still being in Bath . . .*

"Here." Wynn thrust a letter into Bash's hands.

"What's this?" Bash dropped his spoon on the rim of the bowl and opened the missive, scowling at . . . He squinted at his friend's scrawling penmanship. "Is this a list of sorts?"

"Call it a guide to wooing your lady." He grinned, avoiding the mention of Vivienne's name in such a place. "After I left you to your post, I decided that you desperately needed help and wrote a list for you."

The men at the table hooted, stomping their feet, while one tossed a roll at Bash. He caught it and bit into it, glaring at the ensign who dared throw it. "I don't need—"

"You are obviously in love with the lady, and this is the way for you to win her heart." Wynn tapped the paper. "I even numbered it for you."

Bash narrowed his eyes. "You aren't even married or courting a woman. Why would I, or anyone for that matter, take relationship advice from you?"

"It doesn't mean that I don't know how to woo a woman. Because I am a second son, my choices are limited, and besides, I just haven't found the one I wish to woo. You have." He straddled the bench, pointing to the first item on the list. "You said she's a writer. I figured purchasing her some new fancy writing tools would be just the thing to start with as a gift, as well as some of that extravagant paper the Prince Regent prefers."

Why didn't I think of that? Bash frowned and stuffed the note into his pocket before he rose, intending to leave the rest of his meal in favor of privacy. He dug into his satchel, grabbing a handful of surprisingly edible cookies that he had made the other day and brought to share. Baking had become a sort of necessary hobby when it was recently decided that the Yeomen of the Guard no longer be given a table at St. James's Palace for meals. Granted, the yeomen were given a board wage, but he was attempting to save funds, and tavern fare grew old quickly after the spread that had been available to the yeomen at the palace. But he didn't mind the challenge of learning to bake, as he preferred to spend his evenings at home rather than at the gentlemen's club at White's.

He bit into the Shrewsbury biscuit as he glared at Wynn and left the table. He would rather eat these to fill his belly than stay for the stew and be heckled. He did not embarrass easily, but this was a private matter, and the tavern was not the place to discuss anything regarding a lady, even when one did not use a name. He secretly did wish to review the list, but not in front of the group of guffawing guards.

"Aren't you going to thank me?" Wynn called after him, laughing and already sliding into Bash's place to consume the stew.

Bash pulled on his hat and rolled his eyes at the men's continued laughter. He strode home and lit the taper in his small, rather dingy parlor. He hadn't realized how dingy it was until he had begun searching for a London home for Evie. The woman deserved to live in a palace, but the best it seemed he could do was lease a small townhouse. He had two candidates but wanted to write to her first and see which she would prefer. That would require him penning something else rather than getting directly to the point, of course. If he did not say something sweet in his letter now, she might get the wrong impression. He sighed and removed his satchel. *Guess it can't hurt to see what Wynn has to say before writing.* He set aside his weapons and retrieved the list, sinking down at his desk.

> *One, buy her fancy paper to show her that you were thinking of her.*

> *Two, serve her. Find a need and meet it.*

He scratched his chin, the end-of-the-day growth bristling against his fingers. Find a need? She was a lady. If she had a need, she'd summon a servant. What could he possibly offer her? He sighed. He might have to consult Wynn after all.

> *Three, spend time with her doing something she enjoys.*

> *Four, woo her with words from your heart, praising attributes of the lady. Be genuine. Women can smell a counterfeit compliment a mile away.*

He wanted to snort at that, but there was such wisdom in it, he would be hard-pressed to ignore it.

> *Lastly, hold her hand, and when the time is right, kiss her as best as you can. I know you don't have much practice, but it's all in the pucker—*

He stopped reading. He had no need of kissing advice, but Bash took the time to copy the recommendations into his daily log, challenging himself to add one more idea per day to the list on how to get his Evie to fall in love with him.

It was disconcerting to be out where no sounds, other than night creatures, reached her ears. She had never truly been alone before. She had always been near someone, but if gentlemen could do this all the time, she would fight through her fear. She had Brigand and her weapons and the Lord Almighty watching over her. Dressed in Bash's black, she was given a layer of confidence that she did not possess in her muslin gowns.

She didn't know how long she had ridden, but if her derriere was any indicator, she had been in the saddle for approximately two years.

At the trickling of water, Brigand's ears twitched, and he snorted.

"Would you like some water, Brigand?"

He tossed his head, snorting again.

"Bash is right. You are extremely intelligent as well as handsome." She guided Brigand off the road before the bridge. The horse drank deeply, and she patted his neck, not daring to release the bridle for even a moment as she shifted her canteen to uncork it with one hand.

She longed to slide off and stretch her back, but she feared that if she removed herself from her perch, not only would she be too stiff to return, she wasn't confident she *could* climb back into the saddle without some sort of mounting block.

The horse shifted. "I'm sorry, Brigand. I know you are used to carrying more weight than this, but surely Bash would dismount and give you a break."

Voices from the bridge above made her heart skip. The clopping of hooves sounded. She drew back the horse from the river. He snorted in protest. Two men peered over the rail and caught sight of her. *Blast.* She should've just let the horse keep drinking.

"Oy!" a man with a beard called.

"Good evening," she returned, with her manliest voice. She sounded quite like a frog. She coughed. She should have practiced her voice.

"'Good evening'? Do you hear the tongue on him? Sounds like a gentleman." Mr. Beard snorted. "What's a gentleman doing out this late alone?"

"Mayhap we should part the gentleman from some of his coin as a lesson." The second man joined in the laughter.

"Or all of his coin *and* his horse."

She did not wait to be approached. She kicked Brigand, urging him to cross the riverbed. He trotted forward, and to her relief, it was shallow enough to cross in haste. She urged him into a gallop, racing down the road. Bash knew his horseflesh, and Brigand easily outran the two inferior beasts the thieves rode.

She cast a glance over her shoulder, and seeing no one, she slowed Brigand to a trot and then to a walk. She patted his mane. "Good boy. Bash would be proud of you for taking such good care of me."

She nudged Brigand back into a trot for a few miles more until, at last, she spied a tavern in flickering torchlight. Dare she stop and rest her horse? His heavy breathing and flecked chest said that she would do irreparable damage if she did not take the risk. She guided the horse into the yard. The ruckus laughter inside the tavern streamed out, making her knees knock at the debauchery she was certain to encounter at this hour. *Lord, help me get through this night. Save Grandmother. Save me.*

She urged confidence into her shoulders and kept her head down, shielding her features with Bash's hat as she and Brigand approached the stable.

A young man stepped out, eyeing her weapons. "You be needing a room for the night?"

"Nay. I wish to stable my horse for the night and fare for my belly. I will stay in his stall." She dug into her pocket and her gloved fingertips found the coin. She tucked her thumb under it, flicking it to him. It flopped from her hand and landed under her horse's hooves. Brigand stomped the coin into the mud. Heat crawled up her neck, but she laughed, too deeply, like a man who had been in his cups. She clamped her mouth shut, running her gloved hand over her jaw. "I am more exhausted than I thought. Take care of him and another coin shall find its way into your pockets tomorrow."

"Yes, sir." He took the reins.

She grabbed the saddle and prayed her legs would hold her. She dismounted and released the leather, crumpling to the ground.

"Sir!" The man leapt forward, grabbing her elbows and drawing her to her feet.

Her hat's brim collided with his, knocking it from her head and exposing that her golden hair disappeared into her collar. His jaw dropped. To her horror, he knew. Even if she wished to leap upon Brigand and ride for the next tavern, she couldn't. She lifted her hands. "Please do not say a word."

His gaze went from her weapons to her hair and then down to her breeches. His ears reddened, and his gaze snapped up. "What are you about? Are you some highwaywoman?"

Truth, or go with the highwaywoman? Either would be difficult to believe given her current state of dress, but bearing tales had gotten her in this mess in the first place. "I do not want any trouble. I just need to rest my horse before continuing on to London. I have money." *Not much in my pocket, but enough.* "If you allow me to rest in my horse's stall on a blanket and fetch me some food from the tavern, I shall give you a crown." She reached into her pocket and found the right coin with her fingers, holding it up in the lantern light. It was a risk to spend so much, but she did not wish to eat the meager fare she had packed yet. "Agree and be silent and it is yours. Can I trust you?"

He nodded. "I'll fetch your food and then see to your horse. There is a spare blanket in the trunk by the last stall on the left."

She nearly sagged with relief. She made certain her hair remained tucked into the high collar and shoved on her hat. She would not risk anyone entering the stable and seeing her without it. She grabbed the blanket from the trunk and opened the stall door. She wrinkled her nose. It had been freshly strewn with hay, but nothing covered the residual mess left from years of horses.

She laid out the blanket and whistled for Brigand. He trotted up to her and into the stall. "Good fellow. Watch over me while I sleep?"

He tossed his head up and down before nuzzling her, as if promising he would see to her safety. She left her weapons on and had sunk onto the blanket, barely keeping her eyes open, when the man knocked on the stable door. She scrambled to her feet. He had brought her a hunk of bread, cheese, and a tankard.

"I figured you wouldn't like beer. I had them make tea, but I cannot guarantee its drinkability."

She accepted it with a nod. "And just so you are aware, my horse is intelligent and will guard me better than any dog." She drank deeply, coughing at the bitter taste of too-strong tea.

He dipped his head. "I may not be born a gentleman, but my ma raised me to be a man of God. You are safe with me. Coin or not." He held out his hand. "The name is Thaddeus."

She grasped it. "I believe you, Thaddeus."

Chapter Twenty-Five

BASH LEANED AGAINST THE LAMPPOST on St. James Street, waiting outside the gentlemen's club while watching for the stout Sir Thomas to emerge from Boodle's. He had, at long last, returned to London during Bash's shift and had spent his evening gambling, no doubt. Bash rolled his shoulders and crossed his arms against the uncommonly chilly summer night. He supposed it was good that it was cold, to keep him alert.

It had been a long morning searching London for the best situation for Evie, as the other two townhomes had already been let while Bash was attempting to write to her. Bash liked one of the townhomes he viewed today and signed a lease, praying that his bride would love it. She had been on his mind from the moment he awoke to the moment he closed his eyes, and then he saw her in his dreams. Even his fellow yeomen had commented on his distraction during his shift, which had ended at eight of the clock.

Sir Thomas stumbled out, his layered cape billowing out with the gust of wind. His boisterous laughter revealed that he had been deep in the cups, even if his gait was straight as he moved to his carriage.

Bash pushed off the lamppost and followed closely behind, his ebony attire helping him blend into the shadows. Even though he disliked wearing his disguise with the Bow Street Runners near, he had to risk it. It was time to end this blackmailer's threat against the Prince Regent.

Bash counted as the wheels turned, approaching him on the corner. He drew on his mask and bounced on his toes, tensing his body. The carriage rolled toward him, and he leapt, catching the open window of the door and hurtling himself through it.

"What on earth is—" The man huffed, his jaw dropping at the sight of Bash the highwayman.

Bash held a finger to his lips as he lifted his pistol, keeping the barrel pointed at Sir Thomas's feet. "We meet again, sir. I suggest you empty your pockets once more."

He narrowed his gaze. "You are no common highwayman to come all the way to London to approach me a second time. *Who* hired you?"

"I never claimed to be a simple highwayman." He gestured to Sir Thomas's pockets. "The letter, if you please, Sir Thomas."

"W-what letter?" He puffed out his cheeks, his jowls jiggling violently.

Bash tapped the barrel against his palm. "Let us not insult each other now that we are so well acquainted."

Sir Thomas crossed his arms. "I have no idea what you are talking about."

"The final letter." He drew back the hammer, the click sounding like a gunshot in the close quarters.

"Stop. Stop! I'll supply it." The man's voice shook along with his fingers as he lifted his hands and threw himself back against the tufted leather seat. "I won the packet in a game of cards. The fellow said it was worth a king's ransom, so I read the one, which is how it came to be separated from the packet."

"Did you?" He returned the hammer into a safe position and leaned on his knees so that he nearly closed the distance between them.

"B-but there was nothing I can quote from it. I assure you."

Bash narrowed his gaze, deepening his brogue. "Where is it?"

"I'm no fool. After the first time you robbed me, I no longer keep it on my person. It was too valuable to take out of my home."

"Then by all means, allow me to escort you home." He grinned. "I will leap out of the carriage before we reach your door to keep the driver from seeing me. But if you shout, I will shoot you where you stand and fetch it out myself."

"Y-you know where I live?" Sir Thomas blinked rapidly.

"You said it yourself. I am no common highwayman. Go inside and open the window on the ground floor. Recall my marksmanship, if you so much as think of whispering of my presence."

The carriage turned onto Sir Thomas's street. Bash crawled out the window, perched on the sill, and leapt, rolling upon the ground to soften the impact. He raced into the shadow of one of the trees lining the street. The driver pulled back the reins, and Sir Thomas ambled out. The front door closed behind him, and a moment later the scraping of a window alerted Bash to Sir Thomas. He smirked. The coward did not even question Bash's demands.

Pistol drawn, he peeked in the window to ensure Sir Thomas was unarmed. Sir Thomas already had his hands above his head, his jowls jiggling in fear. Bash climbed through. "Take me to the letter."

"Y-yes! It is only just over here." He opened the drawer.

"That is your secure holding—a drawer?"

He pursed his fleshy lips. "No one would dare steal from my desk. I trust my staff." He left the letter on the front corner of the writing desk and dashed across the room to a wingback chair, where he immediately plopped down and breathed heavily.

Satisfied Sir Thomas was not going to pull a weapon on him, Bash snatched up the letter and turned it over, studying first the broken seal and handwriting in the moonlight streaming through the window. The feminine tilt of the letters matched the hand that he had long ago memorized—Maria Fitzherbert. "You said you read it. Did anyone else?"

"We all did, but without the letter, there is no proof, and without proof, no one shall dare speak of it again, lest they wish to visit the Crown's prison." He shivered.

The Prince Regent would be so pleased that he might allow Bash time to return home to collect Evie and Grandmother himself. He stuffed it into his pocket, when he heard the click of a hammer being pulled into place. His gaze darted up to meet Sir Thomas's steady hand and the barrel of a pistol aimed straight for Bash. *He must have had a weapon stashed in the cushion of the chair.*

Bash cursed himself for being distracted, but he eased confidence into his voice. "How certain are you that you can kill me before I can shoot you?"

"I practice to keep myself sharp." He grinned. "I earned my title much like you, Sir Sebastian—in wartime. I may not be as strong as I once was, but I am very confident in my speed *and* marksmanship."

Bash stiffened at the name, and for the first time as the highwayman, true fear stole into his heart. The man was no weakling. "You have me confused with someone else. Why would a nobleman wish to resort to thievery?"

"Because of your duty to the Prince Regent as his closest Yeoman of the Guard." He smirked. "And because of that friendship, we wished to lay a trap for you."

"Trap? What are you talk—" He frowned. "The letters? Those were a trap?" *Was there anything in there that was really of national security?* "But why would the Prince Regent send me to fetch those letters if they were not real?"

"Of course they were real." He snorted. "We never anticipated them being so . . . informative, especially the last letter we kept from the rest, from Maria Fitzherbert, where she recounts her secret wedding to the Prince Regent. It was an invalid marriage, of course, because he was underage and did not marry with the king's approval. However, there were details in there that should not be public knowledge. George had every right to be concerned about the content." He snorted. "We knew he would want them back and, more importantly, who he would send. Capturing you was our prerogative."

"And what could you possibly gain from capturing me? Having me sent to jail? What good would I be to you there?" Bash had to keep him talking while he figured out what to do. He had a dagger in his belt at his stomach, another at his back, and one in each boot. *How to reach them without getting shot?*

"I am no fool, and neither are you. Of course we would not bring you to jail. No, we have a ship ready at the London docks to take you to France, where we will torture you—if you do not comply, that is." He chuckled. "We are not monsters. We only want a few answers from you before we . . . release you from your pain."

The door creaked open, and two men stood with weapons drawn. "The carriage is ready," the taller informed Sir Thomas.

"Very good. Check him for weapons. We will bring him to his apartment and see if the Prince Regent entrusted him to hide anything useful to us. Then we will away from this horrible city."

The men crossed the room, and Bash wrenched out his dagger from his waist, slashing at the shorter of the two while evading the second. A pistol flashed bright in the parlor. A bullet passed Bash's head by a hairbreadth, knocking off his hat.

"Calm yourself or I shall have to graze your leg with a bullet. I would hate for you to die of an infection before you can help us, but that is a risk I am willing to take."

Bash lifted his hands above his head. He could take three to one, but this was not the moment to spring into action. The traitors seized his arms, jerking them behind his back. "You mentioned you wanted answers." Bash grunted. "Such as?"

"Such as the best time in the Prince Regent's schedule to kill him."

The journey to London left her frazzled and heartsore, thinking of Grandmother and how she must have been admitted to the asylum by now. She guided Brigand through the streets, following the directions to Bash's home, which he had left for her along with a small key in case of emergency. She had never thought she would have need of it. She halted the horse in front of the two-story building beside a pub with a stable a few doors down. She climbed down, her limbs weak from the hundred miles in the saddle. But she was prepared this time and braced for her muscles to give. She steadied herself, and when her knees locked, she released her hold and wobbled toward the stable, guiding Brigand. She swallowed a giggle. She would look like a drunk with her uncertain gait. No one gave her a second glance, with the tavern nearby.

"Oy! Brigand, good to have you back, boy." The groom rubbed the horse's nose, eyeing Vivienne. "I haven't seen you before. What are you doing with Sir Sebastian's horse?"

"Obviously, if I am bringing him to you, I have his permission to borrow his steed, do I not?" she answered in a deep tone, which she hoped was manly. She flicked him a copper. This time it flipped through the air into his waiting palm. "Give Brigand a good rubdown. He deserves it." She turned on her heel and strolled out the door to avoid more leading questions.

She removed the skeleton key from her waistcoat pocket and fit it to the lock. The door swung open with a low creak. She narrowed her eyes to see better in the darkened hall with stairs on the left. She locked the door behind her and leaned against it, a sense of Bash filling the very air, and the peace it lent her made the pain in her chest ease. She inhaled a full, deep breath. She would no longer be alone. She need only tell Bash, and Grandmother would be saved.

"Bash?" She doubted he would be home, but if he was, she wouldn't want to surprise a man skilled with so many weapons.

"Bash?" she called once more, and strode into the hall. To her right, a small room in the front appeared to have once been a parlor. Judging from his desk strewn with paper and a stack of books, along with a small bookcase of tomes beneath the window, he now used it as his study. She gasped at the title of the smallest book. He had purchased her debut novel, and judging from the cheesecloth marker, he was halfway through reading it. Smiling, she ran her finger over the desk, imagining him sitting here. She picked up the small clock on his desk. The artistry of the piece was magnificent. She gently set it back down—riding had made her arms shaky. "Best not drop what's sure to be an heirloom."

She ventured farther down the hall to find a tiny kitchen. There was no larder, but there was a cupboard. She found a loaf of bread and knocked on it. "It's soft." She squealed and bit into it, devouring half the loaf while she discovered a bottle of lemonade and a tin of biscuits.

I know he does not employ anyone . . . so does Bash know how to bake? She peered in the cupboard and found the necessary ingredients. "Muriel would be impressed. What else don't I know about you, Sir Sebastian?"

She peeked out the back door, only to find an alley shared with the other townhouses and no place for a lady to venture alone. Bash kept the interior of his home clean, but the malodorous alley threatened the contents of her stomach. She bolted the door.

Her body ached. If she had to wait for Bash to return from his duties, she needed to rest. She removed his hat and trod up the stairs. There was only one door at the top. Bash's room would complete the small townhouse. She well remembered what had happened the last time she'd snooped in his room. She swung it open. A small, plain bed with a burgundy blanket stood in the corner by the lone window with heavy curtains. In the opposite corner stood a serviceable chair with a basin and pitcher atop it. He did not spend much time here, it seemed, but all was clean.

She had heard that in recent years the Yeomen of the Guard were now responsible for their lodgings. Perhaps he did not wish to spare much funds for his rooms when he had a perfectly beautiful manor in Bath. The ancient opulence of the manor house provided fodder for imagination, with its vast gardens and the priest hole in Bash's old room, but she doubted she would see it again. Even with Bash's help, the law was clearly on Alden's side in regard to the inheritance.

She sighed. "What will Alden do to Grandmother's beautiful home with all those rooms?"

Vivienne regarded the bed. Would it be so improper to take a nap in his bed while she waited for him? The room spun. She tested the bed. It was impossibly stiff, as it seemed to be overstuffed with hay. She smiled at his frugality. A nobleman of character who baked his own bread and slept on hay while serving the Crown in palaces. But if it meant that she could stay with Bash, she would choose to live here without a moment's hesitation. *Even without a guest room.*

She ran her hands over the blanket, her eyes heavy. Seeing how she could not fetch Grandmother out alone, she might as well rest. A basin rested atop a dresser in the corner of the room, but it was all she could do to draw back the covers and yank off her filthy boots before falling onto the bed, weapons and all. The scent of Bash upon the blanket lulled her to sleep, filling her dreams with their time together when they were simply Evie and the highwayman.

Chapter Twenty-Six

"ENTER YOUR HOUSE AS IF we are old friends, Sir Sebastian. Remember, I will shoot you if you so much as whisper. I only unbound your hands in case your neighbors happened to be watching." Sir Thomas dug the barrel of his weapon into Bash's back as they crossed the threshold into his modest home.

Bash tossed his hat onto his desk, as he would usually after a long day guarding. His gaze rested on his desk clock. It was slightly out of place. Someone was inside his home. His gaze roved over the room, then he heard a snore above him.

Someone is sleeping in my room? Perhaps Wynn had come to work over the list with him? Or mayhap a drunkard from the pub made his way inside. *But a drunkard would have made a trail.* There was an ally in this home. Perhaps he could escape.

"We aren't alone," Sir Thomas growled. "Bind his hands at once."

The men did so, giving the rope an extra tug or two.

If he moved his hands too much, they would turn purple. "Is this where the torture begins? I must admit, while I may seem strong and all, I am quite averse to pain."

"Another lie. We've seen you practice with the guards. You can take a beating without a word of complaint." Sir Thomas eyed the ceiling, as if he could see through it and find out who was snoring.

"You want us to go check it out, Sir Thomas?"

"Not alone. I want to use Sir Sebastian as a human shield. If the man above is a friend, he will shoot you, but not him." He shoved Bash toward the stairs.

To the man's credit, Bash supposed, Sir Thomas did not have his lackeys act as an added barrier between Sir Thomas and a bullet. Bash slowly climbed the stairs and paused at his ajar bedroom door. He squinted in the dark. A slight man was sprawled out on the bed. No yeoman or guard was so short of stature. Sir Thomas pushed him forward. Bash stepped where the creak of the floorboards would alert the person in his bed. The man jolted upright, keeping the covers pulled to his chin.

"Who are you?" The tall lackey lifted a rapier to the man's neck.

The fellow yelped and dropped the covers, revealing a stream of golden locks that cascaded to the bed. The sight had the lackey dropping his rapier's tip to the floorboards.

"Evie?" Bash dropped to his knees, horrified. "What on earth are you doing here?"

"Bash!" She sprang from his bed and launched herself at him. Her arms found purchase around his neck as her momentum pushed him to sit back on his heels, and she sank into his lap. "Oh, Bash." Her sobs shook her slight frame.

"Whatever is wrong?" Something terrible must have occurred to bring about her being in *his* bed and in *his* clothing and weapons. His throat tightened, the very thought of his Evie in danger burning his insides.

Sir Thomas clicked his tongue. "I see you kept more than just the money in your robbery. I must admit, it takes a lot to surprise me. I did not foresee a romance between the young lady and the highwayman. I had heard of a wedding but did not realize who it was you had wed. Felicitations to you both. As touching as this scene is, we really must be off if we are to make it to France at a reasonable hour."

"France?" She jerked away from Bash, eyes widening.

Under the haze of sleep, had she thought they were Bash's friends who were waking her at swordpoint because they considered her a threat?

"Sir Thomas? W-what is going on?" Her gaze moved from Bash to the men before them, weapons drawn, and at last to Bash's tied hands. "What are you about? Why would you bring Sir Sebastian to France?"

Bash leaned his forehead to hers. "I need you to be brave, Evie. These men know who I am and wish to exploit me."

"And now that you've seen who is behind this kidnapping, you will need to join us." He snapped his fingers, and his men sprang for her. "What fun we shall have using you as leverage."

Bash roared, leaping to his feet and headbutting the nearest as the second lifted a sword to his throat.

She raised both her hands. "Please don't hurt him, Sir Thomas! I will go with you peaceably." She gave Bash a smile that made his heart ache. "Don't fight them, Bash. I'll be safe as long as I'm with you."

If only that were true. Because of me you have never been in more danger. He grunted as the men shoved him to the floorboards.

"How touching to see the two of you have grown so starry-eyed. How did you get such a lamb to fall in love with a lion?" Sir Thomas chuckled. "On the drive to Bath, she hardly spared me more than a few sentences from her book, but I suppose I am not as dashing as I once was."

"And seeing how you are the villain in this story, I have more discernment than I realized," Evie mumbled.

"Perhaps, but then if you did have discernment, I doubt you would have fallen asleep in this man's bed. It is telling about how much she trusts you, Sir Sebastian." He grasped her hand in his and lifted her small finger. "Now, how about you show me something interesting, Sir Sebastian, before this young lady discovers the pain of a broken finger."

She swallowed but did not cry out. The sweet woman lifted her chin, scowling defiantly at Sir Thomas. But Bash knew the man did not make idle threats.

"I vow I have nothing of worth to you. But I do keep a log of my shifts." He nodded to a plank at the foot of the bed. "It's under the floorboard." There was nothing of interest in the log, but as he was private natured, he tended to keep such things hidden—especially when the latest entries were scattered with his thoughts of Evie throughout the day. . . along with that highly embarrassing list from Wynn of how Bash might woo his new bride.

Her wrists chafed after being tied for an hour with rough ropes as they tore apart Bash's home, looking for anything the Prince Regent would not wish to fall into the wrong hands. She longed to be free from the ropes, but she doubted it would happen anytime soon, especially if she was to be on a vessel heading to France soon. And if they were heading to France, how could they save Grandmother in time?

Now lying with her face pressed to the filthy floor of the coach, she held Bash's gaze. Gone was the awkwardness between them as she drank in the sight of him. She did not know what the next hour would bring, but her heart was content to be beside Bash at last. Granted, they were captives of a mad Napoleon follower. No matter the danger, or how foolish it was, she felt safe with the man who knew how to leap from the back of his horse and land with ease atop a racing stagecoach and halt it, who would protect the lady stranger within after she fell out the stage door in a faint at his boots, and go so far as to return her funds with interest. To think she was married to such a man. If she had to be bound, what a man of honor to be tied to for eternity.

When Bash had tried to whisper a question directed at her, Sir Thomas squeezed her arm so hard, she knew a bruise had to be left behind. All they possessed to communicate was their eyes. In her stories, the hero and heroine had entire conversations in silence with only their eyes, but that was to convey love. *How does one communicate through eyes that a dear grandmother is being held in an asylum by a horrible cousin?* She rested her head against Bash's shoulder and breathed in his scent of leather and woodsmoke, pulling her racing heart and thoughts to Scripture and prayer. *Casting all your care upon Him; for He careth for you. Be sober, be vigilant; because your adversary the devil, as a roaring lion, walketh about, seeking whom he may devour.*

Lord, do not let me be devoured by my anxiety. I need to be strong, firm, and steadfast. I give You this situation. Guide me.

Bash nudged her with his shoulder, a question in his eyes. She couldn't tell him everything now. She shook her head and leaned into his shoulder again, praying for deliverance for Grandmother.

The closed coach halted, and the door wrenched open, revealing a massive ship bobbing in the harbor. Men darted about on the deck, readying it to set sail at once. *Is no one suspicious of this activity at this hour? England is at war after all.*

Sir Thomas motioned them out with the barrel of his gun. "Time for your honeymoon trip. How does France sound?"

They scowled up at him but kept their mouths shut as they rolled to standing and Vivienne stumbled out of the coach. Nothing good would come from answering his taunt.

Sir Thomas grasped her hair, an action that had Bash lunging for him. One lackey seized him by the arms, while the second halted Bash's attack with a blow to the eye.

"If you so much as touch her, I will end you," Bash gritted out through his teeth.

"No need for such dramatics." Sir Thomas chuckled as he stuffed Vivienne's hair into her collar, pulled the hat over her hair, and shoved her to Bash. "Best see to it that you remain disguised. If any of my men realize you are a woman and catch sight of your shapely limbs in those breeches, I cannot be responsible for their comments, nor their actions."

She felt Bash tense against her. Perhaps it was foolish, but her fear lessened when she was next to Bash, which was baffling, given her tendency for anxiety. But even in those beginning days with him on the road, her anxiety had not toppled her. It was as if her soul had recognized Bash as safe before she even knew him. God was with her, and He had sent her Bash to aid her. She was safe—no matter what happened.

She followed behind Sir Thomas with Bash before them both. The gentle breeze cooled her hot cheeks. Surely the sweat was causing her ash sideburns to run. Honestly, how did gentlemen wear so many layers? It was difficult wearing stays and petticoats, but they were light compared to all this fabric that swallowed her and the neckcloth that threatened to choke her at any moment. As she strode across the deck, she was thankful that the heavy clothing hid her curves. The crew seemed to all be required to scowl, wear scruffy beards, and have bulging muscles that bespoke no weakness. She fought against a gag as the wind changed. The sailors stunk like fish left in the sun for three days. She had never been fond of seafood.

She followed Sir Thomas belowdecks, the narrow steps and lack of a handhold sending her pulse to skittering. If she tripped, she would break her neck. She took the steps gingerly, timing them with the gentle rocking of the vessel. In the hull at the stern stood the brig, with imposing iron bars forming a single wall. Inside was a cot with bedclothes that looked like they hadn't been washed since the bed was first dressed. She bobbled as the ship swayed, and Bash pressed his shoulder into her to steady her as the sailor unlocked the iron door.

The sailor shoved in Bash and then her. She tripped over the threshold, and Bash tried to catch her with his body, but there was only so much he could do to break her fall without his hands and they crashed to the floor, her atop him.

Sir Thomas grinned, holding up the lamp. "Enjoy your stay aboard. We will be in France by dawn." He tromped up the stairs, leaving them with the single swaying lamp just outside the iron bars.

"Evie? First, are you hurt?" His deep voice rumbled beneath her.

Her cheeks heated as she shifted off the knight and tested her limbs. "My knees and arm are bruised, but I am well."

He exhaled heavily. "Good. Now, why were you in my room in *London*, dressed in my clothes?"

Chapter Twenty-Seven

"Evie?" He whispered as she shook her head again, as if trying to compose herself. Maybe he should kiss her, as he had wanted to on the road, to still her hysterics? *Kissing is always a good idea.* He slowly lifted her chin with his bound hands and claimed her soft lips. He leaned into the kiss, wishing to wrap her in his arms, to run his fingers through her hair. Her breathing relaxed, along with her body. That was too easy. Perhaps a second kiss was necessary to be absolutely certain her hysterics would not return. He deepened the kiss.

He should pull back. He needed to. With a grunt he pulled back, her thick lashes fluttering open and her green eyes focusing on him, clear and desperate. "Evie Poppy Larkby, you tell me right now what is amiss. It must be dire for you to come find me."

"Oh, Bash." She rested her head on his shoulder, nestling into his side. "I cannot bear to tell you this, but you are right in assuming that the situation was dire to force my hand in such a manner."

"Did Sir Josiah approach you?" He clenched his teeth. "Is that why you were hiding in London? Was he so aggressive in his determination to see you as his bride?"

"No." She turned to him, taking his tied hands with her bound ones, the concern in her expression stirring him. "I am here because your grandmother needs you."

He blinked, drawing back as a stab of guilt plagued his stomach. He had not even thought of her being the reason for Evie's appearance. "What happened? Is she . . ." He dipped his head. "Is she—"

245

"She is with us yet. Indeed, she was well when last I saw her, but your cousin was disappointed in her recovery and that she was attempting to give her home and fortune to me. She said she always intended to take care of *your* bride if you ever wed, as Alden would have just gambled it away."

He shook his head. "That does not surprise me. She has always said that she would see to my bride's dowry so that I might marry however I liked."

She lifted her bound hands to her heart. "What a sweet romantic. I only wish that I was not the cause of your cousin's ire."

"Ire?" Bash drew back. "What has my cousin done? What did Alden say to you to cause you to race across England?"

"Oh, Bash. We did everything to stop him, but he contested the will and cast Grandmother Larkby into the asylum in London. He had her declared unfit, therefore allowing him rights to seize her fortune as the so-called rightful male heir."

"He what?" He rose, pacing the room, longing to face Alden and beat him for his vindictiveness toward a loving woman. "He tossed our grandmother into an asylum?"

She nodded. "Nothing would alter his choice. I told him I would take her to my townhouse, but he would not relent."

"The viper."

"He is indeed. We must not allow him to steal her future from her." She rose and studied the bars and jabbed them with her shoulder, as if searching for a weakness . . . or expressing her frustration with the situation. "We have to get out so we can free her."

"Come. I should have done this before I kissed you." He nodded to the ropes tying her hands and set to work on loosening the knots. "Once we get off this ship, *we* are going to do nothing. It is too dangerous for you to come. *I* will go for her." He tossed aside the rope and nodded to his own hands as she silently worked them.

After freeing him, she knelt by the bars, studying them. "No. I have a plan, and you are going to need me."

He squatted beside her and slid his hands down her arms, intertwining his fingers with hers. "I already need you, and I fear that should anything happen to you, I could not survive it." He lifted her hand to his lips, kissing the top.

She smirked and jerked her hand out of his. "You are not going to make me bend to your will every time we disagree by kissing me, are you?"

He grinned. "It has served me well in the past, and you seem to like it just as much as I do."

She whipped off her hat and batted him on the arm. "Well, stop it! We need to think."

"Do you really wish me to stop kissing you?"

Her cheeks flamed, and she pulled her hat back over her ears. He laughed. Apparently she did not. He stood with her, drawing her toward him. "Since we agree that ceasing kissing is not the answer, how about another kiss to settle the matter of my only kissing you when we disagree."

"You are full of nonsense." She shoved past him and craned to look at the bars up top. "We will make things right—together—as the lady and her highwayman."

Bash shook his head at the thought of Evie in *his* clothing riding alongside him as if to battle. "You can hardly be serious. This is your plan? To ride in with me, pistols drawn, after we somehow escape this ship?"

"Grandmother is of strong mind, and next to you, who would dare to question us?"

"My cousin would dare. He has abandoned her in the asylum, no doubt hoping for her death. He is no fool. He will have the staff alerted that she is an escape risk. They will be on guard. I cannot allow you to take such a risk, with you appearing in public dressed as a man. A judge might see you locked behind the very doors from which we are attempting to free Grandmother."

She rested a hand on his chest, stilling his argument. Did the little minx know how her touch swayed him? Of course she knew.

"Don't you think this is why you became the highwayman? This is why you have all those skills as a guard and as the Prince Regent's right-hand knight?" She gritted her teeth. "I know it might take some time, but would the Prince Regent help us?"

"He is preoccupied at the moment with another matter. He would help, but it would take time to see Grandmother free, and that is something that we do not have, with her delicate health."

"Then we best leave now and fetch her out." She squatted again and removed a knife from her boot, wedging it into the hinge, popping up the head, and removing the pin.

Bash's jaw dropped at her ingenuity. "How did you know how to do that?"

"Book research. It's a good thing Sir Thomas didn't think I'd be armed beyond the obvious weapons in my harness." She handed him the knife. "I cannot reach the top. Do you think you can manage?"

He grinned, removed the pin from the hinge, and eased the door from the frame. "You are so brilliant I could kiss you."

"All this talk of kissing when we should be escaping," she scolded halfheartedly.

He grasped her hand, and they darted out from the brig. "We have darkness on our side but not time. We will be out of the River Thames too soon. Are you strong enough to swim?"

She nodded. "Especially now that I won't be tangled in my skirts like last time. I may have to lose the coat though, because it is so heavy."

"You will need it when we fetch out Grandmother." He slid it off her and donned it himself, chuckling at the shortened cuffs. "Follow me. If I stop, so do you. If I tell you to jump off the side, you do it. No questions asked. Understood?"

"I thought you said no questions?"

He rolled his eyes and lifted his finger to her soft lips before clasping her hand. They took care not to make excessive noise as they wove through the hull. Cargo groaned and creaked with the gentle lapping of the River Thames. With tonight's wind, they had precious little time, and without Evie's quick thinking, he would have been far longer in getting them out.

Boots on the stairs had him jerking her to his side, but the sailor only fetched a rope and darted back up without glancing at the brig. Bash felt her sigh. He closed his eyes and listened. They were never going to have a better time than when the crew was distracted in leaving the docks.

"On three," he whispered, holding up his fingers and ticking off the count. He led the charge up the stairs. As he'd hoped, the sailors were too busy with their tasks to see them as they sprinted for the railing. He swept her into his arms and leapt over. Shouts sounded as they struck the water.

He hoped she was holding her breath as he released her legs while still keeping one arm about her waist, kicking as they swam under the water. They broke the surface, both gasping.

"You fine?" he managed as they swam for the shore.

She nodded, teeth chattering.

Even in the summer, the Thames was chilly and smelled horrible, with unmentionables floating past. She followed him, stroke for stroke. She had not exaggerated her talent with swimming and did not complain. By the time they reached the stone steps at the river's edge, the crew had lowered the rowboat and were in pursuit, taking care not to shout and alert all of London to their presence. It was early yet, and they might still be recaptured without anyone else being the wiser. Bash grasped Evie's hand, and they scrambled up—Evie's feet slipping against the slime that caked the first few steps.

"Just a little farther and we can escape them." He helped her over the river wall, and they raced for the alley, winding through the streets of London until at last he dared to stop to gain his breath. He bent over his knees, and Vivienne leaned against the side of the building, panting. She had lost her hat in the water, and with her face clean, there was no hiding her feminine features. He scooped up some dirt and ran it over her jawline.

"Vile!" She pulled away from him.

"What? You've done it before."

"With *known* soot. This is alley sludge." She wrinkled her pretty nose but did not wipe it away. "It smells horrible."

"All the better to play the part of a London thief." He reached into his pocket and drew out his black oversized kerchief, tying it about her head to hide her brilliant hair. "Are you still determined to rescue Grandmother with me? If we get caught, everything I've worked for as a yeoman is gone, which doesn't matter as long as my grandmother is safe, but you, dressed as the highway robber from the newssheets? You would be tried, and God help me if you were taken from this earth too soon. My own life means little if the ones I love are gone, when I could have prevented their loss."

"The ones you love?" she whispered.

His gaze held hers. "Yes. Most ardently."

"I feel the same way."

His lungs squeezed. He had hardly dared to hope that she loved him. He cradled her face with his palms. "You do? Really?"

She smiled up at him. "I have lived most of my adult life without the love of a parent. But when you and your grandmother found me, you both offered me something my heart has been desiring for years. Grandmother has become the mother I always wanted . . . and you, you have become the dearest person in the world to me. You both are my family now. I would not be so bold to admit my affection for you if I did not think there was a danger to this night."

He drew her chin up, searching her wide green eyes. "Do you not know by now how much I adore you, my sweet wife?"

She shook her head.

"Evie, would I have married you to save your reputation if I did not hold you in regard?"

"Tess said much the same thing, but I will answer you as I did her. You are a yeoman—a knight. You are bound to be chivalrous to a fault."

"Kiss me." Her breath caught, but he caught the flicker of desire in her eyes.

"Don't you think there has been enough kissing in one night between two people who were only supposed to be pretending affection, Bash?"

"Kiss me, Evie, and see that my lips will tell the truth."

"To kiss a knight is a proposition that I find I cannot refuse." She rose on her tiptoes and wrapped her arms about his neck, lifting her lips to his.

He lifted her from the ground, their lips parting and breath mingling before he set her down. "What do you know from my kiss, my lady?"

She ran her fingers through his short locks, which were quickly growing back. "That you are trying to sway me with your wiles," she whispered into his ear. "And it will not work." She spun away. "Grandmother gave me the love that I lost. I will not turn my back on her now, even if it seems senseless to enter an insane asylum to rescue her. So you will either allow me to join you, or I shall stumble along behind in an attempt to distract the guards to allow you inside to rescue her."

He grunted. "I suppose there is no way I can dissuade you from this once your mind is made up."

"You do not stand a chance, even with those kisses of yours." She grinned. "Love is stronger than fear."

"It seems that it is also stronger than sanity."

Chapter Twenty-Eight

BASH SNAPPED THE REINS AND glanced sideways at her on the milk cart, which they had paid the owner handsomely to rent for the day. Evie's ebony breeches revealed shapely limbs. He averted his gaze. Even if they had a certificate of marriage, she was *not* his until she said she wished to be his completely. Love was a good place to start. Given time together, he hoped for their relationship to grow. First, he would court her in the manner she deserved, wooing her using that list of Wynn's, which he had thankfully memorized, and learning all he could of her while sharing his memories, feelings, and hopes with her. Then, perhaps one day, she would wish to become more—to raise a family of their own.

They crossed the streets of London, pausing at Wynn's home long enough to bang on the door and ask for him to ride to fetch Telford. Fortunately the barrister was in London for another yeoman's wedding, so Bash gave Wynn instructions to pass along to him. Telford would know what to do and how to look into granting custody of Grandmother to Bash, as well as the legality of his grandmother's fortune being taken. Bash had no need of the money himself, but he hated the idea of his cousin stealing from their grandmother. He prayed that Grandmother's good health would hold.

"And you are going to charge headlong into this asylum with your bride?" Wynn's eyes widened at the sight of Evie in Bash's clothing.

"It's our only option," Evie interjected.

Wynn nodded. "Godspeed then. I will ride for Telford at once."

"If you are caught up in this, you are risking your position as a Royal Horse Guard," Bash warned. "There is more afoot this night than what we were able to tell you."

"I gathered, given that shiner you are sporting. Besides, you would do the same for me." Wynn lifted his hand in farewell.

Bash directed the ancient horse and snapped the reins, hoping the plodding animal would speed it up.

"Where are you headed? The Bedlam asylum is in the other direction," Vivienne whispered as Wynn's home fell behind.

"As Bedlam is a private institution, I have no doubt that he sent her to St. Luke's to avoid paying one farthing for her accommodation."

"Lord, have mercy. He wouldn't." She pressed a hand to her stomach at the name of the infamous asylum reserved for those who could not afford Bedlam's care.

Few visitors were allowed inside, and even fewer patients were ever released. He had little idea of what the inside looked like—no one really knew besides the patients and the staff. Unlike Bedlam, which allowed for visitors, the one free to patients was shrouded in mystery—and any mystery when dealing with the care of unfunded guests left little hope for their treatment. "He stole a widow's home and fortune. He has no moral compass. No, I would bet my position that he took her to St. Luke's, and I intend to get her."

It took a bit longer to reach that asylum, but as they approached Old Street, it was nearing five of the clock, when it appeared that the staff shifts were changing. Her jaw dropped at the sight of the massive wall surrounding the imposing building of clamp brick—about five hundred feet long. It appeared there was only one entrance, at the center, where a guard stood with a pike, poking at cobblestones. Beyond the building to the left, the obelisk spire of St. Luke's Church rose above the buildings, a glimmer of hope above such an ominous prospect.

"Bash, how on earth are we supposed to get inside? I was picturing it being a small building with a few windows and maybe another entrance. This is a fortress."

"A fortress guarded by a sloth." He pointed to the guard standing outside the gate, looking bored. "That's our ticket inside."

They climbed out of the cart, and Bash scowled at her swaying gait. "Walk like a man, Evie! Do you want to draw the eye of every seedy man about?"

"Whatever do you mean? I'm walking with purpose." She gave a sample of her pace.

"You are wiggling." He demonstrated, swaying his hips.

She slapped a hand over her mouth, her shoulders shaking from the effort of keeping her laughter at bay.

"'Tis not a laughing matter." He gently chided as he sensed the banter helped her nerves. He placed his fists on his weapon harness. "Your disguise is the key to our success."

"You are right. I'm sorry. Sometimes in tense situations I find that laughter is better than the fear."

"As do I." He motioned for her to try walking again. "Now, act like a man."

She slouched her shoulders and kicked her legs as she walked. "How's this?"

He ran a hand over his jaw and sighed. "It is a wonder that you escaped your stepbrother long enough to reach Bath if that is the extent of your acting skills."

"It wasn't that hard. You know very well that I was not disguised as a man for that adventure."

"Let us be thankful you were not." He grinned and grasped her hand. "Are you ready, my lady?"

She drew back her shoulders. "Let's free an innocent woman."

He released her and approached the guard, with Evie close on his heels. "Good morning, mister."

The guard frowned as he craned his neck, looking down the street. His replacement must be taking his time arriving. "Is it? I was supposed to be in the cups by now with a wench on me arm." He frowned at the approaching figure. "Where were you, George? You kept me waiting a good quarter of an hour."

Bash tucked Evie into the shadows with him at the man's approach.

George grunted, rubbing the sleep from his puffy eyes. "Doesn't matter. I'm here now, Frank."

"Yeah, and you are going to owe me for keeping my silence about you being late for the third morning this week."

"Have a drink on me." George dug in his pocket and flicked him a copper.

Frank caught it with ease, slapped him on the shoulder, and ambled toward the pub.

Bash turned and followed Frank. "So you are keeper of the keys for the asylum?" Bash said casually as Evie strode beside them, her gait awkward. He fought to keep his expression relaxed.

Frank frowned. "What of it?"

Bash flipped a gold coin in the air, catching it with his palm and tossing it up again. "I have need of your keys. I will give you one guinea now for the use of the keys, one more for direction inside, and two more upon our escape."

His eyes widened. "For such a sum, I could quit my job." He licked his lips, his fingers twitching. It was only a matter of time before he agreed. "What do you and the young man have need of inside?"

Bash flipped the coin again. "Never you mind, but I like you. I shall add another coin for your silence."

Frank grinned, revealing mottled yellow teeth. "Your servant." He tossed him the keys. "Buy me a drink while I draw you a map of the inside."

"With what paper?"

Frank lifted a small book of poems from his pocket and a nub of a pencil. "I get bored on the job and my girl likes it when I memorize poetry for her, so I mark the ones I memorize. Give me another copper and I will tear out the title page."

Bash caught sight of Evie's shoulders tensing, but she kept her face stern to hide her feminine features. "It would be a pleasure, but the lad is rather young to be exposed to such things."

Frank roared with laughter. "If you think this pub is too rough for him, he has no business being inside St. Luke's."

"Fair enough, but we have no time to spare." Bash withdrew another coin, handing it to the man.

He drew a rough sketch, mumbling instructions on where to find the women's ward as he ripped out the title page. "There are about three hundred cells inside. The men's ward is on the left. The women's is on the right. It's pretty straightforward. You bring the keys to the Hare and Hen afterward, along with my money." He shoved the paper into Bash's hands. "If you don't, I'll tell the Bow Street Runners everything I know about you, and you'll forfeit all anyway."

Bash nodded and scooted Evie away. "That was close," he murmured, holding the map out for them both to study.

"Good thing you have all those special skills working for the Prince Regent, stealing from innocent young ladies. This should be child's play for you."

Bash swallowed back the laughter bubbling in his chest. "Good thing you think you have all the skills necessary to join me, based on your writing research." He pointed at the map. "So he said that all staff entered and exited from the main door. No back door. That will complicate things."

Evie nudged him, pointing to a group approaching the gates. "More staff?"

Bash nodded. "They most likely will not change the staff for another twelve hours."

"There's little chance we can sneak inside amongst them, even if we are posing as orderlies from Bedlam coming to fetch a patient."

He nodded to the milk cart. "What if I were a deliveryman?"

"And I?"

He eyed three empty barrels outside the grocers beside the pub. He peered inside. "These look passably clean. I'll purchase these from the owner. Would you like to be my delivery?"

Vivienne was the obvious one to clamber inside one of the three barrels Bash had stacked in the milk cart. Her knees pressed under her chin, and she tried not to think about her confined space, which was already making her limbs ache and smelled faintly of rotten apples. *For Grandmother.*

"Who are you?" she heard a gruff voice ask.

"They hired me last week. The other guard let me inside last time, but we were a bit slower this morning. You are George, aren't you?"

"What's in the cart?" George's voice changed from outright hostility to caution.

"Nothing but lard for the cook."

The guard must have waved Bash through the gate, because the cart rumbled again. The wheels thumped over the threshold, causing her to bang her head on the top of the barrel. She inched her fingers above her head to rub the spot and hopefully block further injuries as she desperately tried to figure out what was going on outside her barrel, but all were speaking low or mumbling, and only Bash's voice rang true.

"Which way to the kitchens?"

She gasped as the barrel was knocked to its side. She braced herself as best as she could as the barrel rolled. Spots dotted her vision, and she swallowed against her churning belly. *Please don't let me cast up my accounts.*

The top flew open, and Bash's arms reached for her. "Sorry it took so long. I had to make it look convincing."

Her legs tingled from being bent for so long, but Bash's arms tightened about her and kept her from collapsing. She rested her head against his broad chest, nearly releasing a sigh of contentment before recalling herself and the task ahead. She shook her right foot, and as the feeling rushed back she gingerly tested it with her weight, wincing at the sensation of embroidery needles poking her. "I think I can manage now. Let's go."

He kept her hand in his as he guided her through the maze of dingy gray halls to the women's ward, using the guard's keys a few times to get past doors to reach the next section of the hall. As they passed door after door, the sounds of despair filled the air, a shriek piercing through every few moments and sending chills down Vivienne's spine. At last they reached the women's wing, which was guarded by a lone man. He sat at his desk, an open ledger before him as he read his newssheet.

Bash approached with confidence, Vivienne following closely behind. She attempted to mirror his stance. *Cross arms, stand straight, and puff out chest.* She glanced down and caved her shoulders in. *Don't puff out chest. Slouch.*

"Looking for Mrs. Larkby. She should have arrived recently."

The man lifted his gaze, sheer boredom in his eyes. "And I care why?"

"We're fetching her. Her family is sending her to Bedlam. Apparently they felt guilty, since they are flushed in the pockets with the old lady's money."

He snorted. "Remorseful, are they? That would be a first." He flipped open his ledger and ran his finger down the list, pausing when he reached her name. "Never seen you two before." He eyed them. "You say you are with Bedlam?"

"We are new." He shrugged. "The other fellow got sick before his shift."

He eyed the kerchief covering Vivienne's head. "Where's your hat?"

"Head lice," Vivienne mumbled.

The man's nose wrinkled in disgust. "She's in cell forty-two on the left side." He tossed him a ring of keys. "Bring the keys back. I do not want to come looking for them when I finally have gotten comfortable on this wretched chair."

Vivienne was at once appalled by the lack of protocol and grateful for St. Luke's incompetence. With the keys and direction, they pressed onward. Someone rammed into the door beside her, and Vivienne nearly jumped into Bash's arms but remembered herself at the last moment. Bash nodded to her, silently asking if she were well. They kept going, only pausing outside the door marked *42*.

"Can it possibly be this easy?" Vivienne whispered in front of the door with a little latched access square at the bottom, which she supposed the staff used to deliver food.

"So far so good." He unlocked it, an eerie creak releasing from the hinges as he pushed the door open.

Vivienne gasped at the sight of the grand lady's silver hair streaming to her waist as she stood barefoot in a thin nightgown, her head lifted to the small barred window set high in the wall, as if waiting for dawn's light to reach her. A small wooden bed with strewn hay was the only furniture. Vivienne's throat tightened over the poor souls condemned to live here.

"Grandmother?" Bash whispered from the doorway.

She faced the window yet and shook her head. "I'm hearing voices now. This place truly is designed to make you mad. I won't be long now, Lord."

Bash held the door, and Vivienne crossed the room. She rested her hand on the dear lady's shoulder. "You are well in body and strong in mind. Do not fear on that score. I told you I would come for you."

She turned and blinked at Vivienne and then Bash. Her lips quirked into a smile. "I would think I was imagining you coming to save me, but the sight of Vivienne dressed in Bash's clothing is beyond my imaginings." She wrapped her arms about them both, her body quaking. "Let us make haste from this place. The very walls cry out from sorrow and abuse. I want to go home—I need my husband's roses about me. I need his roses."

"We will see you free from here," Bash promised, pulling her into an embrace. "But, Grandmother, you must act as if you do not know us. We are supposed to be from Bedlam."

Grandmother's lips pursed. "I see. Well, I was always praised for my skills in tableaux as a girl. This should be no problem."

Vivienne placed a firm hand on her shoulder, as if she were nothing to her, and guided her into the hall, past the many doors, and to the guard's station.

"W-who are you?" Grandmother moaned, blinking rapidly and muttering under her breath. "Where are you taking me?"

Bash tossed the keys to the orderly with a nod of thanks. "Have a good morning."

"Is there such a thing in this place?" The man gritted his teeth. "Good luck with that one. She fought me like a wildcat when I locked her up."

Good for Grandmother! It was a relief that she had fight in her yet. Perhaps the journey to the asylum had awakened her again.

When they rounded the corner, Bash wove his fingers through Grandmother's, guiding them through the asylum. *Thank goodness Bash was able to memorize the path.* She shivered at the thought of attempting the rescue on her own. Even she could not imagine herself capable enough to attempt it by herself.

When they reached the trio of barrels in the hallway, Bash lifted Grandmother in his arms. "My apologies, dear heart, but it is the only way past the guard, as we have no credentials to prove your removal."

She nodded weakly, and Bash nestled her inside and set the lid atop. He moved to Vivienne, his hands at her waist. "Ready?"

She bit her lip, nodding sharply. The idea of being confined again sent her heart to racing. *Lord, help me through this. Let me not give in to my anxiety.* She closed her eyes and focused on the verses Bash had shared from 1 Peter 5. *But the God of all grace, who hath called us unto his eternal glory by Christ Jesus, after that ye have suffered a while, make you perfect, stablish, strengthen, settle you.*

She drew in a deep breath and exhaled slowly, training her focus to Christ and the knowledge that Bash would protect her better than any man since her father's passing.

Chapter Twenty-Nine

LIFTING THE BARRELS BACK INTO the wagon cart was difficult, especially taking care not to jar them while moving as quickly as possible. With a nod to the guard, they rolled through the gate. Bash's heart pounded as he directed the milk cart around the corner and past the asylum. Frank would be livid that Bash was unable to fulfill the rest of the bargain, but Bash had to put a few blocks between them and the pit before it was safe to halt for a moment.

He tied the animal to the side of a building and hopped into the cart bed. After prying open the top of Grandmother's barrel, he reached down for her. Her frail arms wrapped about his, and he held her to him. She was impossibly thin and shivering. He shrugged off his coat, which was still damp from their leap into the Thames. He draped it over her thin shoulders. "We will remove you from the cold as quickly as possible, Grandmother."

"After being in that putrid hovel, the morning air will do me good." She eyed the second barrel, lips parting. "Is your bride still in there? What are you doing bothering to wrap your wet blanket of a coat around me when she's in the dark? Get her out, you nincompoop."

"Nincompoop? Is that what you call your rescuer?" Bash worked on the lid.

She crossed her arms. "Only when he is being a nincompoop."

He pried open the lid. Evie gasped for air, and his gut twisted at her pale cheeks. He grabbed her hands and lifted her out, but given her extra clothing, it was difficult to be gentle. "Did I hurt you in the escape?"

She shook out her arms, releasing a shudder. "Confined places are not my favorite. There's nothing wrong with me that a cup of tea cannot fix."

"My apologies, dear. He was being an overly concerned nincompoop." Grandmother patted Vivienne's arm. "He will do better next time."

"Next time?" Evie frowned.

"Between the two of you getting into ridiculous situations, I have no doubt there will be a next time." She winked.

Bash squeezed Evie's hand before settling Grandmother in the cart bed. "We must take the back roads to my residence. I'll send someone to return the cart by this afternoon."

"But won't that be the first place Sir Thomas will look for you?" Evie whispered to spare Grandmother, but her soft snores already sounded.

He grinned as the cart rumbled forward. "That's why it is perfect. Sir Thomas will know it is too obvious a place for me to hide, so he will not even bother searching there. He knows how I work. He will think us halfway across England by now." He winked at the unfeasibility of that fact, but the sentiment was true. Sir Thomas thought Bash the highwayman capable of the impossible.

They rolled through the streets of London, where the squeak of rats and the men plodding down to the docks kept Evie close to his side. At the corner of the street where his house stood, he halted the cart.

"I do not want to leave Grandmother, but I cannot rightly waltz up to the front door without checking for danger first."

Evie nodded, hopped out of the cart, and darted off.

"Evie!" he protested.

But she sauntered to his house and glanced through the front window before she scampered back, confusion stamped on her expression. "There is someone lounging in the chair as if he is quite used to doing so. He built a fire."

"Did you recognize him?"

"No. He has black hair and is quite broad in the shoulders."

"That's Telford." He scooped Grandmother into his arms and sprang from the cart, hurrying to the front door.

Evie grasped the door handle and pushed. The barrister rose at the sight of them as Wynn came out of the kitchen with a plate of biscuits in hand.

"I sincerely regret handing out keys, as it seems my home has become an inn," Bash teased, nodding to his friends. "Allow me to see Grandmother upstairs. Have you searched the house?"

"It's safe." Telford crossed his arms, squinting at Evie, as if trying to place her.

Bash climbed the stairs with Grandmother, laying her in the bed while sounds of Evie rummaging about his kitchen reached him. She no doubt was searching for tea. He tucked Grandmother in as she murmured about her roses. Smiling, he stroked her coarse silver hair from her cheek and pressed a kiss to her temple.

He trotted down the stairs as Evie brought out a tray with sliced bread and four glasses of lemonade. He crossed the hall to her.

"I couldn't find the tea." She shrugged apologetically.

He relieved the tray from her. "It's in the top cupboard. You probably couldn't see it, but it is for the best, as you are less than proficient at making tea."

She grimaced. "You speak the truth, unfortunately."

He set the tray atop the desk in the front room. "What did you find, Telford?" he asked as Evie handed them each a glass.

"Alden went through the proper channels. Mrs. Larkby's fortune is legally his. I am drawing up the paperwork on having Mrs. Larkby placed in your care, and I doubt anyone will object to the proposition. However, you should know that by the time her fortune may be called to attention in the courts, I am certain Alden will have her funds properly tucked away into the estate and untraceable."

Bash ran his hand over his jaw. "I could keep her here."

"In London? Her home is in Bath." Evie removed her coat. "She told me she could not live in a place so far from her husband's roses."

The barrister gasped. His eyes widened as he turned his back on her to face the fire. "Y-you're a woman?"

Wynn chuckled at Telford's reddening neck. "For a man who can look death in the face multiple times a week, you are clearly morti-fied."

Evie smiled, placing her hands on her hips. "I have been dressed as a man this entire time. There is hardly any immodesty draped in this bulky attire."

"I beg to differ," the barrister muttered. "Seeing as you are not prop-erly attired, it is time to take our leave. Wynn!"

Bash rested his hand on his friend's shoulder. "All is well here, Tel-ford. She is my wife."

"Your wife?" He blinked. "My congratulations, Sir Sebastian and, uh, Lady Larkby." He dared a glance to Evie and nodded, returning his gaze to Bash at once. "I shall be working through the day to secure your guardianship over Mrs. Larkby. She is safe enough with a knight of the Crown and a lady who would dare so much for her. It seems the lady you have chosen is a match even for you, Sebastian, which I suppose is how she captured your heart so thoroughly."

"She has indeed. Thank you, my friend." He shook Wynn's hand as well. "I appreciate the risk you took."

"Anytime." Wynn leaned forward and whispered, "Seems that you took my advice and were quite creative with number three."

Bash rolled his eyes. "Yes, it was the most quality time we have had since we first met. You should start an advice business."

Wynn's eyes sparked. "You'd be my most devoted client."

"Get out of here." Bash chuckled and shut the door behind them. They were alone at last.

Evie extended her fingers to the flame. "You have some most de-voted friends. We owe them much."

"I owe you everything, Evie." He stood beside her and unbuttoned his waistcoat, desperate for warmth after the plunge in the Thames. "If it hadn't been for your quick thinking, Grandmother's and my stories might not have played out so well." He shook his head. "To think of Alden going through all her things . . . and mine, preening in his suc-cessful coup."

"I nearly forgot." She reached into her waistcoat pocket, removed a small leather pouch, and dropped two items into his palm. "I smuggled them out in my reticule. I thought they might be of value to you. It is a good thing I used your leather pouch, because one of them is paper and would have been ruined in the jump into the Thames."

He lifted the necklace to his lips and kissed it. "I didn't think I would ever see it again." He lifted up the turquoise diamond-shaped gem and smiled at her. "This was my mother's. I remember it well about her neck. Would you do me the honor of wearing it?"

She pressed her hand to her lips. "Are you certain, Bash?"

"It graced the neck of a woman I loved. I wish for it to do so once more."

She removed the neckcloth and turned. He fastened it about her neck.

She looked to the age-spotted mirror above the fireplace, smiling. "It's lovely. I am honored to wear something that was your mother's."

He turned the second item, a folded paper, over and over in his palm.

"Might I ask what is the paper?"

"I'm afraid it is a secret." He tucked it into his pocket.

She accepted his refusal with a nod. "With this new turn of events of Sir Thomas knowing of our connection and of Grandmother being without a home, I believe it might be best that Grandmother and I return to my townhouse in Bath so I can care for her, far from the London port. We do not want you to worry about us being abducted. Perhaps I can purchase some rosebushes from Alden to place in decorative pots for the front stoop of our home." She gave him a sad smile. "It is for the best. We shall both still have our dreams, while Grandmother is happy in the town she loves best."

But what if my dream has shifted since meeting you? It had long been his dream to work for the Prince Regent until he was crowned king. Then Bash would gain significant power in his position, but what was power without having the woman he loved to share his life with? Certainly they were bound for life, but if he were to leave her in Bath with Grandmother, he felt his window of opportunity might shut and he would never again have the chance to woo her—to have a true marriage. *But what does she want?* "Very well. I will cancel the lease on the London home before we depart. We will leave first thing after we rest and break our fast properly."

She stretched. "Thank goodness. I desperately need to sleep for a few hours at least. Do you have any more blankets?"

He crossed to a small closet in the corner of the room and retrieved two serviceable blankets, stacking them on the ancient settee. "These are not elegant, but they will keep you warm."

"And for you? What will keep you warm?"

He motioned to the hearth. "I can sleep on the floor beside the fire. I am used to sleeping wherever I can lay my head, and a fire is luxury enough for me."

"I am well aware how well you can sleep without comfort." She held out one of the blankets to him. "Take one, and I can sleep on the ground, as it is your home."

"I learned from our first adventure that you do not sleep on a hard surface very well." He flung the blanket wide, spreading it on the floorboards. "You talked in your sleep too. I'm not sure I will get much sleep, even if I'm not on the floor."

She rolled back her shoulders. "I have changed much since then."

"But the talking will never cease. Sleep on the settee for both of our sakes, please." He led her to the piece of furniture.

She laughed softly and curled up on the settee that had been left from the previous owners. Within moments her soft snores filled the room.

Lord, what am I to do? Should I release my calling as a Yeoman of the Guard? Guide me. He rolled to his side and studied her face in the flickering firelight. He gave up trying to sleep after a half hour, and by noon he'd had an errand boy return the milk cart to its owner while he prepared a feast of his entire supply, packed his few belongings, bought two ready-made gowns that he thought might work for his women, and procured a private coach to arrive by one of the clock before waking Evie.

She was thrilled to change and even gave him a peck on the cheek in thanks that sent his heart to soaring.

He left Brigand tied to the coach, as he knew the trip to Bath would be arduous since Grandmother had already been through more than any lady should bear. It was hard seeing such a strong woman weakened from circumstances, but with Evie's gentle, comforting hand, Grandmother rested off and on the entirety of the trip. He could have pushed the coach to finish the drive in a single day, but he decided, in the end, that he needed to take it slower for Grandmother's sake. At the inn at the halfway point, he ordered two rooms and nearly regretted doing so, as it separated him from Evie. But he supposed he had better distance himself, lest the sudden break crush him if she refused to allow him to live with her in Bath.

Vivienne suppressed a yawn as the coach halted before her terrace home. With the need to house the servants, Tess, and her new family for a few nights at least, she knew it would feel much smaller than it had when she had lived here with her father.

When Ladd opened the door, Vivienne sighed in relief that they had made it safely despite Alden's fury. But with Bash at her side, she felt that she would have been protected no matter what. She nodded to the butler and handed the hideous bonnet that dear Bash had purchased for her journey to Brexton, who was waiting just inside. "Where is Miss Hale?"

The footman bowed and extended her a folded note. "Apparently she departed late last night. She left a note for you, my lady."

She frowned and read the note. *Called away. Love, Tess.*

"Hardly a note at all." She shook her head at Tess's habit of writing only the barest of letters. *At least the guest room is now free.* She would eventually have to sort through Father's things to free that room as well, but not yet. "Please see Mrs. Larkby to the green room."

He bowed and extended his arm to Grandmother.

Her shoulders stooped from the exhaustion of the drive, but Grandmother gave Brexton a brilliant smile. "And who are you, my handsome fellow?"

Vivienne waved Bash into the parlor. "I suppose we need to make our plan now that we have some privacy."

He cleared his throat. "Yes. I've thought of little else."

"I too." She pulled the bell cord before recalling that the footman was upstairs. "Have a seat please."

He pulled at his neckcloth.

"It is unbearably hot, is it not?" She moved to the windows, struggling with the latch.

"Allow me." He stood behind her, arms on either side of her as he moved to assist her in opening the window. She turned, intending to move away so he could better open the window, and found his head inclined toward her, their lips nearly touching. The draw to close the distance between them was nearly palpable.

"Evie," he breathed, his arms still on either side of her.

Her eyes moved upward to focus on his golden-flecked ones. "Yes?"

"I find myself questioning our latest arrangement."

Her heart skipped. "Oh?"

"I vowed to you that I would not waver, that I would not ask for more nor abandon you. I will ask but this once. I have no wish to part from you. I've decided I will retire from my position as Yeoman of the Guard. I have been thinking of St. Luke's and where we found Grandmother. I am not certain how yet, but I want us to find a way to help those poor souls inside—I was thinking to take a page out of Telford's book and become a barrister and give a voice to those who need it most. Until I can earn that position, I have savings enough to provide for us here in Bath. I want to live as a true husband and wife and build a life with you—to have children with you." He lifted her hands to his lips. "Do you dream what I dream?"

A single word flitted to her lips, desperate for escape. How much her life could change in an instant. She could keep her first dream of a quiet life, or she might choose adventure with Bash. "Unequivocally."

He drew her into his arms, pulling her up against him. His lips found hers, gentle at first, then growing more passionate with each passing moment. She melded into him, kissing her knight again and again, never wanting this moment to end. And now it did not have to.

Epilogue

"Look! There it is." Vivienne gasped, pointing at the bookshop's window.

"*The Highwayman and His Lady*?" Bash laughed, his arm encircling his wife's waist. "'Tis a good thing I no longer have clandestine missions in my future, with you turning my work into that of a romance. You'll have to find a new muse, as the Prince Regent sent word this morning that I am to retire the highwayman after solving the blackmail issue."

"Such a pity! But you forget that I can inquire about your past adventures too. It's one of the dangers of being married to a writer." She rose on her tiptoes and pressed a kiss to his cheek. "And my writing about our adventure proves that I love you most, so unless you can provide proof, I win."

He withdrew the shilling-shaped folded paper and held it up between two fingers. "Consider this your proof that I loved you first and, therefore, the most."

She gaped at the paper. "You said that was a secret!"

"It was, until I needed to share it with you." He unfolded it and extended a scrap of blue material to her.

She gasped. "This is muslin."

He grinned, enjoying her surprise. "Indeed. Do you remember it?"

"From my ruined skirt when you captured me?" She ran her fingers over the torn material.

"When you ran through the woods, I plucked it off a bush and tucked it in my pocket so as not to leave a trail, should anyone come looking for you. I found it later in my pocket, and I could not bear to throw it away . . . because my heart had already been stolen by you, and if it was all I had left of our time, I wanted to treasure it all my days." He lifted her hand to his lips. "I win."

"Oh, Bash." Her eyes filled. "You are such a romantic."

Grandmother stepped out the shop's door, lifting her copy of the scarlet book with gold lettering. "I wanted to be the first to purchase your new book. I had better be in this one after the trouble I went through to see you two married."

Vivienne and Bash looked to each other and then to her. "Pardon?"

"Oh, you well know that I figured out you weren't married after a few moments of you two interacting, so don't pretend that I didn't have a hand in your romance! I know destiny when I see it, and you two were meant for each other, so I determined to see you thrown together." She patted Vivienne's cheek and handed her an envelope.

Vivienne gasped at the amount inside.

"I didn't have much left after Alden took my funds, but I sold a piece of jewelry that you managed to save and secured you two a trip to Scotland for your honeymoon. Not without selfish reasons, as I expect to have some great-grandbabies within the year. Twins run in the family, so I shall allow you two some time to court without me getting in the way." She winked. "After all, it's my handiwork that saw you two married in the first place."

"Your handiwork? Pray tell, what was that?" Bash grinned.

"Getting Vivienne to kiss a knight was harder than it looked. Now for heaven's sake, woo your lady, Sebastian. I'm not getting any younger!" Grandmother swept into the carriage, tapping her cane to the roof. "Sir Sebastian and Lady Larkby will stroll home via the scenic route."

Bash lifted Evie's hand to his lips as the carriage rolled away. "Shall we, my lady?"

"We shall, my highwayman."

Author's Note

DEAR READER,

I am thrilled you decided to read the second book in the Best Laid Plans series. I hope you loved my story of an honorable highwayman and a runaway-bride romance writer, along with their tendency to break the carefully laid rules of the ton. As with all my novels, I attempted to stay as close to historical details as possible, but sometimes for the sake of story, I like to write heroines who break the rules to a degree and therefore find themselves in trouble . . . or in the arms of an impossibly handsome mystery man who just happens to be a knight.

If you are curious to see for yourself the historical places Vivienne Poppy visits, such as the Pump Room, the Assembly Rooms, and Sydney Park in Bath, check out my Pinterest board for pictures I collected in my online research, at pinterest.com/grace_hitchcock. When I discovered that Sydney Park had its first hot-air balloon take flight in 1802, I *had* to send Bash and Vivienne to the skies. A bit of fiction that I added to the Pump Room scene is the selling of pastries.

While Sebastian Larkby is a fictional character, the Yeomen of the Guard was an elite group composed of only handsome young men of tall stature. Their dress consisted of white wigs, white stockings, and a scarlet uniform that was in the Tudor style. They were the Prince Regent's closest guards, and it was considered a high honor to be a yeoman.

Maria Fitzherbert had been twice widowed when she wed Prince George in a secret ceremony on December 15, 1784. It was considered an invalid marriage because he was underage and did not have the king's approval. The two wrote letters to each other, which inspired Bash's part in retrieving stolen ones with sensitive information.

Do you want to read *To Kiss a Knight*'s alternate opening? Join my newsletter on gracehitchcock.com to get the alternate opening, updates on where I am in the writing process, behind-the-scenes news, and exclusive giveaways.

Stay tuned for Tess Hale's journey to love in *To Win a Wager*, the third book of the series. Think highlands, secrets, mayhem, and a dashing nobleman in search of reclaiming his family's fortune that was stolen from him. Happy reading, friends!

Acknowledgments

To my knight in shining armor, Dakota. You are my inspiration for heroes. I could not write without you, and let's be honest, it would be a lot harder to get the kissing scenes written correctly without you. Flappings and flutterings forever!

To my sweet babies—thank you for being mine. I love you!

To my family: Dad, Mama, Charlie, Molly, Sam, Natalie, Eli, and nephews—thank you for always being so supportive of my writing.

To the reader—thank you for reading Vivienne Poppy's story! I hope you thought the romance dreamy and you got a few chuckles and cringes at some of the extra cheese I am so fond of adding. It can't be helped.

To the team at Kregel, Dori Harrell, and all my amazing editors— thank you for all your hard work in bringing Vivienne's story to further life! You are wonderful, and I am thrilled to be a Kregel author!

To exclamation marks, for capturing my excitement in this acknowledgments section!!

And to Jesus—thank You for loving me forever. I will never stop praising You for all that You have done!

About the Author

GRACE HITCHCOCK IS THE AWARD-WINNING author of multiple historical novels and novellas, including the Aprons & Veils series. She holds a master's in creative writing and a bachelor of arts in English with a minor in history. She lives on the Northshore of New Orleans, with her husband, sons, and daughter in a cottage that is always filled with the sounds of sweet little footsteps running at full speed. When not writing or chasing babies, she's baking something delightful and can usually be found with a book clutched in her fist.

Sometimes the only way to outsmart a scandal is to find a crown big enough to silence it.

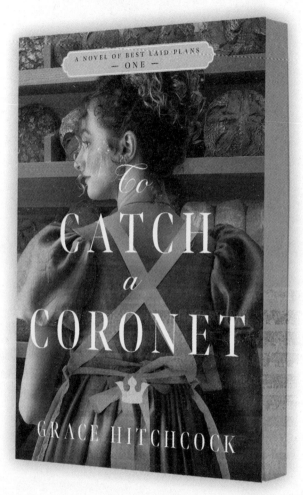

"Perfect Regency! This hilarious novel has it all: sparkling dialogue, a spunky heroine with a penchant for baking, and a dreamy hero who loves her in spite of her antics. I loved it and highly recommend!"
—Colleen Coble, *USA Today* best-selling author of *Fragile Designs*

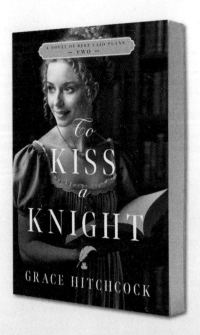

YOU CAN KEEP THIS BOOK MOVING!

Give this book as a gift.

Recommend this book to a friend or group.

Leave a review on Christianbook, Goodreads, Amazon, or your favorite bookseller's website.

Connect with the author on their social media/website.

Share the QR code link on your social media.

2450 Oak Industrial Dr NE | Grand Rapids, MI 49505 | kregel.com

  Follow @kregelbooks

Our mission as a Christian publisher is to develop and distribute—with integrity and excellence— trusted, biblically based resources that lead individuals to know and serve Jesus Christ.